More praise for
Etched on Me

"*Etched on Me* is one of the first authentic, searing portraits of a young woman's all-out fight for her sanity since *I Never Promised You a Rose Garden*. You will not forget Lesley, or her trials and triumph."

—Jacquelyn Mitchard, *New York Times* bestselling author
of *The Deep End of the Ocean*

"*Etched on Me* is an emotionally raw and fiercely written novel, exploring a young woman's struggle to survive in the midst of tumultuous circumstance. I couldn't put it down."

—Amy Hatvany, author of *Best Kept Secret*

"Jenn Crowell has written a miracle of a novel, full of grit and grace; her Lesley Holloway is a character for the ages—wry and whip smart and achingly real. This book will forever be etched upon my heart."

—Gayle Brandeis, author of *The Book of Dead Birds*
and winner of the Bellwether Prize

"There's such warmth here: the very best and the very worst of which human beings are capable. The narrator makes delightful and engaging company (I'm kind of a bit in love with her) and the story is utterly compelling. I just HAD to read on to find out what happened in the end; it really mattered to me because Crowell made it matter, and that's what great writing can do."

—Clare Allan, author of *Poppy Shakespeare*

"A harrowing and riveting story of a young woman struggling against inner and outer destructive forces to find peace, equanimity and connection. Crowell has written a moving psychological thriller that offers us deep insights into the legacies of trauma and the difficulties of moving forward. It's a wonderful novel."

—Leonard Chang, author of *Crossings*

"In Lesley Holloway, Crowell has created a protagonist whom I wish I could meet off the page. Confronted with abuse, stigma, and shame, Lesley takes real risks to do more than survive her circumstances: she changes them. Along the way, Lesley draws strength from a small but hardy cast of supporting characters we'd also all benefit from knowing in everyday life. In the hands of an author lacking Crowell's skill, the novel might risk falling into stereotype and caricature. But Crowell deftly maintains control—unflinching, authentic, and empathic—throughout."

—Erika Dreifus, author of *Quiet Americans: Stories*

"*Etched on Me* reinvents the 'coming-of-age' novel by making the body of a young woman the center of the drama. . . .

As Lesley beats back the abuse from her past and the self-destruction driving her, she discovers there is something alive in her bigger than her rage and hurt. What she has to fight for next will break your heart—just as it should—because what we tell females about themselves is a story that can indeed make or break them. Jenn Crowell will open your eyes with this tale of how the body and heart of a girl can, on her own terms, become that of a woman."

—Lidia Yiknavitch, author of *Dora: A Headcase*

"Readers will cheer for Lesley's progress in this against-all-odds, sometimes grueling, suspenseful, and character-rich tale of individuation. Bringing to mind Susanna Kaysen's memoir *Girl, Interrupted* or Jeffrey Eugenides's *The Virgin Suicides*, Crowell's novel darkly fascinates."

—*Library Journal*

Also by Jenn Crowell

Necessary Madness
Letting the Body Lead

Etched on Me

A NOVEL

Jenn Crowell

WASHINGTON SQUARE PRESS

New York • London • Toronto • Sydney • New Delhi

W

Washington Square Press
A Division of Simon & Schuster, Inc.
1230 Avenue of the Americas
New York, NY 10020

First Washington Square Press trade paperback edition February 2014

WASHINGTON SQUARE PRESS and colophon are registered
trademarks of Simon & Schuster, Inc.

For information about special discounts for bulk purchases,
please contact Simon & Schuster Special Sales at
1-866-506-1949 or business@simonandschuster.com.

The Simon & Schuster Speakers Bureau can bring authors to your
live event. For more information or to book an event contact the
Simon & Schuster Speakers Bureau at 1-866-248-3049
or visit our website at www.simonspeakers.com.

Designed by Leydiana Rodríguez-Ovalles

Manufactured in the United States of America

10 9 8 7 6 5 4 3 2 1

Library of Congress Cataloging-in-Publication Data

Crowell, Jenn
   Etched on me : a novel / Jenn Crowell. — First Washington Square Press
trade paperback edition.
      pages   cm
   (ebook) 1. Survival—Fiction. 2. London (England)—Fiction. I. Title.
   PS3553.R5928E83 2013
   813'.54—dc23   2013014712

ISBN 978-1-4767-3906-9
ISBN 978-1-4767-3907-6 (ebook)

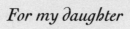

For my daughter

1

Have you ever wanted something so much, it's not a desire so much as a beacon? Have you ever prayed for it so hard, your fingernails curl into your palms and your eyes squinch shut and your whole body just hums?

My daughter is that simple, shining thing. Taken from me under bright lights in a white room, my stitches still raw. I fought so much they put me in hard restraints. I screamed so loudly they shot me up with sedative.

When I resurfaced, the blood had soaked through my hospital gown. I wanted to cry but couldn't. It was as if my body was weeping for me. Just like before, only this time it wasn't me who was making it happen. I felt floaty and exhausted. Closed my eyes.

"Come on, Les, stay awake." Immi, shaking my tied-down arm from the left side of the bed. "Your solicitor's going to ring soon."

I opened my eyes again. Stared at the opposite wall's watercolor portrait of a budding rose, its outlines like those of the mandala coloring book pages Clare and I used to fill in at the Phoenix.

Shit. Now I *was* crying, flapping my tethered hands in useless flail.

Behind me, I felt Gloria's hand stroking my hair. "All right. Shh. Just try to stay calm, sweetheart."

Yes. Calm. That was what I needed to be, so I could get unbound, so I could reach for the phone when it rang, hold it in my own grip. I've grown pretty used to extreme highs and lows in my twenty-two years of life, but that had to be the nadir: aspiring to have my restraints taken off in order to take a call from my solicitor to discuss my child protection case.

They'd just untied me when he came on the line. "It's a temporary order, not a long-term arrangement. We'll demand full visitation rights whilst she's being fostered. Battle this all the way to the European High Court if we have to."

Six months later, we're still battling. In silence. I can't say a word to the media now, no matter how much I might want to go back on breakfast TV, no longer mild-mannered and plaintive but a warrior mum instead. One public statement, and my face could wind up in a mug shot taken at a North London women's prison. So I keep my mouth shut, and wait in drafty corridors, and scribble notes on my solicitor's cast-off pads. Some of them are to him *(Mention positive parenting evaluation? Ask for evening and weekend visit hours?)*, but most of them are for me, and for her. No sappy "Dear Daughter" missives, just fervent snippets: *I want to bury my face in your fuzzy hair until the end of time. If I win, it'll be for all of us phoenix-girls.*

I hadn't wanted to write this story down at first. Some of it I didn't have words for, and other bits just made me convinced I didn't deserve her. Hardly needed more fuel for that fire, right? So I stopped for a while. But then I thought (a tiny thought, dangerous but powerful): What if we go all the way to the European High Court, and they still shake their heads and say, "No, so sorry, birthday cards and photo exchanges once a year it is, thanks very much for playing, Miss Holloway"? What of the massive silence that will descend then?

Not just massive, but final. Either I get her back at our next hearing, or I lose her forever.

I'd like to think, of course, that her adoptive parents would be sensitive and respectful, but what if they aren't? If they put on syrupy, rueful voices and sigh, "Oh, darling, your mummy loved you so very much. She just had some . . . well, some *issues* with her mental health, and couldn't take care of you properly"? You'd best believe I'm sneaking a letter into the birthday card, just in case. Not talking smack about her new mum or dad, of course. I've been a team player all through this (not that it's got me anywhere), and I'm not about to do anything that will make my girlie think poorly of me. I just want her to know someday, when she's old enough, if it comes to that, that I was meant to be her mother. That, fully admitted "issues" aside, we were both robbed.

2

Whenever I talked to the press or went on telly, back when I was pregnant, the journalists and program hosts would always lean forward with an expectant, awed posture and ask, with an attentiveness so studied it would have made me laugh if I hadn't been scared shitless, "So, Miss Holloway, how did this all begin?"

Behind their solicitous open-ended act, of course, they just wanted the lurid basics. And so, like Clare tending to one of her famous French reduction sauces, I had to boil the complexity of my life down. "Well, it started when I ran away from home at sixteen, because my dad . . ."

I slept in the park that first night, on a bench near Islington Green. Thank God it was August. Universe cut me a flipping break. Woke me with chirpy birds, to the softest sunlight ever. I sat up, rubbed my aching neck. So sore it popped, but I felt brilliant, because I'd gotten *out*: of that claustrophobic tiny flat, of that hall closet into which Dad had shoved me in order to have his way with me.

I stared down at my hands. Brought them to my face, ran them over the bridge of my nose. Grinned into my palms. I couldn't believe I'd actually gone and done it, made the impossible escape, sprinting down the stairs of our building at two a.m. like a skittish greyhound, an overstuffed rucksack jostling against my burdened back. Nothing's impossible when you're pushed to your limits, though. Just a single shove, and I was a fucking rockstar.

One in dire need of breakfast. I took my grumbly stomach down the road to a manky café and spent my last five pounds on a greasy plate of sausage and egg. While I chowed down, I pulled the slip of paper I'd been hoarding from my pocket. Smoothed the creases with my thumb till the scrap lay flat on the table. My talisman.

I'd found the phone number a month before, on a bulletin board at the library, just below leaflets advertising Mummy and Me storytime. Those featured cheery primary-hued logos, but the poster that caught my eye was all grayscale solemnity, earnestly inquiring: *Worried About a Child?*

I wasn't a child anymore, and worry didn't even begin to describe it, but I grabbed my book renewal reminder slip for *A Pictorial History of Women in Rock* and jotted those digits down on the back. Nothing but the numbers. Last thing I needed was him discovering the words "Children's Services Team" and busting my lip open.

As it was, Mum almost caught me, coming up behind with her armful of crap romance novels, making me jump. "Bit old for storytime, aren't we, Les?"

I swallowed hard. Tried to imagine myself plopped down in her lap, eagerly watching the pages turn, waiting breathlessly for what came next.

And then: tried not to.

"Just looking for study groups," I said. "Make sure I'm extra-prepared for autumn."

That made her beam. Ever since I'd gotten a scholarship to a posh girls' school for the coming year, she'd been bragging on me left and right: not just to people it'd be understandable to share the good news with, like our neighbors, but also to complete strangers. Talk about mortifying. I mean, not saying I wasn't proud of myself, or shouldn't have been, but come on. It's not like the checkstand girl at Tesco's gives a fuck.

Right then in the library, though, I was beyond grateful for that cover-up. I tucked the receipt in my pocket, where it never left for the next four weeks. Once, it almost fell out while he was yanking my jeans down. I'd learned to stop screaming years ago, but in that moment I was so petrified that I had to bite my tongue so I wouldn't shriek.

At night, afterwards, I'd lie in bed, all sleepy and sore, and just gaze at the phone number. Didn't take long for me to memorize it, so I could have easily done away with the evidence, but there was a real sense of comfort in being able to look at that crumply piece of paper and know there was a whole team who potentially had my back.

I finished my breakfast now, and went outside to a phone box. I'd have used my mobile, but I'd turned it off so as not to hear the barrage of rings I knew would jangle throughout the day. I smoothed my talisman again against the glass window. Deep-breathed, and dialed.

The social worker who answered was called Francesca, and she was ace. "Of course we can help you with emergency accommodation."

Her first available appointment was later that evening. I didn't know where to go until then, and the only thing I had left in my wallet was a transport pass, so I rode the tube all day, transferring off the Northern Line as soon as I could in case my parents had gone looking for me.

Sitting on the train, rucksack in my lap, hair rumpled, I suddenly felt like what I had always thought of as "one of *those* people": the kind you don't make eye contact with, lest they go off on a paranoid rant; the kind you step around, even if it means giving up a seat. My first taste of public otherness.

In the afternoon I rode out to Middlesex and got off at the stop nearest my new school. I had no idea whether I'd be able to go now, and part of me didn't care, but another wanted desperately to catch a glimpse of what might still be possible.

As I peered through wrought-iron gates at the cluster of brick buildings and broad expanse of lawn, I pictured myself in a maroon uniform, gliding jauntily down the main hall's front steps. The very thought made my eyes sting. Who the fuck was I kidding?

No, I told myself. *Don't think like that. You're a rockstar.*

A tired one. A queasy one. A scared one.

Francesca met me by the automatic doors of the social services office at five o'clock. She was younger than I'd expected, midtwenties maybe, her face soft round the edges, her gaze warm.

"I'm so glad you rang," she said as we stepped into the lifts. "That took heaps of courage."

On the way to the conference room, I ducked into the ladies'. I'd wanted to change my clothes that morning, but the café's toilets had been so dodgy I didn't dare. I knew I didn't have enough time for a full ensemble change now, but I also knew my dignity hinged upon my ability to walk into that meeting with clean underpants on.

I locked myself in the disabled stall so I'd have more room, and stepped out of my grass-smudged summer jeans. The knickers I had on were turquoise, my favorite color. I yanked them down. Wadded them up. Thought about shoving them into a pocket of my rucksack, but then I saw the dried stains and smelled the sour scent of him and knew they had to go.

The replacements I stepped into were white briefs, boring but comfy. I put my jeans and sandals back on, tossed the defiled turquoise scrap in the bin, and headed down the corridor.

Round the conference table sat my new best friend Francesca, some other lady from Children's Services whose name I forgot soon as she told me, and a police constable. The fact that he was a man didn't bother me since I reckoned he'd be on my side, but Francesca was super-sensitive about it all, reassuring me that we could reschedule the interview with a woman if I'd rather.

I said it was fine, but then my voice started to quaver, and I stammered something like "Th-thank you, though," and my eyes got wet enough that Francesca jumped up and fetched me a tissue, and my stomach growled so loudly that her colleague nipped downstairs and got me a packet of crisps and a soda and a paper cup of water from the office cooler, and they all watched me rip into the bag and swig like a wild animal, devouring the sweet salty coldness—terrible manners, I knew, but I couldn't help it, Christ, it was all so good.

Once my blood sugar drop and damp eyes had been taken care of, it was time to get down to business. Here the constable was kind, but not messing about. "We understand this is difficult for you, but it's a quite serious allegation, and we'll need extensive details." I nodded, because of course it was, and of course they would.

The questions were easy enough at first, vague enough to be safe, like when did it start (soon as I was old enough to fill out a bra) and how did it progress (feel-ups first, then more), but when things got into the mechanics department and they wanted an itemized list of who shoved what where, I went straight up to the ceiling like a rogue funfair balloon, leaving them peering, bewildered, into my ethereal-eyed, rigid face.

The ceiling is a weird concept to explain to normal people, who are used to dwelling completely anchored in their bodies. And I never intended to check out of mine. But around the time I learned to stop screaming, I also found out that I could leave my physical self shoved up against the hall closet's hatboxes and drift into a whole other sheltering, liminal space where I didn't have to feel the press of him on me or the thrust of him inside me.

The nice people across the table, of course, knew none of this, and I could hardly articulate it in five easy steps at that moment. So they just kept asking, gently, tentatively: "Lesley? Are you all right?"

I reached my hand across the table. "Let me write it down," I said, in a hoarse voice that didn't feel like it was sounding from inside me. "Only way I can say it."

"Of course, of course" came a chorus of murmurs, as Francesca slipped her notepad over to me and placed the pen in my hand.

I wrote so fast and so hard the pen stabbed the paper. My letters, neat and rounded at first, oozed into angry shapes, chaotic as a ransom note, angular as hieroglyphs. I signed my name in a furious swirl, then slid the pad back.

"Do you mind if—if I run to the loo for a minute?" I whispered.

"Not at all, not at all" went the choral murmurs.

Nausea punched me in the gut soon as the door slammed behind me. I sprinted for the nearest sink. Leaned over it just in time for my stomach to clench like a fist and my mouth to spew the bilious lava of crisps and carbonated syrup. Even after I'd finished retching, I spat until every last drop ran clear.

Back in the meeting room, they'd moved on to the logistics.

"What about your mother? Is she aware of what's going on?"

I thought of our disastrous putting-on-airs afternoon at Harrods for high tea. Tower of cucumber sandwiches and scones set atop a pink-draped table. "Perfect day for a mother-daughter date, innit?" *Yeah, Mum, real improvement over the father-daughter dates.* My confession tumbling out, inadvertent but urgent. Her face flushing red as if I'd slapped her.

Now, two years later, my mouth puckered in a *don't fucking cry* knot. I braced my palms, hard, against the bare table edge.

"Yeah," I choked out. "Mum knows."

The three of them exchanged solemn glances.

"Have you any friends or relatives you could stay with?" Francesca asked.

I shook my head. My family was pretty much the thermonuclear sort (no siblings whose safety we needed to worry about, thank God), and my friends and I had grown apart once they heard I was headed off to a snobby school and leaving them behind.

"Well, then, can you think of anything specific you might need?"

Someone to stroke my hair, and tell me the worst was over, and bring me supper on a tray like I was a sick little girl.

"Umm, let me think," I said, my words edging perilously close to babble. "I have this library book I left back there called *A Pictorial History of Women in Rock* that needs to be returned. And I'll need a new mobile number, and a September tube pass, and a school uniform." I paused. "Assum-assuming I can still go?"

"Absolutely, you can," Francesca said. "I'll have a chat with the headmistress and sort it all out."

"What about tonight?"

Soon as I asked, Francesca went rambly-mumbly apologetic. "Well, you see, we've not got any available foster carers at the moment, so we're going to have to put you up in a hostel."

I pictured cheery bunk beds and common areas with Internet kiosks. "You mean, like for foreign backpackers?"

"Erm, not exactly. It's a hostel for adults who are . . ." Long pause. "In transition."

Middle-aged men lounged against corridor walls, their stained fingers clutching cigarettes, their eyes skimming the neckline of my sleeveless summer blouse. A few rooms down, a bleached-blond woman in a miniskirt kicked at a closed door, screeching "Let me in, you wanker!"

Francesca linked her arm through mine in sisterly rally, all *Come, let's march bravely through hell,* but when one of the lechers opened his gap-toothed mouth to blow a hard puff of nicotine and leer "Hey, pretty," I burrowed into her in terror.

"Your room's right here," Francesca said lightly, pulling away from me to retrieve the key from her trouser pocket.

"It has a lock." My words were a huffed gasp.

Francesca glanced at me with a bemused look. "Of course it does."

When she handed me the key, it was all I could do not to kiss the damn thing, to run my tongue along its serrated, rusty edges in worshipful relief before turning it. My room, *my* room, with a lock, and a—

Dingy linoleum floor, and threadbare blanket, and peeling wallpaper, and exposed bulb.

"Oh, dear." Francesca surveyed the room and sucked her

lips between her teeth. "We'll have to speak with the maintenance staff."

My shoulders slumped a little. I ran my hand over the nearby desk-slash-dresser. Yanked my fingers away to find them covered in dust.

At the gritty feel of it, I immediately pictured my old room, with its fluffy turquoise duvet and Björk posters and stacks of plump pillows and strands of twinkly lights trailing round the windows. For a moment, I wanted to sneak back and burrow into all that soft goodness, but then I remembered there was nothing good or soft about a lockless sanctuary.

You have no right to be a diva, I told myself. *Francesca pulled this together for you last minute, when she could have been out saving little kids. Show some flipping gratitude.*

"It's totally fine," I said. "I'll manage."

Francesca promised to return the next day and left me with instructions—kitchen and laundry facilities on the ground floor, spare towels in a cupboard by the bathroom—and some cash for food in an envelope. After she'd gone, I sat on the creaky single bed, my knees drawn up to my chin, my forehead on my knees. In the next room, I could hear the muffled groans and wails of a couple either fighting or having sex, I couldn't quite tell which.

Frantic for a way to block the noise, I reached down into my rucksack for my beat-up portable CD player. He'd offered to buy me an iPod for my "sweet" (ha) sixteen the previous April, but I'd told him the only thing I wanted was for him to keep his fucking hands off me. That earned me both his palms around my neck the next time we were in the hall closet, but it was worth the choke hold just to spit those words like bitter seeds.

I put in my cheap earbuds now and pressed PLAY. The CD I had going was a mix I'd made called "Best of the Screaming Women," mainly to annoy the shit out of my mum, but also because I reckoned that if *I* couldn't scream, the next best thing was to let some other woman with a strong voice do it on my behalf.

First up was some stuff from that ancient Kate Bush album with her about to kiss Houdini on the cover. The song about letting the weirdness in I could deal with—not like I couldn't relate to that idea, right?—but when the track came on where she howls and stutters about locking all the doors in her house to keep an evil spirit out, I felt like I was going to vomit all over again, so I punched the forward arrow quick till I got to some Portishead.

There we were. Dark but chillaxed old-school trip-hop, like what I imagined I might hear once I'd moved out the hostel and was finally dining at a hip bistro with candles in wine bottles, waiting for my salad and balsamic-glazed salmon to materialize on a plate delivered by a tattooed wait-ress. *(Nobody loves meeeee, it's true, not like youuuuu do.)* I drew my knees back up to my chin, and rested my forehead back on my knees, and rocked to and fro until I felt nothing ex-cept the soothing sway of the motion.

By the time I came down from the ceiling again, my ear-buds were as silent as the hall outside. I got up and opened the door to check. Empty. Finally safe enough for a sneak towards the shower.

As I pulled my pajamas and toothbrush from my ruck-sack, my mobile skittered out across the floor. When I powered it on, I found fifteen voicemails, each one from him. I didn't even listen. Just turned the phone off again, draped my fresh T-shirt over one arm, slipped my sandals back on, and sprinted for the linen cupboard.

Its towels were scratchy and thin as my new blanket, but thankfully clean—unlike the bathroom's sinks and toilets, in which cigarette ashes floated. *You're just getting a head start on university,* I told myself, fighting to convince myself both that I would eventually go and that every coed residence hall of course stank of burnt curry and urine. On my way to the shower, I chucked my now-permanently-silenced mobile into a bin.

Behind the stall's scummy vinyl curtain, the water ran blissfully, blessedly hot. I stepped under the surprisingly vigorous spray and warily eyed the plastic soap dispenser (exact same model as in the psych wards I'd stay on later). When I pressed a button, the machine spurted a multipurpose pink goo that smelled of flowers soaked in antiseptic.

I tipped my head back, luxuriating in the steam and the sting. I knew I risked complaints from my fellow hostel-mates, but I didn't care; I was going to run that hot water all the way down even if it caused a riot.

When I reached for another gel pump with which to tackle the grimy soles of my feet, I felt a sudden twinge in my belly, far too low to be a harbinger of more nausea. I glanced down, glimpsed a smudge of blood on the bruised inside of my thigh. My shoulders dropped—not sinking at the feel of dust, this time, but sloping in relief. As a clot hit the rusted drain with a smeary dissolve, I pressed one slick hand to the wall to steady myself. Shook my head like a dog under the droplets, all curved-back grin and hysterical laughter, my whole body quaking with prayers to every off-kilter deity I could name: *Thank God, thank the Screaming Women, thank the bare lightbulb above my new bed, thank the bistro candles flickering in their ersatz vases,* I wasn't, thank them all, wasn't pregnant.

3

True to her word, Francesca came back the next morning. I was ridiculously glad to see her—at least until she told me about the doctor's appointment the police wanted to schedule in order to "gather physical evidence."

Even that mannered phrase made my guts churn.

"Will they make me go?" I whispered.

Francesca shook her head. "You don't have to do anything you don't want to, Lesley. Not anymore."

My mouth almost fell open in amazement. I curled onto my side on the bed, pressing my cheek to its pitiful, lumpy excuse for a pillow, hugging myself. "Seriously?"

"Seriously."

"But it would help my case if I went."

She nodded. "I'll make certain you've a female doctor. And stay with you. If you'd like."

Yes, yes, yes, please.

"Okay," I said.

Pelvic exams aren't fun even on a good day, but having my very first one under such crappy circumstances meant I was already shaking and blinking back tears before the gyno even got her gloves on.

"You can tell her to stop at any time," Francesca said softly into my ear, from where she sat perched on a stool next to me.

I felt the doctor grasp the inside of my knee, gently but firmly.

"Go slowly," Francesca said to her. "Please."

I looked over at Francesca. "Can—can I hold your hand?"

It seemed like a weird thing to ask, seeing as how we barely knew each other, but I'd seen enough of her to know that her soft fingers wrapped round mine would help.

"Of course you can." She leaned against the padded table. Clasped my hand in that same rallying fashion in which she'd taken my arm the night before. Her grip delicate yet solid.

When the metal slid into me, my shoulders tensed and my neck clenched and my head lifted off the crackly exam-room paper. Strangled whimpers leaked from my lips no matter how hard I tried to bite them closed.

"Take a deep breath," the doctor said.

"Or take a break," Francesca said, glancing at her.

"No," I gasped, sinking back down onto the pillow. "Let's get it over with. I'm good."

For the rest of the exam, I longed to ditch that clinic in favor of the ceiling, but I also wanted to stay with Francesca, who was being so sweet, cheerleading about how well I was coping, reminding me over and over that *I* was the one in control.

"Do you have any idea how brave you are?" she murmured, as a particularly bad poke made my womb cramp. "I'd have called it quits back in the reception area."

I couldn't help smiling. "Yeah?"

"Mmm-hmm. But you, you're a tough one."

Rockstar. *Don't fucking cry.*

She saw the moistness in my eyes, I knew, because she gave my hand a good long squeeze. And then I did retreat up to the ceiling for a while, 'cause it was just too hard to let her see me like that. But when it was over, as I was slowly sitting back up to the feel of all that cold jelly-glop between my thighs and the light, steady guidance of her hand on my back, I glanced over at her and said hoarsely, "Thank you."

Her face went pink with pleasure, as if she weren't used to hearing those words from a client. "You're so very welcome," she said.

Even harder than that exam, though, was the reunion with my mum. We'd got a court order saying that my dad couldn't have contact with me at all, but she wanted to see me, and part of me wanted to see her. I say "part of me" because, honestly, given the way it'd all gone down so far, I knew my chances of having a real hugs-and-happiness reunion were zero. Hell, even a simple heartfelt "Oh, Lesley, I'm sorry I didn't take this seriously before" was in the realm of minor miracle. So I had to be realistic, and not let my strength get sapped by sick-little-girl-supper-tray hopes. But the hopeful little girls inside you die hard, and so Francesca arranged a meeting in the same conference room where I'd given the police interview.

We made an awkward triangle, me and Francesca on one side of the table, Mum on the opposite. All we could do was cagily eye each other.

Mum looked so pretty. Wan, but put-together. Wearing a little flower pin I'd made for her in art class ages ago, and a cardigan with pearly buttons. The room was so cold—that business-office air-conditioning, always cranked too high—and I could see her hands quivering from nerves and chill. I wanted to hold them so badly. I wanted to rest my cheek against the cardie's wisteria-hued cotton and stroke the nostalgic chipped glaze of the pin, and close my eyes just in time to feel the precise plant of her kiss atop my head. *Oh, Lesley-lovely,* she would say, like I was three again. *I was so daft not to believe you. And now look at you, my brave bold girl. You must be knackered. Rest now, the car's running, we'll go back to Margate on holiday, just us. Leave him with nothing but divorce papers. Run along the seaside with the gulls, till we're strong and tan! Sleep in till noon and have ice cream for lunch. How's that sound, sweetness?*

Like the best plan ever. I leaned towards her, all my hope-caveats evaporating.

Soon as I did that, she began to cry. Ugly, sloppy tears, her face twisted with pain whose source I couldn't place. Her gaze on me both liquid and hard.

"Mummy?" I said softly.

Snuffly gasps. "You know, I can understand why . . ."

She understands! I smiled at her, gently, as if to say, *I understand, too. I know it's been hard.*

"Why . . ." More sucked-in sniffles.

Francesca slid a box of tissues across to her. "Here, Aurelia. Take your time."

Mum straightened up. Slid her chair back, away from me. When she spoke now, her voice was crisp.

"I can understand why you mightn't want to live at home, but leaving like that, without even a note, on our *anniversary*?"

There'd been eighteen roses, one for each year. Mum had buried her nose in them, giddy. "You've outdone yourself, Liam!"

When she said that, he made a big shameless show. Full-on kissed her in front of me, just minutes after he'd coiled his tongue around mine. And I stood there, regulation celebratory card in hand, knowing we all knew, knowing beyond a doubt that, bad timing or not, it was time.

"I didn't mean to hurt you," I said now.

"Then why are you pressing charges?" Furious eye-dab. "Please, Lesley. Don't do this to us."

To *us*? I wanted to lunge across the table and spit in her face. I could feel the saliva writhing in my mouth, all indignant slosh.

I looked over at poor Francesca, who was stuck playing neutral. She gave me a soft *bon courage* glance back.

I could tell Mum noticed, because she sighed and crossed her arms. "We work ourselves to death, your dad and I. Do you have any idea what this will do to us if —"

"What? He gets held responsible for what he did?"

Mum turned her head away, towards a poster that read *You CAN Break the Cycle of Violence.*

Did I? I wondered. *Can I?*

"Mum," I said, "I'm still going to that school. I'll make you proud."

Her head whipped back. "After all this shame?"

"Mrs. Holloway," Francesca said delicately, "many, many women struggle to come to grips with incest in the family. And I don't mean to make light of your difficulties. But right now, your daughter is in great need of—" She glanced over at me again. "Well, why don't *you* tell us just what it is you need, Lesley?"

My Björk posters and my fluffy duvet and supper on a tray and Mummy and Me storytime.

Mum stared down into her lap. Picked at her lavender nail polish, as if it were a scab to be flaked off.

Two could play that game. I sat up. Crossed my arms. Looked away towards the Cycle of Violence. Blink-blink-blinked, so barely I knew only Francesca would see.

"I need for this to be over," I said.

Back in Francesca's car, I wanted nothing more than to cry while she held me, but instead I ranted and raged, imitating Mum. "'How could you *do* this to us? Why must we bear this *shaaame*?'" And then, pounding my fist on the passenger-side door frame: "Fuck that fuck that fucking fuck that."

Once the adrenaline wore off, I brought my hand down and glanced sheepishly at Francesca. "Sorry," I said.

"It's all right," Francesca said.

No, it isn't.

"You think she'll ever come around?" I asked.

Long pause. "I don't know."

"She can't even be proud of me," I whispered.

Francesca reached across the gearshift and put her hand over mine.

"Maybe not," she said, "but I certainly can."

I swallowed. "Thanks."

She gave my hand a little pat. "What do you say to some post-debrief ice cream?"

Yes, yes, yes, please.

We sat and ate it on "my" bench on Islington Green. She slid her tiny manicured feet out of her adorable ballet flats. Rolled up the sleeves of her fitted blouse whose silvery-gray print looked like tears turned to blossoms. "Bit better, at least?" she asked.

I nodded. Licked the cone so hard my teeth hurt. Willed myself not to lean my head on her shoulder.

The rest of that summer was a seedy, anxious blur. I took a job at a fish-and-chips shop, evenings and weekends, to supplement my meager allowance from social services. At night, I'd trudge greasily home, not to the foster family Francesca had hoped to procure for me but back to my shabby now-permanent hostel room, where I'd devour my employee ration of newsprint-wrapped cod while longing for one of Mum's sit-down Sunday dinners.

My time at Hawthorn Hill, the posh school, was a blur at first, too. Mainly because I was so bloody tired from all that work: proving I'd deserved my scholarship, frying fish, avoiding middle-aged men in the hostel corridor, taking a middle-aged man to court. So much for jauntily gliding down steps (I took them two at a time to catch the bus to the tube to the hostel) or making new friends (I could barely stay awake, much less endear myself to girls whose biggest problem was deciding whether to go to Mallorca or Ibiza for winter holiday). But I kept soldiering on, all sleepwalky day long, because come the afternoon, best saved for last, there it was, the hour that made it all worthwhile: literature class with Mrs. Kremsky.

A lot of the other girls didn't care for Miss, but I thought she was brilliant. For one thing, she looked like a slightly more schoolteachery version of PJ Harvey, her dark hair rustling round her shoulders, her pale, starkly striking face framed by silvery earrings whose angular shapes made them look like mini-sculptures.

She was fierce, too. Whenever the class ringleaders, Gemma and Bettina, gave her shit, she'd give it right back. Like the time they mocked her American accent, never mind that it was nowhere near a twangy sitcom one, and subtle enough to show she'd lived here a long time and knew how to walk the map-edges of a lot of different worlds. Maybe that threatened those girls, or maybe they did just think it was funny.

Either way, Miss wasn't having any of it. She spun right round from the chalkboard, and did the most perfect imitation of the bastardized Cockney they liked to put on: "Better to be a born-and-bred Yank than pretend I grew up in Shoreditch to boost my street cred, innit?" Just enough to call them out, but not so much as to be truly mean. Flipping fabulous. I about fell over.

Another time we were supposed to be working on our essays, and the girls in the back were whispering and giggling about their debauched weekends instead, thinking nobody could hear, but I knew that Miss's finely honed bullshit radar was about to detect.

Sure enough, she glanced up from her desk, casually graceful, her Tate Modern earrings going swingity-swing, and said, in her sharpest *I'm so not messing around* voice, "Ladies, last time I checked, tallies of who boffed whom weren't part of the National Curriculum." And then, just before the girls could get all squawky and miffed, she flashed them a sly little smile to let them know that, yes, she was vexed, but she also remembered what it was like to be sixteen and had no doubt had some debauched weekends of her own.

She was clever like that, Miss, but also challenging as a teacher. Some of the other instructors at the Hill were known for going a bit easy, especially on the girls whose parents had donated to the school's endowment, but Miss wasn't having any of that, either. I mean, talk about rigorous, she had us reading *Ulysses* in Lower Sixth. Everyone else moaned about it, but for me it was a nightly ritual: get home round about ten after closing the chip shop, huddle under my ratty blanket, put my Screaming Women on, crack open that dusty, hulking monster of a book, and crawl right into Leopold Bloom's head.

I'll be honest, most evenings I did a skim, but when I got to the part at the end, with his wife, Molly, going on about being a flower of the mountain and the hillside and the seed-cake, my jaw went slack with amazement. The thought of an actual question, heavy as fruit with desire, hanging in the air *(May I? Will you? Will we?)*, the very idea that you could be asked, be worthy and cherished enough for someone *to* ask, not just take—God, that was heady enough. But then, to think that you—that *I*—would want to say *yes*, and not just say it but murmur it, whisper it, moan it? I couldn't even imagine.

Well, all right, sometimes I imagined, but I only got about thirty seconds in before the blackness closed over my head and I became closet Lesley, of the shoved spine and musty hatboxes and uninvited knuckles and forcibly twined tongue, and that part of me didn't want a damn thing to do with *yes*. The fingers of her hand went right up in a paparazzi block, curved straight into a preemptive punch; they never slid down anywhere warm, or opened any blouse ribbons for an eager suitor. The only leaning she—no, say it right, *I*—did was away, pushed up against the wall I'd built for myself, repeating: *No. No. No.*

I wouldn't reach *yes* until Clare. But there in my room, underneath a dog-eared book by a dead one-eyed Irishman, a little catwalk between *no* and *yes* started to take shape, to scaffold.

And it freaked me the hell out. As did going to school and watching honey-haired girls move their lithe, buttery-limbed bodies through space like they deserved every good thing the world had to offer.

On top of that, I had to give a deposition, which is an interview, carried out by the opposing side's legal team, that's designed to make you feel so intimidated that you either screw up your story or cave from the pressure of the interrogation. And when I say "interrogation," I'm not at all exaggerating, because that torture dragged on for six hours. Six bloody *hours* of a microphone clipped to my blouse, of wires plugging me into their dirty machinery, of a court transcriptionist's keyboard *clack-clack*, of a video camera's voyeur lens recording my every lash-blink as my dad's so-licitor asked crap like, "How many sexual partners have you had?" *(Just your client, and it wasn't exactly a partnership.)* Or, my favorite: "Any chance you wanted to get back at your father for something?" *(Umm, other than the fact that he couldn't keep his privates private?)* Fishing around for every last crumb of stale bread that could point a trail back to *Lesley's a skank, Lesley's a liar.*

I wanted to pound the table, give them a "Fuck that fuck that fucking fuck that," shout back every cheeky answer that popped into my head. But I'd been told by my own solicitor to "refrain from engaging" with their attempts to wind me up.

"Don't worry," I told him. "I'm a disengagement pro."

And indeed I was. Ceiling to the rescue. Not a single sniffle. Which of course Dad's solicitors jumped on: "In all candor, Miss Holloway, you don't look the least bit trauma-tized."

I bit my lip. Felt the ceiling cave.

Can we stop, please? I scribbled to Francesca on her note-pad.

She read my query, then raised her hand. "Pardon me, gentlemen, but I believe your time is up."

And just like that, it stopped. She took me down the hall to her office, with its orchid plant on the desk and its corkboard with postcards from Venice and its little dishful of candies, which she let me unwrap, one by one by one, so my hands would have something to do other than uncontrollably shake.

"Sorry," I kept saying. "I'll refill it."

"Don't waste a second worrying." Francesca reached for a toffee. Popped it into her mouth. Worked its chewy center down to nothing with impressive demureness, then leaned forward towards me, so close I could glimpse the red glints she'd recently got put in her hair, tingeing its brunette ordinariness with sparks of spitfire.

"This will be over soon," she said.

And then it'll get better, I thought. *The girls at school will stop calling me "Scholarship Suck-up," and I'll buy new turquoise knickers and string some lights round the windows in my room at the hostel, and my dreams will stop being freak-show mash-ups where I feel his fingers yank my hair and watch my own fingers stroke shiny tresses until the wires cross and the blackness closes over my head and I wake up and thud my fist, slam slam slam, into my pitiful pillow.*

But the dreams weren't through with me yet. That night, when I startled out of their familiar terror, I got up and went down the kitchen, grabbed a pair of shears, and hacked off every inch of my own shoulder-length mousy blond hair.

All that earned me was an earful of snickers from Bettina and Co. the next morning, but I didn't care, imagining myself as . . . well, not butch, so much (I hadn't an awareness of what that meant yet), but definitely blunt-cut indie cool.

At least until lunch, when I went into the girls' toilets and stared in the mirror at myself and conceded that yeah, I really did look like shit. The rough yet flyaway fuzz atop my head, the harsh angles of my cheekbones, the recent resurgence of acne spots angrily dotting my face all made it clear: I was nothing but a scruffy waif. I reached out a finger, jabbed it at my reflection. In my head, backed by demented carnival music, Kate Bush was singing *"That girl in the mirror, between you and me, she-don't-stand-a-chance-at-getting-anywhere-at-all,"* her words precise yet slurry. I was suspended between a sob and a snarl.

Just then Mrs. Kremsky came out of a stall and noticed me standing by the sinks. "Hey, Lesley," she said, all chillaxed, as she rinsed her hands under the tap.

Indie cool, Les, indie cool, I told myself. "Hi, Miss."

She glanced over, still matter-of-fact, but I could sense a tautness to the way she looked at me. Like she'd figured it all out: me, feeling like utter crap, but also thoroughly invested in my game face.

"Short hair really suits you," she said.

I swiped at a smudge on the mirror. "Oh. Thanks. Reckon my stylist went a bit overboard, though."

Miss turned towards me, her arms loosely crossed, her head lowered with that crooked *been there myself* smile. For a moment, I pictured her as a teenager in a shadowy kitchen, her black-fingernailed hand poised for glinty-bladed attack.

"You know," she said, "I could try to even that out for you, if you wanted."

Of course I wanted. The idea of Miss smartening up my botched fury sounded like the best serendipitous gift since finding the Children's Services Team's phone number.

She nipped out to the supply closet and came back with a pair of scissors more delicate than the ones I'd used, but still substantial. "Wet the front for me?"

I dipped my hand beneath the faucet. Ran my dampened fingers through what little front I had left. Stood still as I could as she stepped up behind me, near enough to reach the tufts at the back of my neck, but not so close that we jostled each other. She was way taller than me, and I felt more than a little awed. "I didn't realize you did hair, Miss."

"Oh, I was a Manic Panic fan in a former life," she said, snipping at the bits by my ears. "Don't mind a modified Chelsea cut, do you?"

Ha, so she *had* been punk.

"Not at all," I said, closing my eyes so she could trim nearby.

When I opened them again, she tilted her head to appraise me. Made a contemplative *hrm hrm hrm* noise. "Little more, I'm thinking." Two decisive snips, and then she gestured for me to turn back around. "There. Have a look."

I looked. Raised my hands to my mouth in amazement. My sharp face and its bothersome bumps were still there, but she'd transformed my ragged cowlicks into something cropped and smooth enough to befit an edgy pixie.

"Holy shit," I said.

Bless her, Miss didn't bat an eyelash. "You might have to spike it into submission in the mornings," she said, "but other than that, totally low-maintenance."

I couldn't help grinning. "Loads better. Thank you."

"No problem." She turned to leave. "Exam on Eliot this afternoon. You ready?"

"Studied like mad."

Quick glance over her shoulder at me, along with a grin

back. "Good, because I outdid myself on the essay questions this time."

A few hours later, I strode into lit class with both a newfound swagger *(Say good-bye to "Scholarship Suck-up," Mallorca twats!)* and an insatiable need for a nap. Between the final reckoning of the till at the shop the night before and all that *Waste Land* reviewing, I'd not got to bed till two in the morning. As Mrs. Kremsky passed out our exams, I felt a yawn coming on and hurried to hide it with my palm.

"Ahh, no falling asleep on the dawn of modernism, now." Miss said it teasingly, but my face still burned.

While I scrawled out answers, I propped my head up on my left hand. Paused to drum my pencil atop the page, in the hope that its rhythm might keep me awake.

At the desk in front of mine, Gemma turned round in petulant whisper. "Some of us are trying to *work* here, if you've not noticed."

"All the more reason to save your grievances for the after-party," Miss said from the lectern.

My delight at that smackdown kept me going for another paragraph or so, but then my chin commenced slumping and my eyelids began to flutter.

Next I knew, I was lolling my head back up like a shit-faced turtle, just in time to see the others file out of the empty classroom and find Miss crouched down on her heels beside me.

"Ohmygod," I mumbled, rubbing my fingers over the bridge of my nose and my eyes. "I'm so sor—"

"Don't be. It's all right."

No, it wasn't. Not with a big blob of drool on my unfinished exam, and wisps of my freshly cut hair scattered all over the desk.

Miss reached over and put her hand on my arm. For a minute or so, we just stared at each other, silent. A welcome change from my weekly meetings with Francesca, whose cheery kindnesses filled up every spare space, whose staccato bursts of questions (not that I could fault them; she had to ask) came rapid-fire: "Do you feel safe at the hostel? Are you keeping up at school? Do you need me to liaise with your solicitor? With your mum?" (*Please. No. Just sit here, and be with me.*)

Around Miss, I felt I didn't have to talk. Which, strangely enough, made me want to.

"I work," I said. "Eats up all my evening. And the trip out here on the tube, it's an hour and a half, easy."

"Where are you commuting in from?"

"Islington."

Her mouth turned down in a grimace. "No rest for the weary on that Northern Line, is there?"

I shook my head.

"Listen," she said. "I can give you a ride here and back."

I bit my lip. Stared down at my half-finished exam.

"And I won't be offended if you think that's too weird."

"No, no," I said, looking up. "I just hate to make you go out of your way for—"

"It's not out of my way. I live a few blocks from Angel station." She gave my arm a squeeze, then let go. "Think about it, okay?"

• • •

I didn't have to think long. Come the next Monday, I was standing outside the hostel with my schoolbag on my shoulder, watching Mrs. Kremsky's dark-gray Volkswagen pull up to the front door.

"Nice, very nice," she said from the driver's seat, with a nod towards my spiked hair. "Have you had breakfast yet?"

I shook my head.

"Well, then." She reached over and plucked a paper bag from atop the dashboard. "Take your pick."

I peered inside to find a pair of scones. Cranberry-orange and chocolate chip.

"Aww, bless," I said. "You didn't have to."

"Yes, I did," she said, smiling. "No way I'm braving the congestion zone without a Costa Coffee run."

She gestured towards one of the plastic-lidded cups nestled near the gearshift. "I hope hazelnut with copious amounts of cream works."

A real flipping latte. I lifted it in both hands, inhaling.

"*Oh*," I said after the first sip, my voice unfurling in a satiated sigh. "It so does."

She glanced over at me. Smiled again. "Good."

We drove the rest of the way in silence, sipping at our drinks, brushing crumbs from our laps. I'm not one to go in for thoughts about the afterlife, but let me tell you, that trip was heaven, from the roomy leather seat with the internal heat that kept my spine toasty to the warm flaky sugar that dissolved on my tongue.

Next day, it was the same thing: hello, coffee, pastries,

conversation-less inch northbound. You had to hand it to Miss for being down with that level of awkward reticence. I mean, she very well may have had an inner Francesca popping up like an overeager student, waving her hand, going, "Ooh! Ask Lesley about her tragic situation! Educate her about literary theory! Make small talk about weather, or traffic, or school!," but if so, she did an excellent job of keeping her quiet.

Which isn't to say that we didn't communicate at all, because we did plenty. Mainly through Miss's CD collection, which was a remarkably ecumenical glovebox stash ranging from punk to classical. She'd take a sloshy swallow of her coffee, glance over. "What'll it be today, Les?"

"Vivaldi," I'd say, if I wanted to lean my head against the window and doze. "The Clash," I'd suggest, if I had an exam that morning and needed to get pumped up.

One day I brought "Best of the Screaming Women" along in my bag, just for the hell of it. When I handed it over to her to play on the drive home, Miss took one look at the marker-drawn label and gave me a thumbs-up.

"Oh my God," she said, chuckling, when the first Kate Bush track came on. "Last time I heard this, Maggie Thatcher was still in office and I was holed up in Bloomsbury, writing a thesis on my boy James."

"You moved here for university?" I asked.

She paused for a moment, chewing her lip as if debating whether to say more, then nodded. "Nineteen years, this country's been stuck with me."

"Well, it ought to be grateful."

Her chuckle bloomed into a full-on laugh. "Campaigning for a shorter book assignment for next month, are we?"

"No," I said. "I mean it."

She reached over like she was about to give my arm a squeeze again, but then her mobile rang, and she scurried to turn down the music and answer.

"Hey, you." I could tell from her tone—breezy but alert—that it was her year-older-than-me son phoning. "Mmm. And whom are you going with? . . . No, it's fine, I just wanted to know. . . . And you've got money for dinner? . . . All right. Have fun, darlin'."

She finished with him and turned the CD back up just as the song about the evil house-invading spirit came on, all bellows and wails. I drummed my stuttery fingers along the armrest on the passenger side, in time to the door-slammy percussion. Felt myself leave myself.

By the time I came back down, Miss had already turned onto Liverpool Road. "Still with me, Les?" There was an endearing smudge of lipstick on her front tooth, from her pensive what-to-divulge gnawing.

"Yes," I said.

You'd think that those casual-but-warm hours spent in Miss's car would have given me a glimmer of hope, a bright spot, same as my nascent *Ulysses* catwalk, but they didn't. Every time her son rang, I felt a prickly skin-crawl of envy, a different flavor of desire: to be called "darlin'," to be offered dinner money that wasn't dispensed out a government envelope, to have someone "just want to know" for reasons other than a Children's Services file update.

And then I'd get out of the toasty car with my gone-cold

coffee, wave good-bye to Miss like she was merely my colleague, and take that longing with me, wrapped round my shoulders like a moth-eaten cloak while I swept up the chip shop or sat at my desk-slash-dresser eating my dinner of instant noodles, fighting the urge to . . . what? Cry? Stomp about? March into the hall and fling myself at the first Pervy McPerv I saw, in a desperate, misguided attempt at procuring some affection?

The conventional wisdom, dispensed via countless young adult novels, goes something like this: Our fragile-yet-fierce heroine, in a desperate, misguided attempt to procure some dulling of her pain, stompmarched down the kitchen, dodging a phalanx of Pervy McPervs, and reached, not for kitchen shears this time, but for a knife with which (tears rolling down her cheeks all the while) she numbed her unspeakable agony with one deftly executed forearm slash.

To which I say: *Complete and utter bollocks.*

My even having the knife was an accident. We were working on paper projects in art class, wending our fine blades along dark pages to craft shapes and symbols, leaves and faces. The teacher called mine "winsome and affecting," and was keen to chat with me about putting them in the school magazine, but I had to politely edge past, because I had English next, and I'd be damned if I was showing up late for that. "Dead flattered, really," I said, scooping up my books, inadvertently stuffing the capped blade in my cardigan pocket. "Have to dash."

To be honest, I wasn't just brushing her off for Mrs.

Kremsky; I was also dodging doling out the information I had to give all my teachers, based on what Francesca had told me the last time we'd met for lunch at Pret.

Miss, I reckoned, would be the perfect person to test the explanation waters on, so I ran like mad to get to her classroom. Could have talked about it in the car that morning, sure, but I didn't want a brief FYI to turn into a Serious Conversation, even with her.

"London Marathon's not till April," she said, laughing a little, as I came barreling in.

"So, umm," I said, pausing to gasp, "I need to let you know that I'll not be in class three weeks from Thursday."

"No?" Attendance was a big deal at Hawthorn Hill. There were allowances made for the Mallorca/Ibiza crowd, of course, but overall the headmistress was pretty obsessed with racking up stellar statistics to present to her funders at their annual gala.

I shook my head. "No. It's an excused absence, though."

"Everything all right?"

"Yeah, I just . . ." Seeing the ringleaders sashay in, I leaned in a little closer, lowering my voice. "I have to testify in court. For —"

"Mrs. Kremsky," Bettina announced, slamming her Mulberry purse down on her desk, "that piece you had us read for today was rubbish."

"Spoken like a true *Times Literary Supplement* reviewer," Miss called to her before turning back to me and touching my shoulder. "It's fine, Lesley."

* * *

When we got in the car that afternoon, Miss didn't start the engine or load a CD for the drive, but instead sat there for a moment, her right elbow propped against the window as she ran her fingers nervously over her chin.

"Listen," she said. "Whatever's going on with you and this court case—"

"Don't worry. It's not *my* trial."

She looked over at me. "You," she said, shaking her head, "are the last person I would suspect of criminal behavior."

Who you putting your money on, then? Bettina? I wanted to shoot back, but all I could do was pose a shy question. "How . . . how much did Headmistress Fallon tell you?"

"Just that you live on your own, and that your social worker is your emergency contact."

I let my breath out slowly.

"Oh, good," I said. "I keep thinking she's sent around a memo, telling the faculty—"

"All your business? No, and I'd have had a concerned chat with her if she had."

Whew. Miss was still on my side.

"Now, having said that," she said, "if you ever *∂o* want to talk, I'm more than willing."

I rubbed a loose thread on my skirt, twirling it.

"Totally your call. I know from experience that sometimes you need to tell, and other times you need people to stop asking."

Shut up, I thought. *Shut up before I lean my head into your lap and bawl.*

"I'm good," I said. "But thanks."

• • •

On the way home, Miss put in a classical disc, one I'd never heard before. All cello solos, so gorgeous I could feel them resonate in my chest.

"God, that's ace," I said.

"Isn't it? I think it has something to do with the fact that cellos are the closest instrument to the human voice."

"So it's like it's singing to you?"

"Yeah. Of course, it could also be because it's my mother playing."

"On here? No way."

"Mmm-hmm." She handed me the case, whose graceful, curving letters read *Darkness/Brightness: Selections by Caroline Merchant*. Beneath the title was a photo of a classy older woman sporting frosted-blond hair and a string of pearls, her cello tucked demurely between her long-skirted knees.

"Wow, she looks nothing like you," I said.

Miss laughed. "She's not much like me, either." That very well could have come off like a dig, but the way she said it was tender, as if their differences were a long-standing source of affectionate amusement for them both.

As we reentered the congestion zone, a light rain began to spatter on the windows. I huddled tight inside my coat, feeling relieved when the CD's final poignant note drifted into silence.

When Miss pulled up outside the hostel, I made no effort to move. Didn't even unfasten my seat belt. Just sat there, watching the moistness sluice down the glass.

"Okay, so," I said. "The trial's about my dad. He's the reason I ran away. And my mum's standing by him, even though she knows everything he . . ." I couldn't finish.

Miss turned to face me, her gray-eyed gaze intense.

"You're not the only one," she said softly. "I'm an escape artist, too."

"What do you—"

"College wasn't the only reason I left America." Her voice was strong, her head held high; nothing in her shook or quavered, but I could tell she was taking a huge risk, opening up to me like that, and knew it.

"Your dad," I said.

She nodded. "I couldn't take it anymore. All those hungry glances."

"And your mum?"

"Checked out. In denial. Dreaming of a symphony chair."

"Did you press charges?"

She shook her head. "There . . . there weren't official grounds to—"

"So he didn't actually fuck you."

"Excuse me?" Her voice was hard now.

"No offense," I said, "but if he didn't sneak into your room at night and yank off your knickers, you've no right acting like you understand."

She put up one hand. "Okay, look, you're absolutely correct that emotional incest isn't the same thing, but—"

"What?" I said, undoing my seat belt with a snap. "You want me to sit here and say, 'Oh, thank you for sharing, Miss, I'm so glad we're kindred spirits'?"

She shifted back so that she faced her window. "No," she said, sighing. "I just wanted to —"

"Don't bother." I wrenched the passenger door handle, jumping up and deserting her with a slam.

Upstairs, back in my room, I tore off my jacket and paced round the room, fuming — not at Mrs. Kremsky, but at myself. Never mind her right to say those things; *I'd* had no right to mouth off at her like that. Stupid, stupid, stupid.

I sat down on the bed and flipped open my geometry book, trying to distract myself with hard angles and precise measurements, but it didn't work. Minutes later, I was up again, stride, turn, stride over the linoleum, my fingers raking the gelled spikes of my hair.

You idiot, I told myself. *She was the closest thing you had to a mentor, nearest thing you had to a friend.*

My right hand reached down into the pocket of my cardigan. Found the X-Acto knife. At first, my thumb merely toyed with its cap, but then my skin did a little dance, worming under the plastic, playing along the edge of the blade, anxious little tic, fiddle, fiddle, fiddle, while I paced. I thought of Miss's elegant, poised face, her carefully chosen words, her gift of her younger self's vulnerability, offered up to me as solace.

I sat down on the bed again. Slipped the knife from my pocket. Wrenched the cap off. Shoved my left sleeve up. Poked the metal tip into my wrist. Prick prick prick, delicate and precise as pointillism. Little punitive droplets, like the ping of rain. Take that, and that, and *that*.

Didn't make me feel better, but it at least calmed me down enough that I could prop up on my pillow and have another go at geometry. In the morning, I woke shaky and nauseated, mentally replaying every pointed word and bitter shout of my argument with Miss. The thought of facing her in class made my stomach churn even worse than when Francesca told me about the gyno appointment.

I had to make it out of bed somehow, so I reached down and grabbed the recapped knife from where I'd been using it as a placeholder in my textbook. Didn't take more than a minute of poke-poke-poke to get my feet swung over the mattress and onto the floor.

When I was finished, I tucked the blade inside my bag's side pocket. Promised myself I'd return it to the art workshop closet at lunch, but I never did.

4

I wouldn't call self-harm an addiction, but I have to admit that once you start, it's incredibly difficult to stop. Mainly because it serves a crucial function: it *works*. Otherwise, without any payoff, there'd be no reason to keep doing such a bizarre, terrible thing to yourself.

And when I say "payoff," I'm not talking about feeling good, like a drug high. I mean, there's a certain level of endorphin rush, sure. A relief so swooping you might mistake it for rapture, when in reality it's a mechanism for survival.

Well, make that multiple mechanisms. Most people assume, of course, that there's one overarching reason for why every self-harmer does it. A bespoke explanation, tailored to each individual silent sufferer, perhaps, but still a conveniently packaged, singular summation of motive and result and need:

She does it in order to feel.

She does it to regain control over her own body.

She does it to punish herself.

She does it so that, in its aftermath, she can nurture herself.

(Check. Check. Check. Check.)

For me, once I got going, compulsive self-harm was like an emotional utility belt. I cut myself when I couldn't stop crying. I cut myself when I couldn't cry. I cut myself when I thought of my mum or Mrs. Kremsky, and how I'd (inadvertently or deliberately) hurt them. I cut myself so that I could roll my sleeve back down and stroke my sore arm and whisper "There now, Lesley-lovely." I even cut myself because I was angry at myself for cutting.

By the time my dad's court date rolled around the first week in November, I was doing it several times a day. Just enough to take the edge off, easy to cover. Not like anyone would have noticed; Francesca was busy flitting from client to client, and Mrs. Kremsky had decided (after apologizing for "overstepping" her "bounds") that it wasn't a good idea for us to commute together anymore.

During the trial, I had to leave my X-Acto knife at home because of the metal detectors, but I managed. My solicitor arranged for me to give my testimony remotely, so I wouldn't have to see my dad, and the Victims' Services people got me all set up in a nice comfy room with a leather couch like a giant marshmallow, and a TV, and heaps of soda and crisps in a little towel-lined basket. How surreal, but also comforting, it was to kick back and pop in a comedy DVD and get the giggles along with Francesca, who kept pouring and refilling and reassuring me that all I had to do was get through the day.

When my solicitor came in to tell me I'd be going on the

satellite link to the courtroom in a few minutes, I imagined myself beamed in from Hollywood—a distaff Flavor Flav, perhaps, sporting gold chains and a giant clock. *(What time is it, y'all? It's Ceiling Escape Time, bitches!)*

"I'm gonna rock this," I said to Francesca.

She smiled. "Of course you will."

I sat up straight in the mauve Topshop blouse she'd helped me pick out. Laced my hands in my lap so I wouldn't reach for her.

You are not a skank, I told myself. *You are not a liar.*

But then the camera's beady eye clicked on, and I froze, tongue-tied by Mum's shame. *Umm. Err. Ahh.*

My paralysis ascended into panic. My hands slid apart. Bunched into fists.

Fuck that fuck that fucking fuck that.

I blew out my breath. Forced my gaze to go soft. Let the edges of the walls and my body blur so that I could answer the barrister's questions.

Yes, he said he'd kill me if I told.

Yes, he'd haul off and hit me across the face if I didn't get on my knees.

Yes, he threw out my birth control pills because he was convinced I was sleeping with a boy in my class.

Yes, I got the pills because he didn't care what might happen.

They sentenced him to five years in prison. Afterwards, for the few seconds I saw her outside, my mum gave me the telling-off of my life. Tottering down the courthouse steps after me in her heels, roaring with a fury I'd never heard emerge from her mouth before. "You little bitch. Are you happy now?"

Francesca put an arm around me. "Come on, Lesley," she said. "Just keep moving."

But I couldn't. I turned around to face her. "Nobody won, Mum," I said softly.

"How could you just sit there, Lesley?" she sobbed. "How could you say all that so calmly, like none of it mattered?"

I hadn't the time or the words to explain that the reason I looked so numb and cold was because it *did* matter to me, so much I couldn't bear it.

That night at the chip shop, as I poured hot oil into the deep fryer, I pictured myself plunging my arms in there, too. I could sense my brain ramping up, tuning its off-kilter orchestra, the keening sounds all Darkness, no Brightness. Soon as I got home, I scrabbled in my schoolbag pocket for the blade. Sliced a little deeper than usual on the inside of my forearm. Slipped my silky blouse down carefully so that it wouldn't stain.

After that, I thought I'd be all set for sleep, but instead I tossed and turned. I tried to relax by putting my headphones in, but soon as Kate Bush came on warbling "Mother . . . stands for comfort," I flung the CD player across the room, my head echoing with both the thunk and a thought: *It's not over. It'll never be.*

I ended up pacing first my room, then the hall, in nothing but my T-shirt and knickers. No one came out and saw me, thankfully, but I wouldn't have cared if they had. In my insomniac stupor, I felt both invincible and broken. My mind was on the ceiling, but my body whimpered to be found: not by the Pervy McPervs, but by a cool, gentle hand that would clasp mine and lead me back down the corridor, accompanied by a voice murmuring, *Come now, let's tuck you into bed.*

By morning, my exhaustion had graced me with a fierce, almost feral, caginess. I stompmarched my way through the tube turnstile, down the escalator, and onto a packed train. Bristled along the corridors of Hawthorn Hill with a detached haughtiness so unlike me that Gemma and Bettina glanced at each other, bewildered and (I imagined, I hoped) impressed.

Round about lunchtime, though, I began to crash. The lights above my head took on blurry, menacing shapes; the dining hall's Friday afternoon chatter echoed so hard it hurt. I felt like a tuning fork struck too hard, the hum in my chest all agitated buzz.

On my way to the toilets, I passed Mrs. Kremsky, who glanced at me with a look of concern. "Feeling all right, Lesley?"

"Yeah, sure." I put one palm up, waving her off as I smacked the loo door open with my other hand. For a second I was afraid she'd follow me, but she didn't.

Inside, the stalls were empty, the room quiet except for the thump-hiss of a radiator. I went for the disabled toilet and sat down on the floor to dig in my rucksack. Once I'd snaked my blade out of its side pocket, I shoved the bag under me as a cushion. Reckoned I'd be there a while.

Leaning back against the tiled wall, I shrugged off my cardigan. Unbuttoned the wrinkly cuff of my school blouse. Rolled it up all the way to my elbow.

My fingers shook as I flicked the cap off the knife. I tipped my head back. Closed my eyes. The loo door swung.

My eyes flew open. I sat still and silent as I could, my breath held.

Clack, clack went a pair of high-heeled boots. *Click, click* went the latch of a stall. I could hear whoever was in there humming a poppy chorus, its melody miles away from the discordant sounds of the Screaming Women. Flush, *click*, another *clack*, another swing and, oblivious, she was gone.

I got out my CD player and put in my headphones. Closed my eyes again. Let the blade play lightly, breaking nothing, as the opening scritchy-scratch of "Sour Times" merged with the radiator's bang.

Wasn't more than a matter of seconds before I was up on the ceiling, floating in a warm, languid space, all toasty spine and sugary mouthful, soft maternal hand leading me back to crawl under my fluffy turquoise duvet.

I didn't realize how long I'd been working the blade until I felt a gush, vague but sticky with ooze. I opened my eyes, stared down at my left arm, and almost fainted.

From my wrist clear down to the middle of my forearm, the skin was a jagged gape, like one of those rubber coin purses right when you've squeezed it open to slip your money in.

I dropped the blade to the floor. Hurried to press my cardigan sleeve to the wound. When I pulled the fabric away to check its flow, I was greeted with a fresh spurt that arched like a tiny fountain.

Shit. Shit. Shit.

Dizzy now, I crawled to the stall door and pulled myself up by its latch. Staggered out to the sinks, my gait wobbly. I couldn't look in the mirror. Couldn't look down at the dribbly trail I knew I was leaving. All I could do was yank paper towels from the dispenser on the wall. Stupid of me, I know—I mean, if thick wool wasn't stopping anything, rough little paper scraps were hardly going to save the day. But still I pulled and pulled, dabbed and dabbed, until my knees buckled under me and I fell to the floor.

My gaze went gray and prickly. Off in the distance, coming closer, I could hear Bettina teasing Gemma about her date for the Bonfire Night fireworks over the coming weekend. "*That* wanker? Are you out of your head?"

As she opened the loo door, her snicker turned to a scream. "Oh my God. Look."

Terrified, hiccupy gasps. Retreating feet.

I stared up at the ceiling lights. Watched them flicker. My pulse felt like bored, anxious fingers tapping against my neck. I rolled over onto my back, draping my bad arm over my chest as Gemma and Bettina burst back in with Mrs. Kremsky.

"I've no idea, Miss. Gem and I just found her like that."

"Is there anything we can—"

"Get the nurse. I'll stay with her."

My eyes flickered closed. I let out a little moan.

"Lesley." I felt the slender warmth of Miss's knees next to my head. "What happened?"

"Ceiling," I mumbled. "Went too far."

Her fingers clasped mine, gently extending my hurt arm to the side for a better view. She let out her breath. "Jesus."

I heard the whip of fabric, then felt the press of starchy linen wound around and around in a tight, efficient circle. My arm throbbed so hard I tried to jerk away.

"Don't." She held my arm fast, raising it high at an angle above my head.

I opened my eyes to see her crouched there, bare-shouldered, in a white camisole, her long-sleeved blouse re-purposed as a tourniquet.

"You're ace, Miss." I closed my eyes again. Felt myself drift.

"Don't go anywhere, Les." She shook my shoulder.

"Not going," I said. "Just sleepy."

She cupped her free palm against my cheek. Her skin was so warm, so dry, next to mine's clammy sweat.

"I know, honey," she said softly. "But you need to stay awake, okay?"

Yes, closet Lesley nodded.

Door swing. "Miss, Nurse Kennedy is ringing for an ambulance."

A whole audience now, their feet shuffling side to side in twitchy fear.

"Cold," I said hoarsely.

Miss, in her best *I'm so not messing around* voice. "Give her your cardigans."

One by one, the girls nervously stepped up. Gemma had snot dotting the hollow under her nose; Bettina's mascara was tear-smudged into raccoony half-moons. As they draped their cardies over me and Miss murmured for me to stay with her, I wondered: *Had* I died? Was this some sort of motherless-daughter heaven?

For a moment I drifted again, comforted, but when I heard the squeaky roll of a trolley coming closer down the corridor, every soft place in me went rigid. Blurry-eyed and shivering, I looked over at Miss. Mouthed the word *scared*.

Soon as I said it, her brows furrowed with a sorrowful cramp, her face melting into empathetic softness.

Nurse Kennedy flung the door open. "Stand back, girls."

They huddled obediently by the disabled stall as two male medics pushed the trolley inside. Soon as I saw its black webbed straps, I completely lost it, shaking my head back and forth, babbling *nonononono* as the medics motioned Miss back and squatted, one on either side, to unearth me from beneath the pile of woolens and pick me up.

"Just relax, love," one of them said. I wanted to spit at him, but my mouth was too dry.

"Any of you coming with?" the other asked.

"I am," Nurse Kennedy said.

"No." My voice spiraled higher. "I want Miss."

Over by Gemma, I saw Miss bow her head and swallow.

"Lesley," Nurse Kennedy said, "I'm required to accompany any student who's injured on school grounds."

I struggled to sit up, swatting at the medics, who were trying to fasten the straps over me. "Stop. Stop it. I'm not going without her."

Nurse Kennedy and Miss glanced at each other, and then Miss broke through the throng, edging over to take my outstretched hand. I lay back. Let them buckle me tight.

They pushed the trolley so fast Miss had to run to keep up, her hair flying free of its topknot, her shoes' heels scraping the front steps in time to the wheels' rocky bounce. I lifted my head off the pillow for a second, taking in the school's brick grandeur for what I sensed would be the last time.

Inside the ambulance, the medics stationed Miss at my head and cranked my mattress all the way down. As it creaked backwards, as I fell backwards, the terror rose in me again.

One of the medics grabbed my good arm. Swabbed it with antiseptic. The muscles in my neck clenched.

"Don't hurt me," I whimpered. "Please please please don't hurt me."

The other medic shook his head. "Flipping hell. Nearly severs her own artery, and she's worried about *us*?"

"She's an abuse survivor," Miss snapped. "And you've got no right to speak about her like that." She leaned her mouth down to my ear. "He's just putting a drip in, sweetheart. No one's going to hurt you. I promise."

When the needle pierced my skin, I squeezed my eyes shut. On my other arm, I could feel the hurried unspooling of Miss's blouse, followed by the shock of air and gauze's rough sting. I let out a small, sharp cry.

"Shh, shh." Miss leaned over me, cradling my head in her hands. "Let them help you."

As she ducked down, her long, loosened hair fell around me, smelling faintly of rosemary shampoo, ushering me behind a dark veil.

When I awoke in a room at the Accident and Emergency department, it was to the startling sight of a clear bag full of blood dangling from a pole above my head. *They fixed me*, I thought. *It's all over*.

But then I felt a stiff ache in my shoulder, and the heat of an examination lamp's glare. I turned my head to see my bad arm splayed across a small metal table, beside which a male doctor sat perched on a rolling stool.

I glanced to the other side of my bed. "Where's Mrs. Kremsky?"

"You mean that half-dressed American who came in with you? Out in the corridor, on the phone."

When I heard the plasticky snap of his pulled-on gloves, the fingers of my pulse drummed along my neck once more. "What are you—"

"Suturing this mess you've made."

I turned my head to see him reach back onto the counter for a paper-draped tray. As he swiftly brought it down to rest next to my elbow, I glimpsed the neat lineup of instruments: tweezers, scissors, an elongated needle threaded with what looked like hairy black silk.

I was just about to rear up from the mattress in fright when Miss swooped back in like a superheroine. They'd given her a blanket, which she'd draped loosely around her shoulders like an ecru shawl. She looked tired and rumpled, but still beautiful and badass, as she shot an appraising glance at the doctor. "You're giving her anesthetic, aren't you?"

"Waste of drugs." His face and his voice were one massive sneer. "She's obviously fine with pain."

My chin jerked from the tray to the doctor to Miss as my mind stuttered. *Oh my God oh my God oh my God, they really are going to hurt m—*

"One quick call to her social worker," Miss said. "That's all it would take to open a malpractice investigation."

The doctor blanched. "I'll have a nurse bring in a seda-tive." Balky pause. "And a local injection."

"Thank you." Miss scraped a chair up next to me, sat down, and reached a hand through the bed's slats to hold my good one. I squeezed so hard her wedding ring dug into my fingers, no doubt hurting both of us, but I didn't care.

A nurse brought me a Valium in a paper cup, and the doctor a syringe. When he loaded it up and my chest began to tighten, Miss moved her chair closer. "Deep breaths, Les," she said. "Just keep looking at me, all right?"

I nodded. Felt the searing squirt of liquid, and then numbness. Every few seconds there came a faint tug, fol-lowed by the creepy sound of a tied-off ligature's snip. Each time I wanted to yank away or cry out, I fixed my gaze on Miss's steady one.

My tranquilizer kicked in well before he finished up. When I emerged from the chemical haze, I found my arm encased in a sturdy bandage that looked like white-and-red Christmas paper.

In the pushed-back chair next to me, Miss was dozing, her chin bent down onto her shoulder at an uncomfortable-looking angle.

"Miss?" I said.

She lurched up with a snorty start. "Huh?" Dazed eye-rub. "Whoa. Sorry. Didn't mean to nod off there."

"S'okay," I mumbled.

She pulled her chair in close again. Leaned over the bed. Reached a hand down to the collapsed spikes of my hair, brushing them back from my forehead more softly, more sweetly, than anyone had in as long as I could remember.

Part of me wanted her to stop so that I wouldn't break in a million pieces, and part of me wanted her to keep doing it forever. She must have seen the conflicted look on my face, because she slipped her hand away, letting it hover above my scalp, questioning. "What is it?"

I swallowed. Blinked fast. "Hurts," I managed to croak out, just before I burst into tears.

Her face melted again. "Oh, lovey." She pushed the guardrail down so that there was no metal gate separating us, and hoisted herself onto the mattress to enfold me in her arms.

Wet-faced and mewling, I sank into her. She drew my cheek against her shoulder with one hand, rubbing my back with the other as she rocked me.

"I'm sorry," I sobbed, lifting my head. "I'm so sorry."

She took my face in her hands, tipping it back to wipe my damp eyes with her thumbs. "I know you are," she said. "But the only thing you need to worry about right now is getting better."

She leaned over to pluck a wad of tissues from a box by the sink. "Here. Blow your nose."

Dutifully, I blew. "They're—they're not going to keep me here, are they?"

She bit her lip. "Well, I'm not sure. Francesca will have to talk things over with the doctors."

"She's coming?"

Miss nodded. "Soon as she gets out of a meeting."

"And you'll . . . you'll stay with me until—"

"Of course I will." She drew her arm around my shoulder, and I leaned back into her.

"I don't want to go into hospital," I whispered.

"Nobody does, darlin'. Especially not for something like this. But it could be the best way for you to—"

I pulled away. "You don't know that."

"Yes." Her voice was grave. "I do."

My brows furrowed. "What—"

"It's a long story." She stood and motioned for me to lie down again. "Here, get comfortable while we talk."

I expected her to duck back to her chair, but she returned to the edge of my bed.

"Not long after I moved here," she said, spreading her blanket over me, "I fell in love with an English guy. We got married young. Had our son, spent ten obscenely happy years together, and then he got cancer. Dead at thirty-one."

"God, Miss," I said softly. "I can't even imagine."

"Well," she said, "I had a couple months of self-absorbed sleepwalking, and then my mother flew over to help me out—"

"Wait, the clueless cello player?"

She smiled. "Yeah. We patched things up so well that I decided to move back to America and take a big-shot headmistress job at an international school in Washington, D. C."

"So you got yourself sorted out."

She shook her head. "Oh, no. That was just an overachiever prelude to my real crash, on the first anniversary of his death. I spent the day in back-to-back meetings, so busy I barely had time to think about it. Dropped Curran off at a sleepover. Came home, went in the bathroom to get ready for bed. Figured I'd brush my teeth, crawl under the covers, and have myself a good cry, but then . . ."

She glanced away for a moment, then turned back to me, her gaze solemn but solid.

"When I looked up from the sink and stared in the mirror, I saw a complete stranger. Who was she? Who was I? I literally had no idea. So I tried to orient myself by looking down at my hands. Tilted them from side to side. I could see their movement, but I couldn't feel the motion. I had no idea where the air ended and my body began."

I stared down at the pale-blue diamond print of my hospital gown. Thought of the ceiling.

"I know what that feels like," I whispered.

Miss gave me a soft nod of affirmation, and continued. "I put my palms up to the glass. Slid them along the outlines of the face staring back. I tried to conjure up the me whose mouth had kissed him, whose fingers had stroked her son's hair. But I couldn't. And so I started slamming my hands against the mirror, trying to break my own reflection."

I pictured blood and glass, shards and splinters. "You didn't—"

"Oh, no, no." Her mouth turned downwards in a fearful frown. "Is this too much for you, sweetheart? Hearing about it? Because I can stop if you—"

"No," I said. "Go on. I want to hear."

She relaxed into relief. "Just then," she said, "my best friend called me from London. I managed to pick up the phone, but all I could do was ramble. 'Lost my edges, lost my edges,' I kept repeating." She swallowed. "And then I started babbling about needing to hurt myself to find them.

"At that point, he begged me to go to the hospital. I kept protesting, saying I couldn't, that no way was I leaving

Curran for that long. And he kept pushing back, saying: 'No. You need to be safe. Curran needs you to be safe.' When he told me that, I felt myself, the mother in me, rise up, just for an instant."

Her voice shook a little. "I've done a lot of difficult things in my life. I've held my husband's head over a bowl so he could retch from chemo. I've told an eight-year-old his father was gone and never coming back. But that was, without a doubt, the hardest thing I have ever done."

"Were you afraid?"

"Oh my God, yes. I had no idea what an inpatient unit would be like, so I imagined the worst. Plus I felt like such a failure."

"A failure?" I repeated.

She nodded. "I'd sworn up and down I'd never be like my father."

"Was he ill?" I asked. "I mean, other than the fact that he—"

She nodded. "Committed suicide not long after I came over here."

Wistful, I closed my eyes. "I'd be throwing a flipping party if my dad did that."

Her tone was measured, with just a hint of a challenging edge. "Would you?"

"Oh, yeah. I mean . . ." I opened my eyes again. "Weren't you glad?"

"No," Miss said softly. "But I *was* angry."

She glanced away again, as if embarrassed. "At the time, it seemed like such a pathetic, selfish thing for him to do. I just assumed that sanity, that stability, was a simple matter of sucking it up and not giving in."

She looked back at me. "But that night, going up to the triage window and telling the nurse I needed a psychiatric evaluation, I — I realized it had nothing to do with being strong enough, because at that moment, what was happening in my mind was far, far bigger than I was."

"Did they section you?"

She shook her head. "I admitted myself voluntarily. Took a few hours for them to find me a bed, so I wound up waiting in a glass-walled cubicle."

"What — what did you do all that — "

"Huddled under the blankets and stayed on the line with Jascha until our mobile phones went dead. Last thing he said to me was 'You're brave as fuck, and I love you.'" She ducked her head shyly. "We're married now. Five years in December."

The thought made me smile. "What was your wedding like?" Normally I didn't go for that daydreamy, girlish crap, but in the moment what I longed for was a delicious distraction.

"Well, we had a Russian Orthodox ceremony. Mainly to keep my mother-in-law, Vera, from disowning us, but — "

"What did you wear?"

"Oh, that was a matter of much debate, let me tell you. *My* mother, of course, found some prissy lavender number she was gunning for."

I made a face.

"Yeah, that's what I thought, too. Threatened to dress

like a Soviet-era prostitute if she didn't stop going on." She tucked her blanket tighter around me. "We eventually settled on red velvet."

I imagined Miss walking down the aisle of some Gothic, icon-studded cathedral in the dead of winter, silvery snow crystals dusted in her upswept black hair. Smashing. "Did you wear combat boots?"

She chuckled. "Matching heels."

"Damn. And your flowers?"

"Pale, pale roses."

I could almost inhale them, their silken sweetness mingled with the sharp waft of incense. "Pretty."

From outside my door came the rumble of a food cart. I smelled meat and starch and gravy, and my stomach, empty since breakfast, let loose a roar.

"Your stunningly mediocre dinner is served." Miss pulled over one of those bedside tables that swing out like a bridge across you, and set down my tray: grayish Salisbury steak, a pallid plop of potato mash, and a cupful of pears floating in gelatinous syrup.

She was right about it being blah, but I didn't mind—at least not until I spied the cellophane-wrapped set of plastic cutlery. Even tucked inside a paper napkin, the inept knife both beckoned and tormented me.

When she saw my stricken face, Miss grabbed the packet and hastily tore it open. "Shall I cut that up for you?"

Not like I could do it, anyways, what with one numb hand and another taped with drip lines, so I nodded. Miss bent down with matter-of-fact efficiency, her hair swinging to the side to reveal her bare shoulder blade, on which the red-and-purple-inked image of a phoenix gleamed.

"Your tattoo is ace," I said. "Did it hurt?"

She slid one finger under my milk carton's tab to open its bland mouth. "Like hell."

"Was it worth it, though?"

A hint of a smile as she loosened a straw from its paper casing. "Oh, yeah."

I'd already devoured the anemic steak and was tucking into my fruit cup when I heard voices in the hallway.

"You do understand that . . . doesn't cooperate . . . have to section her?" Another male doctor, older sounding than Mr. Stingy Anesthetic.

"Yes. Of course." Francesca.

I set my spoon down. "Miss," I said, my voice trembling.

Miss turned from where she stood stretching by the end of the gurney. "Hmm?"

"When you went into hospital, how long were you there?"

"Just three days."

A long weekend. I tried to picture myself back at school on Tuesday, my battle scars hidden, but couldn't.

"And did it . . . did it help?"

Miss ran her hands over her bare arms. "Yes," she said. "It did."

A few minutes later, Francesca came in, crisp and bustling in her aubergine-colored suit, carrying a bin bag full of my clothes. When I saw her flustered face, my shame rose, swift and potent as my earlier panic.

"Francesca," I said, my lips quaking. "I didn't mean to be any trouble, really, I —"

"Don't apologize," she said, patting my good hand, which had just got freed from its drip. "You've been through so much."

I glanced at the bag. "What's that for?"

"Well, I've had a chat with the psychiatrist on staff," Francesca said, her voice brightening back into its usual *Hello, my name is Francesca, and I'll be your bureaucratic hostess this evening* tone, "and we decided it'd be best if you stayed here for a bit. Just out of concern for your —"

"Give me the paperwork," I said.

Francesca looked surprised, as if she'd been expecting me to throw a tantrum. "Good on you. What a trouper."

After I'd signed the consent form, Miss smoothed my blanket and Francesca switched off the overhead light so I could rest. When I drifted this time, it was into the softest of sleeps, brief but beatific. I rolled awake to glimpse Miss and Francesca sitting next to each other, their faces shadowy in the dim crack of light beneath my room's closed door. Francesca had lent Miss her blazer to keep warm, and they both held the remains of sandwiches in their laps.

Soon as they saw I'd awakened, they set their cellophane wrappers aside and resumed their posts next to me. My guardian angels. One dark, one bright.

"They're almost ready for you, love," Francesca said. Her voice was gentle, but her proclamation sounded ominous. I pictured predators hungrily licking their lips, awaiting my arrival, ready to devour.

When a male orderly came in and pulled my trolley towards the door, I reached with my good hand for Miss as she and Francesca walked me to the lifts.

The orderly punched the UP button. Francesca squeezed my shoulder. Miss kissed me on the forehead. The descending lift's bell dinged, the juggernaut rolled, and then I was both a meek body constrained and a mind bobbing wildly on a metal ceiling.

5

I didn't come back down until I heard the scrape-turn of keys in a lock. I opened my eyes to see another orderly holding open a heavy door, whose small window's glass was obscured by a typed sign that read *WARNING: ELOPEMENT RISK*. I pictured star-crossed lovers on the run, jumping turnstiles and sprinting across train tracks, their fingers laced.

The orderly behind my head rolled me into the unit's main hallway and parked me by the nurses' station. A female staff worker in her forties, whose expression was so flat it made me wonder if she shouldn't be a patient instead, helped me sit up and slide off the trolley.

I looked down at my gown, so skimpy it left my legs bare to the upper thigh. "My clothes," I said hoarsely. *My blanket too*, I wanted to add, but I knew the fact that Miss had wrapped it around my shoulders didn't make it mine.

Trolley-pusher tossed my bin bag to the nurse. "You'll need to check it for contraband."

Contraband? I thought. *What is this, a prison?*

And then I realized: *Elopement risk.* Not of brazen lovers, but of broken people. I looked towards the door. Watched it swing open, then slam shut, as the trolley disappeared. Something in my body listed, as if I were still that greyhound racing across Islington Green.

"Careful there." Nurse Ought-to-Be-a-Patient steadied the same shoulder Francesca had squeezed, and guided me towards a private toilet across the hall.

"What—"

"Body search." She held the door open.

"I, um, I . . ." Tears welled in my eyes. "Please, can't you just—"

"Go." She waved a hand towards the sink. Sat down atop the toilet lid and uncapped a pen, drumming it against the metal teeth of her clipboard. "Take off your socks, please."

Socks. That was benign enough, right? I grabbed the sink edge to steady myself, yanking each fuzzy wad of hospital-issue gray cotton from my feet and flinging it in a ball on the yellow-and-white tile.

"Stand up and untie the back of your gown for me."

My shoulders clenched. The face in the mirror, gaunt knife-edge pixie, wavered somewhere between a gasp and a glower, her narrow eyes hard.

"Miss Holloway, if you don't cooperate, I'll have no choice but to bring in more staff."

I thought of the male orderly who'd held the door open. My good arm reached up, hesitated for one stubborn moment, and then fumbled to unknot the strings.

I heard the squeak of the toilet seat as the nurse stood. In my reflection, I could see her behind me, tilting her head in that same *hrm* motion Miss had while she was cutting my hair.

"Take your knickers down."

Shit shit fucking shit *no*.

"Excuse me?" I said.

"I have to check inside all your clothing. In case you're concealing any—"

"What—what would I hide in my underwear?"

"Oh, you'd be surprised." Her face crinkled a little in equally surprising sympathy. "I know this is awkward, dearie, but let's just hurry and get it over with, shall we?"

I nodded. Bent down and slid my knickers to my ankles as fast as I could, widening my stance and opening my knees just enough to show her that I wasn't packing heat or smuggling heroin.

"There's a girl. Turn round?"

I yanked my knickers back up and spun, my thinly clad behind thwacking up against the hard porcelain of the sink. The nurse stepped in close, so close that I could smell the pungency of her breath, all cinnamon chewing gum and nicotine.

"I'll need you to take your gown down in the front as well."

I forced my shoulders to drop. Shimmied the fabric down for her to appraise my breasts and belly.

"All done."

I lunged for the coarse cotton scrap, pulling it up to my shoulders, hugging it to me as the nurse hefted my bag with all the care of a rubbish collector. "We'll sort through this in your room."

Hostel déjà vu, right down to the desk-dresser combo, only with two major differences. One: this room didn't have a lock. And two: it did have a security camera. Little beady eye, just like the courts' satellite feed, right up in the corner, giving me a surreptitious wink.

"Is that on all the time?" I asked.

"Wouldn't serve its purpose if it weren't." The nurse sat on my bed and gestured for me to join her. I wished she'd have gone for the chair, given me a bit of space, but who was I to ask for such things? Locks, privacy, breathing room — those liberties were for people who could be trusted to refrain from cutting open their arms, not me.

"What about the toilets?"

She jerked her thumb in the direction of another door behind her. "En suite bath. You can dress in there."

Thank God. Oh, thank God.

While I was offering up silent prayers of gratitude for my ability to hairwash and shit in peace, Nurse Ought-to-Be was rummaging through my bin bag like an emaciated rat, tossing each scrap onto the blanket and sorting the lot into piles. Tracksuit bottoms: yes. Drawstring hoodie: no. Bras went into an ambiguous third pile. "We'll let you have those once you've got through your twenty-four-hour observation period."

At that point, the surreality of the situation began to thoroughly sink in. I was, by my own volition, sequestered in a place where lingerie was considered a weapon.

I pulled my legs up to my chest and draped my arms loosely around them, rocking back and forth as if I were back at the hostel with my headphones.

The nurse gave me an authoritative glance. "You look a bit agitated," she said. "Would you like a PRN?"

"A what?" I asked, my question muffled by my lowered head's brace against my knees.

"Medication for anxiety. You can ask for it as needed."

What I need, I thought, *is my schoolbag and my blade and* Ulysses. But wasn't any way I was going to get those—even assuming Nurse Kennedy or the girls had salvaged them from the stall. Might as well take what I could get, even if it was a chalky tablet that would make me feel ethereal as the spun candyfloss my dad had once bought me on the board-walk at Margate.

"Yeah," I said. "That'd be good."

Once re-dressed, I edged my way into the dayroom, where a motley crew of men and women sat on a cluster of couches watching telly. I'd been placed on an adult unit since the ward for young people was full, and I felt horridly out of place: tiniest, loneliest, most adrift.

I went over to the kitchenette area and poured myself a few sips' worth of cold water from the tap. On the cracked beige laminate level with my eyes, a former patient had af-fixed a long strip of masking tape on which he or she had written, in spiky print, the words *RISE ABOVE*.

I emptied the pill I'd been given into my palm. Pressed my palm to my mouth. Swigged. Swallowed. Turned around to see a salt-and-pepper-haired gent take his place before the telly, switching it off.

Mumbles and groans ensued, but he kept his cool. "All right, now, this will only take a few minutes."

He wasn't kidding. The primer on nutter-hostel civility went like this: "Please bathe, at least for the benefit of your fellow patients. Decide mutually on the genre of the evening movie. There will be no viewing of porn or ordering out of pizza, so please don't ask."

While he ran down the etiquette column, another man, the patient closest to me in age (early twenties, maybe?), paced back and forth in front of the coffee machine, inches from where I stood.

He glanced over at me, his eyes darting up and down my body, his voice a husky mutter. "Hey, baby."

I tore down the hall to my room. Grabbed a chair and dragged it up against the door with my good arm. I knew the blinky eye would catch me barricading myself, but I didn't care.

I crawled onto the bed and curled up in a fetal position, covering my face with my hands, breathing hard into my cupped palms. *Not where I belong,* I thought. *Not not not not no.*

I gasped my way through the shudders and rolled over onto my stomach. Rested my face against the waffle weave of the blanket. Tried not to long for the identical one that Miss had draped about her own shoulders, then tucked around me.

Two days later, Francesca worked her magic and found a rare open spot on a residential unit up in Nottingham that specialized in girls like me. A ceremonial returning of my bra and shoelaces, and off I went, past the *ELOPEMENT RISK* warning and down the civilian stairwell, Miss on my one side, Francesca on the other.

Neither of them could leave work to come with me for the long trip, but just having them there to see me off at St. Pancras was comfort enough. Right before I got on the train, Miss handed me a care package: my schoolbag, with my CD player and copy of *Ulysses* tucked inside. I flung my arms around her waist beneath her coat, and hung on for what felt like forever.

6

I'll never forget my first glimpse of the ward: a giant wall mural of a firebird, dead ringer for the one on Miss's shoulder blade, its mouth breathing out the words *WEL-COME TO THE PHOENIX UNIT* in a huffed line of curvy script. Later on, I'd find out from my records that the place's full name was the Phoenix Unit for Severe Adolescent Personality Disorders. Later on, Clare and I would shorten its title to the Phoenix, trying to make it sound edgy.

But right then, standing there bewildered and amazed, I had no idea I'd ever need to pull my records in my own defense, or that I'd even meet Clare. I just figured all that resurrection action was a good omen.

Meanwhile, Kath, the unit director, was bustling me down the empty hall, pointing out a maze of classrooms: art workshop, yoga studio, ADL kitchen. Wait, huh?

"Activities of Daily Living," she explained, upon seeing my stupefied look. "You know, cookery, cleanup."

Oh, yeah. That mundane stuff regular people did. "Got it."

She led me into a cute common area with floral couches and hardwood floors. In one corner stood a white upright piano; in another, a large oak bookcase. "No telly?" I asked.

"It can be distressing for some patients, and besides, we want you all to stay engaged." She tapped a corkboard on which a weekly schedule was prominently posted.

I stepped closer to read the chart. Groups galore, from eight in the morning till eight at night.

"Where's everyone right now?" I asked.

"They've gone out to the shops for the afternoon. Another ADL training."

For fuck's sake, I wanted to snort. *I'm sick in the head, not so stupid I need lessons on how to navigate the aisles at Tesco's.* But I figured Kath, being a teen girl wackjob specialist, had some method to her own therapeutic madness, and so I just nodded and said, "Oh, nice."

"Let me show you your room."

Still no door locks, I noticed, but then again, there'd not been locks anywhere. "It's an open ward?"

"Yes. We're all about personal responsibility here."

Sounded good to me, at least until I saw the pair of beds. Crap.

"Your roommate is in our eating disorders track"—Kath said this brightly, as if it were a career path—"so I'll have to ask you not to keep food in here."

I nodded again and sat down slowly on the bed across from the window, which I assumed, thanks to its duvet's lack of adornment, was mine. On my absentee roommate's bed, a teddy bear watched me with glass eyes cloudy as cataracts. The sight of its milky, soulful stare, coupled with its neck's rakish gingham bow, made me want to simultaneously punch it and cry.

I slid back on the bed, scooping my bags into my lap. "You don't need to search these, do you?"

Kath shook her head. "We've not got contraband lists here."

Whoa. Now I was intrigued. "Any other rules I should know about?"

Kath grabbed a chair and cozied up next to me.

"We prefer to think of them as guiding principles," she said, "but yes, there are a few."

I leaned back against the wall, waiting for the etiquette litany.

"First one is individual accountability. We do our best to keep this a safe and supportive space, but we also want you to own up to your choices and manage your own behavior."

"Which means . . . what?" I asked.

"Well, for starters, you'll have much more freedom than in most hospitals. You'll chop with regular knives in the kitchen and use regular scissors in the art room, just as you would at home."

My stomach dropped. I couldn't decide whether to feel terrified or ecstatic.

"Those areas will be locked in the evening after lights out, but otherwise we don't play nanny."

"So what's—"

"The catch?" Kath's voice dropped into a lower, almost Miss-esque register, like feathers floating down onto hard ground. "A zero-tolerance policy towards destructive behaviors."

"*Zero*?" I whispered.

Kath nodded. "One incident of self-harm—cutting, purging, anything at all—is grounds for immediate discharge."

Holy fuck.

"Okay," I said. "What else?"

"We don't permit romantic relationships between patients."

That gave me pause. Not because I thought the rule was unfair, but because I couldn't imagine that even being a problem. "Other girls have . . . taken up with each other?"

"A few times. Many patients here struggle with poor boundaries."

Now, when I think of the answer she gave, I want to slap her. Not saying people like me always have their boundaries sorted out, or that the Phoenix hadn't the right to make rules, but the way she said it made it clear she believed that there was only one plausible reason two mad girls would get together.

Back then, though, I wasn't planning on hooking up with anyone, so I just gave her my automatic response to any dictate: "Right, sure, I understand."

Kath smiled. "It's lovely to see someone so motivated. I think you're going to do brilliantly here."

For my first six weeks, Kath's prediction proved right. She'd designated that time as an "assessment and adjustment" period, which meant that I didn't have to go to therapy, just participate in the fluffier stuff like collage group. That was run by a gauzy-skirted woman called Lora, who wore a bloodstone pendant and called herself a "holistic health" nurse. She'd hand out textured pieces of art matting the size of big postcards, and we'd sit for an hour round a table with glue and real, not rounded, scissors, clipping pictures we liked out of magazines.

Simple primary school stuff, right? But then it got wacky, 'cause this wasn't just any collaging: this was a view into "The Soul." Every time Lora said that in a reverent whisper, it was all I could do not to fall about laughing at the idea of the National Health Service paying God knows how many thousand pounds a year, and Francesca working God knows how many miracles, for me to find my existential bliss in a copy of *Hello!*

"Just wait till your six weeks is up," my roommate, Dara, warned me one night, twirling in long-limbed pirouette atop her duvet. "Then they baptize you in flipping fire."

"Meaning what?" I asked from where I sat at my desk, fingering my stack of *Introducing . . . Lesley Holloway's Soul!* postcards.

"Individual therapy. Trauma work."

The very word *trauma* made me want to run for the kitchen and rummage around for a paring knife. Which I very well could have done, seeing as it wasn't curfew yet, but I didn't. Not out of any commitment to responsibility or accountability or any of those other "abilities" Kath expected us to magically possess, but out of sheer terror at the prospect of being kicked out.

Sure, the whole program was twee and jargon-riddled, and my twelve other wardmates (yeah, that made me Lucky Thirteen) were even more gaunt and greyhoundy than I, but the Phoenix had one massive, marvelous thing going for it:

safety. Not once did I have to mince down a hallway, stealthy and scared; not once did I have to barricade my door while in the throes of panic. I slept without nightmares and woke without flashbacks. My rigid shoulders relaxed.

When Christmas rolled round, though, my relief gave way to uninvited pangs of homesickness. I tried to quell them by telling myself that it hadn't been much of a home anyway, but my mind wouldn't quit: reminiscing over every awesome present, replaying every holiday special Mum and I had watched together, cuddled up on the couch in front of the telly. Funny how easily my memory committed sins of omission, cleverly leaving out the year when he'd done me so hard I had to lower myself gingerly onto my chair at the dinner table, forgetting that time when I'd gone out on the balcony and dry-heaved into my hands while he nibbled Mum's ear under the mistletoe.

Other girls at the Phoenix had shitty parents, too, but they at least showed up, bearing grudges and gifts, shouting and hugging, making our normally unearthly calm unit if not festive, then at least fierce with shared history and fumbling attempts to care. Me, I'd have settled for a cheap card bitching about how I'd ruined Christmas forever, but apparently Mum couldn't be bothered.

Thankfully, Miss could, because she made the three-hour pilgrimage up from London to visit. Not on the actual big day (she had her own family, after all), but close enough to it.

She brought me a store-bought container of Christmas pudding nowhere near as good as Mum's homemade, which can only be described as epic (perfect ratio of raisins to currants, easy on the orange peel, with a splash of high-end brandy). Still, it was the thought that counted, and I eagerly tucked into a bowlful at the Phoenix's communal dining table, on the lookout for the traditional tokens hidden inside. Those, Miss said, *were* homemade, crafted by her sculptor husband. "So that explains your smashing earring collection," I said, grimacing at the taste of metal.

I spat the charm into my palm. Saw it was a ring, and snorted. "Right, like anyone's going to fall in love with me."

"And why wouldn't they?" Her voice was as indignant as if I'd suggested James Joyce shouldn't be part of the National Curriculum.

"Come on, Miss. You know." I swept a hand around the room.

She reached for a napkin with which to blot her mouth. "Psychiatric hospitalization is hardly a romantic death sentence, Lesley."

My envious gaze drank in every inch of her subtle, effortless cool: Doc Martens, black velvet blouse, hair gathered up into a bun with one of those burnished thingies that looks like a posh chopstick.

"Maybe it wasn't for *you*," I said.

"And it won't be for you, either." She twirled her fork round the edge of the pan to scrape up one last bite of pudding. "It might take a while, but you'll find someone who's down with the damage."

"If you say so," I muttered, pushing my chair back. "Hey, wanna make a soul card?"

In the art workshop, Miss raised an eyebrow at the shelves full of scissors and paper trimmers as I pulled down Lora's shoebox and flipped through it. "What color's your aura? We've got the whole rainbow in here. Burgundy, chartreuse —"

"Lesley." Serious case of *I'm so not messing*.

I looked over. "Yeah?"

"You're not still injuring, are you?"

I shook my head.

"And you're keeping up with school in the midst of all these groups?"

"Well, not exactly," I said. "I mean, they have a school here, but it's only for the younger girls. No A-levels."

She sighed.

"What?" I said, spreading the cards out on the table. "Francesca says this place is the best in the country. You think she's talking shit?"

"No," Miss said carefully, sitting next to me to finger the fanned-out hues.

I watched as she selected a hunter-green one. "Not black?"

"My soul abhors clichés. How about yours?"

"It's feeling a bit lemony today," I said, choosing a tart yellow card from the pile.

We worked in silence for a few minutes, sliding magazines back and forth, swapping our glue bottles when they got too dried out. Every so often, Miss would murmur to herself, "Oh, now *that* was genius of you, Glor."

"Normally you get an hour," I said. "But this is the abbreviated version. Soul speed dating."

"Well, then, let's see yours first, expert."

I showed her my card, which read *DAFTSCARED-SACREDSTRANGE* in large, akimbo letters.

Miss's face came close to doing the melt, but she dialed it back to a soft smile. "Mine's far less bold."

She held it up to reveal a circlet of immaculately glued images:

An open book, gilded by a nearby lamp.

A sunlit wooden spoon, nestled in a bright blue porcelain rest.

The sound hole and burnished body of a guitar, its strings gleaming.

A woman's head, lowered against her shadowed lover's shoulder.

A woman's hands, cupping the ripe curve of her pregnant belly.

Mesmerized, I reached for the card, staring at it for what seemed like ages, my breath held. The feeling the pictures gave me wasn't inspiration so much as awe, heavy and huge.

"Okay," I said quickly, and shoved the card across the table in her direction. "Now you have to fill out the paperwork."

She laughed. "You're kidding."

"Nope," I said, leaning back to grab one of the worksheets Lora kept in a stack. "It's"—I crooked my fingers into claw-like quotation marks—"'reflective practice.'"

As I watched her scan the instructions, I could tell when she'd got to the "image dialogue" part by the sound of her disbelieving laughter.

"You want me," she said, "to ask a piece of photo matting . . . a *question*?"

I grinned. "That's how it works."

Her brows went all furrowy. "And you find this . . . use-ful? Meaningful?"

I shrugged. "It's okay. Nice brain break."

She shook her head. Plucked a pen from a crammed-full coffee jar. Bent intently over the paper for a moment, then passed it back to me.

Along the typed lines, under the question *What is this card trying to tell you?*, she'd written in gorgeous English teacher script:

1. *That Francesca really needs to get on this place about upping its academic standards.*
2. *That (even though Lesley doesn't believe it, not now, not yet) all these things and more are possible.*

"Here," she said, handing her card to me. "Keep it."

7

On New Year's Day, Amal, one of the strictest staff members, caught Dara with her fingers down her throat, which meant that (true to Kath's word) she was sent packing within hours. Which meant that I wound up sitting in my room, staring at an empty bed, feeling the dull ache of aloneness yet again. Which meant that Kath decided it was my turn for the fire baptism.

The therapist she assigned me to was a willowy forty-something woman called Bethan who watched me with an unnerving composure, her knee-high boots crossed at precise angles, her scarves knotted in elegant, drapey perfection. When she spoke, her voice was maddeningly muted, but her deep-digging questions, coupled with the close quarters of her windowless office, made me so anxious I either flitted to the ceiling or answered with snarky diffidence.

"What do you think brought you here?" (Her first query.)

"The fact it was on the schedule."

No hint of a frown. God, I wanted her to frown. "Actually, I meant what brought you to the unit."

"What do you think?" I rolled up my sleeve, revealing the angry knot of barely healed tissue on my bad arm.

"But you came voluntarily. Which suggests to me that you recognized you had things you needed to sort out."

"I just wanted to get out of everywhere else I'd been."

"You wanted to feel safe."

Supper tray, storytime, fluffy duvet.

"Um, *yeah*."

Still no frown, but a subtle shift in her posture. "I'm noticing a lot of tension, a lot of defensiveness, in both the way you're speaking and the way you're holding yourself right now. Is that an accurate impression of how you're feeling?"

"I'm not feeling anything."

"Physically, or emotionally?"

I crossed my arms. My gaze went so soft and unfocused the glow from the lamp on her desk began to smear. Lightness in my head, ethereal as the second before you faint. Emptiness in my chest, like a cored-out apple.

"Both," I said. "Yes."

"Can you think of a possible reason why you might be dissociating at the moment?"

"Disso-*what*?"

"Dissociating," Bethan repeated. "Checking out. Leaving your body."

My eyes narrowed. "How'd you know about that?"

"It's very common in people who've experienced abuse."

"Really?" I said. "I thought I just had a weird brain."

Bethan smiled. "Not weird, smart. It protected you from things too hard for you to handle. Helped you survive, even."

Thanks, brain.

"Huh." Pondering this, I chewed my lip, as if that might bring me back to my body. But my eyes couldn't stop flitting to her office lamp, and every time they did, I went dizzy and empty again.

"So, now that you know what dissociation is, any idea as to what—"

"I don't like your office," I said.

"Because you don't fancy coming here."

"No. It just freaks me out."

"Does it remind you of something?"

Hall closet. Bare bulb. Knuckles punching my mouth. Fingers jamming inside me. Hands pinning my wrists.

My guts turned inside out, remembering. I slid off the chair and dropped down to the rug, bent double on my knees, my fingers digging into my scalp as I rocked back and forth.

"Lesley." Bethan's voice rose a touch. "Tell me what's going on."

I shook my head over and over.

"Try to stay grounded. Take some deep breaths."

I lowered myself all the way down. Gasped a few stuttery sucks of air.

"Now sit up slowly."

I sat up slowly. Good girl. Look. Good girl, I am.

"Open your eyes."

Tentative slit-flutter.

"Let's do some reality testing. Have a look round the room. Pick a few objects that are specific to here, that aren't in your old memory."

I jerked my chin from side to side.

"Got them?"

I nodded.

"Brilliant. Tell me what they are."

"Clock. White noise machine thingie. Ugly painting."

Another small smile. "Are you feeling calm enough to come back up and talk?"

I shook my head again.

"It's all still there, floating about, isn't it?"

"Yeah."

"Then let's see what we can do to box it up tight. Remember how we learned about containment in group?"

Vaguely. Sorta.

"Yeah," I said again, hoisting myself up from the floor.

"Well, that's such an abstract thing to wrap your mind around that it helps to make it concrete. Let's come up with an image you can picture and call up when you need it."

"Like a real box?"

"Just like. Have you any ideas?"

"One of those sealed-off drums for toxic rubbish," I said.

"Mmm, well," Bethan said, adjusting her posture into perfect equilibrium, "we want it to be a container you can open again later, so that you have the option to examine those old memories further."

Oh, fuck that fuck that fucking fuck that. No way was I becoming a hall closet archaeologist.

"It can have a lock, right?"

"Absolutely."

I thought for a second. "Fireproof safe. With fifteen codes to crack."

"Perfect. Go ahead and draw it the next time you've art workshop. Make it detailed as you can."

After I'd agreed and she'd let me go, I stumbled back out into the commons, shaky and exhausted. If this torture was how I was going to recover, I reckoned I'd take a pass on healing, thanks, and staggered off to the unlocked kitchen to scavenge.

When I got there, I found a new girl standing at the counter, chopping vegetables on a wooden board. Compared to the dancers and drama queens with their liner-rimmed eyes and glistening claret mouths, she looked downright plain, her dark, curly hair suppressed inside a tight plait, her ample figure a mere suggestion beneath her oversized pullover and long, full denim skirt. When she glanced over at me, I could see the glint of her glasses' frames, bright teal, and the doughy tenderness of her makeup-less face. I felt unmoored, unsure; part of me wanted to hug her in welcome, part of me wanted to mock her seeming serenity, and another part . . . well, it didn't have words for what it wanted yet, but there was something there that made my gaze keep flickering to her bare mouth.

"Lesley Holloway?" she asked. Her voice was girlish and high, but soft.

I took a step backwards, even more unmoored by the fact that she'd figured me out, but also strangely pleased at the idea of her already knowing me in some way.

"Yeah," I said.

"They told me I'd recognize you by the hair," she said shyly. "Or lack of it."

At that point, I was seriously butch. Pixie cut whittled down to a buzz.

"Yeah," I said again, and then asked, like the biggest idiot in the universe, "Are you new?"

She nodded. "We're roommates," she said, wiping her hand on a towel before extending it to me. "I'm Clare Manning."

"Lesley Holloway," I said, squeezing her hand more tightly than I meant to. Soon as I realized my social skills were failing me, I let my hand drop. "Right. Umm. You knew that."

She smiled, widely enough that I could see a chip in her top front tooth. I wondered how a person could smile like that, without faking it, and still be fucked up enough to earn a place at the Phoenix.

I sat down at the table. "They give you the tour already?"

"And the groups list."

"Out of control, innit?"

She shrugged and turned back to dicing. "I don't mind."

So she was glad to be there, too. I thought about asking why, but didn't. Instead I watched the angle of her broad fingers, perfectly poised as Bethan's suede boots, and the quick efficiency of her chop.

"Have you a special diet or something?" I asked, watching her swirl a glug of olive oil in the pan and scrape the mushrooms and spring onions and matchstick carrots off the board.

"No, I just enjoy cookery," she said. "Calms me down when my mind starts going dodgy places."

"You ought to have a show," I said. *"Going Dodgy Places With Clare."*

It's a wonder she didn't slam the hot skillet down on my head, but she didn't. In fact, she giggled. "Could start with here, couldn't I?"

"Yeah. You'd be psychiatry's answer to Nigella Lawson."

"Oh, please." She shook her head, dismissive as I'd been when I'd gotten the ring in the Christmas pudding.

"No, I'm serious," I said. "You even look a bit like her. Dark hair, and curvy, and all that."

I'm not sure why I said it, really; I wasn't aiming to be flirty. I guess I just wanted to see that chipped smile again. Which I got, along with a blush that made me warm as her face, warm enough to completely forget I'd originally come in the kitchen for a sharp knife.

To hear Phoenix staff talk, you'd think that seconds later I grabbed her and pulled her to the floor and wormed my face inside her sensible skirt, taking her from repression to ecstasy while the sauté pan burned.

Well, I hate to disappoint the casting director of *Suicidal Schoolgirls Gone Wild*, but that's complete and utter bollocks. Honest. We were courteous roommates for days, and good friends for weeks, before things got intense, before things got real.

A good bit of the slow buildup was due to all the Phoenix's

daily requirements. That, and the fact that Clare and I weren't particularly alike.

Take the tops of our dressers, for instance. Mine was a loose, messy constellation of talismans (*Ulysses*, CD player, Miss's soul postcard, my never-gonna-happen-in-a-million-years ring token), while Clare's held a neat, sparse stack (Phoenix worksheet binder, devotionals and school textbooks, a version of the Bible I'd never heard of), so staged it was like she'd arranged it for show in case her parents came in. Which they did, each weekend without fail, and when they weren't visiting in person, they were ringing her on the hall phone every night. Not just to check in or send their love, but to pray with her, their sessions going on so long that Amal or Kath would have to walk over and point at her watch to hurry Clare along.

Now I'm not one to dismiss the need for divine intervention ('cause I've prayed harder than Mr. and Mrs. Manning over the last six months, let me tell you), but the whole dynamic seemed odd to me. Particularly because Clare, though she never spoke poorly of her parents, seemed utterly detached from it all, her dutiful adherence to their beliefs neither begrudging nor reverent.

We never talked about why we were sick or what we'd done to land on the Phoenix; unlike the other girls, Clare and I weren't into brainstorming the best ways to get food out one orifice or another, or comparing self-inflicted tissue damage, or competing for the worst hospital admission story (even though I could have easily won on those last two counts). We poked fun on the surface, but we also sensed in each other a common commitment to survival, whether that entailed chopping aubergines or refusing to sneak from the cutlery drawer.

Solidarity aside, the proper dance towards desire really started with Enya and her Smartie-crapping unicorn.

About a month after Clare arrived, Lora the soul-gazer got sacked—our guess was that she joined a cult, but staff never said. To replace her, they brought in a chill art therapist called Andrea, who'd set out the supplies and put on music and let us do whatever the fuck we wanted. Patient-directed expression for the win.

Only problem was, she played the same Enya CD over and over. Which is all right if you've gone to the spa for an hour-long massage, but day after day? That's enough to inspire suicidal ideation in a totally stable person.

Eventually Clare and I got so bored we started making up an imaginary film for which the awful thing would serve as soundtrack. Plot-wise, it was lightweight fantasy, but the production values were brilliant: drunk fairies, an army of warrior dwarves clad in toddler-sized Doc Martens, and of course Enya herself, riding a unicorn across misty hills of green, wearing a velvet cloak and holding a scepter and commanding her loyal subjects to "Be serene, damn it!"

"Of course she'd have a minion," Clare said. "To scoop up all the magical turds."

"Nah," I said, reaching across Chloe for the colored pencil box. "It's such a magical world that the unicorn craps something smashing."

"Like what?"

"I dunno, Valium?"

"Dulcolax," Nina chimed in.

"No," Clare said firmly. "It craps Smarties."

"I take it you'd like me to bring in a different CD, girls?" Andrea said, shaking her head as she unrolled a fresh sheet of butcher paper on the table.

I offered to play "Best of the Screaming Women," but Andrea thought it might be too disturbing, so we had to make do with her copy of Norah Jones instead. A bit snoozy, but still heaps better than the alternative.

Midway through the first song, Clare lifted her head from her mandala coloring book, and sighed, and said, just loudly enough that I could hear, "Oh, Norah. You'd never wonder why you didn't come if you'd gone home with me."

Well. Suffice it to say I was floored. Not only by quasi-devout, thoroughly private Clare outing herself, but also by the possibility of her sly remark being intended as a hint to me.

I decided it was best to play it cool, both for her sake and mine. "Eh," I said, sliding the pencil box down towards Parvati. "She's not really my type."

After that little exchange, I had a few more dreams in which my hands tangled in long hair—dark and wiry this time—but otherwise it was business as usual: prim, fully dressed pilgrimages to and from the shower, followed by group group group group pajamas (again, donned in the bathroom) lights out good night.

At least until Clare's six weeks of assess-and-adjust were up. She came back from her first therapy session with her head down and her shoulders bristly, clomping about the room as she slammed the armoire door, then her dresser drawers, scrape bang scrape bang.

"Sorry," she kept muttering. "Sorry."

"It's cool," I said from where I lay on my bed, flipping through my notes from containment group. Wasn't just saying it to be polite; I knew what it was like to crave clamor, blare, vibration, blood. Whatever it took to wear your inside on the outside.

"No," she said. "No. It's fucking *not*."

Whoa. Cheeky as she could get, Clare never let loose even mild swear words, much less an f-bomb.

I sat up just in time to watch her raise her hands to her face. At first I thought she was covering it, gearing up to cry, but then I saw her fingers curl, their nails clawing over her forehead and down her cheeks.

"Hey, hey," I shouted, as I jumped up and ran over to grab her wrists.

Once cut off, she struggled mightily, pounding her fists against the air.

"Stop it." I shook her. "Clare, stop."

"Why?" Her voice was a clenched growl. "So they won't kick me out?"

"No," I said. "Because you're flipping beautiful."

Her head and shoulders went still. I felt her hands relax. Brought my own up to cup her cheeks.

"Liar," she whispered.

I stroked her hair. "It's true."

"True you're lying?"

"*True* true." And to prove it, I duck-dove in and kissed

her. My mouth was closed, but it was hardly a peck, either, our lips shifting against each other, feeling their edges.

As I stepped back, I could hear the low, breathy leak of her slow exhale. Behind her glasses, her stubby lashes blinked furiously.

"I—I suppose we should go to dinner," she said, her voice hoarse.

All through our chickpea curry, I kept my head bowed. We walked from the dining table to the couches for nightly group meeting in silence, our paths diverging, as if by unspoken agreement, when Clare took a seat next to Nina and I sat by Chloe.

All through the to-me-irrelevant discussion of family visits, though, I caught myself sneaking glances at Clare. She sat slumped on the sofa cushion, as if she'd been shoved down there and abandoned, but her chin was lifted high. On someone else, the expression might have seemed affected or imperious, but on her it just looked pert and plucky. I uncrossed my legs, then crossed them again, pressing my thighs tight against each other, forcing myself to look away and listen to Kath's lecture on how to set reasonable limits.

Yeah, I admonished myself. *You'd best take damn good notes on that.*

We were all about to get up and pick out a board game for our final activity of the evening when I heard the clangy *brrring* of the hall phone.

"Grab it before the devil smites you, Clare," Nina said, snickering, as she leaned up to the top shelf of the bookcase for a tattered Trivial Pursuit box.

Clare gave a nonchalant *oh for pity's sake* head-shake, but the corners of her mouth did a terse little crumple so heart-breaking it made something inside me crumple, too.

"Leave her alone," I said to Nina after she'd left.

"Reckon you'll want her on your team, Lesley," Parvati said from where she sat setting up the board.

Chloe fingered the dispenser of quiz cards, making their top edges snap. "Why even put her on one? We'll be finished before she is."

I had to admit she was probably right, so I settled in grumpily next to Parvati.

Five minutes later, my team was just about to answer a question in Entertainment when out into the commons came Clare, as shy and tentative as that pink, quavery feeling in-side me, a tiny smile now curling her lips upward. When she sidled over and took the empty seat next to mine, it was all I could do not to pull her closer in giddy gladness.

"Lesley's about to save us," Parvati announced.

Clare's smile went even deeper, till it was dimply. Crap. Now I really had to bring it.

Of course, the question would be about some ancient song, from like 1975. No flipping clue.

Nina snorted. "Useless, you are."

"No, she's not," Clare said.

I felt my face do the melt, like Miss's, only blushier. Reached a hand over, put it on Clare's forearm, casual, like my fingers were telegraphing nothing more than *Thanks for the vote of confidence, mate.*

By the time Chloe's team had trumped us, it was edging dangerously close to lights-out. I busied myself sorting the pieces and tidying the cards, fiddling around so much that by the time I set the box back up on the shelf, everyone else, including Clare, had filed down the corridor.

Way to scare her off, I thought as I opened the door to our room.

Sure enough, no sign of Clare inside. I went to my dresser and pulled out a pair of ratty black yoga trousers and a heather-gray T-shirt with a hole at the seam where the neck met the shoulder. Hurriedly I scrambled out of my jeans and polo and into the makeshift pajamas. I was about to shove my balled-up clothes in the hamper when the door squealed open.

I turned around. Dropped my bra, and then the rest. "Jesus, you scared me."

Clare stood there in her long nightdress and flip-flops, her hair still braided, her own wad of clothing tucked under her fuzzy-fabricked arm.

"I—I'm sorry," she said, in the tiniest, most choked voice you could imagine.

"It's okay," I said, because it was.

We tossed our dirty clothes into our respective hampers, and slammed our armoire doors closed, like automaton twins. Then we turned towards each other.

"Hard day, innit?" I said.

She nodded. I could see the muscles in her throat working, forming a small, ripply knot.

"That first therapy session sucks. But it gets better. Or at least not so shitty." My face burned. "Not exactly putting your mind at ease, am I?"

A demi-pause, just long enough for her pluckypert chin to assert itself again.

"Actually," she said, "you are."

I brought my forearms up across myself, rubbing their bare skin. "Well, umm, good. I'm glad."

She gave a stuttery glance round. "We really . . . Miranda's going to be knocking on doors in a minute, so we should—"

"Yeah. Don't need the curfew telling-off."

Her arms were at her own waist like mine now, only bent stiffly, her fingers bound together in fidgety lace. Twirl, twist, twirl.

"Hug good night?" I said softly. "Or would that be too w—"

In answer, her hands flew up and apart like a spray of confetti, and then she was barreling towards me. Unmoored again, I wrapped my arms round her waist, both to steady her and to steady myself.

She rested her cheek on my shoulder as I rested my palm against the back of her head. We stood like that for a minute—her huddled, me hardly believing—and then I felt her shift, just enough to make the press of her full breasts deliberate.

She turned her head to the side and pressed her mouth to the tiny hole in my T-shirt. Not even her whole mouth, really, just her lower lip, whispery little pucker, then a pull back.

Emboldened, I rubbed her back, first in compact circles with my fingertips, then with my flat palm, up and up and up and down, just far enough to skirt the ribbed elastic ridge of her knickers.

I felt Clare lift her head from my shoulder. Her eyes were heavy-lidded, her brow framed by an escaped, traily lock of hair, her lips parted, ever so slightly. Waiting for me.

For *me*. I couldn't believe it, that someone would stand and wait, expectant, craving me, daftscaredsacredstrange, hands hair teeth tongue, *my* tongue, parting her mouth, reaching in hungrily to lick the chip on her front tooth, to swirl round till it met hers. Me the one moving, instead of the one moved into. Nothing to do with power, just elation: at the small moan she made in the back of her throat, at the taste of mint toothpaste and warm spit, at the folding of her body into mine like batter, egg flour cream sweetness, spun.

So shaky and surprised, I was, that I could barely walk backwards, but somehow I managed it, my mouth still on her, and then I was lying down, no, more like flopped down, on my bed, with her straddling my hips, and that was just, well, that was just not going to happen, let me tell you, not even with plain halting lovely Clare. I inched my way up, till I was sitting with my back against the wall and she was balanced in my lap with her legs wrapped round me, and then I was taking her hair out its plait, and smoothing it with my fingers, and murmuring inside her mouth.

When I drew back for air and opened my eyes, Clare's face in front of me had turned smoky-sultry gorgeous, thanks to the double effect of her glasses being off and her hair having gone loose and unkempt.

"My knees," I gasped. "Can you —"

Clare's face went red. "Sure, yeah," she said, sliding off my lap.

I turned down the top edge of my duvet and slid under. Wriggled up against the wall. Patted the patch of exposed sheet.

My bed was so narrow we both had to lie on our sides, clutching each other so she wouldn't fall off onto the floor. Every so often she'd threaten to tumble, and I'd have to lurch forward to grab her, and then we'd shift round, re-arranging limbs till we'd gotten it right.

"Lesley," she said, so quietly I almost didn't hear. "Do you think you're going to get better?"

"In here?" I mumbled drowsily.

"No. At all."

"Bound to happen someday, innit? If we work hard enough in therapy."

I felt her shake her head. "Maybe for you and the rest. But not me."

Thanks to my conversations with Miss, I knew how to handle that one. "And why not?"

"Because I'm evil."

The thought was so laughable I couldn't help but burst out. "Who the fuck told you that? Kath?" Then I realized, and shut up. "*Oh.*"

"They think I'm damned," Clare whispered. "Not sick."

Against my back, I could feel her hand tremble. Under my leg, I could feel hers clench.

"That's rubbish," I said. "Anyone who thinks that about you is the damned one."

Her shoulders were shaking now, so hard I knew that every argument I'd put forth would fail.

"Before here, they tried sending me for a . . ." She hid her face in my shoulder to muffle the words. "An exorcism."

"Oh, Clare. Oh, shit, honey. *Clare.*" I pulled her to me tighter. Kissed her head a million times.

"I was their miracle, right? Little two-pound baby, gift from God. They debated whether it was messing about with His will to hook me up to all those tubes and save me, but reckoned I was special, I was meant to be here. Always told me my life was extra precious. Went on about how suicide was a sin. I can only imagine what they'd say if they figured out the rest."

"They haven't any idea you like—"

"No. And it's got to stay that way."

I stroked her hair. "Then I won't kiss you in front of them at visit weekend."

She drew back. "Don't even joke, Les. We can't let on to anyone."

"But that rule's just a 'guideline.'" I put on Kath's bright breathiness. "Not like the other about harming, where you're out of here after one strike."

The mattress shrieked as she sat up and swung her legs over the side of the bed. "Yeah, well," she said, "I'm out of here soon as Mum and Dad decide I am."

"Wait," I said, sitting up behind her. "How's that even—"

"I'm not sixteen till May."

I ran a hand over my face. "Fuck. So they could just—"

"Ship me off to one of those evangelist boot camps for wayward teens in America?" She stood up, her bare feet slapping onto the linoleum floor. "Yeah. And they would."

"Clare," I said slowly, "if you just want to stop, right now, I—"

She turned to face me, shoulders squared and resolute.

"No," she said. "I'm done swallowing it down with aspirin bottles. I want to *start*."

"With . . . with me," I said dubiously, like that was akin to dating a serial killer.

In answer, she bent down, put her hands on my shoulders, and kissed me hard on the mouth.

"Good night, mistress of the obvious," she said, dashing back to her side of the room just before Miranda arrived for curfew bed check.

I thought there'd be no way I could possibly sleep after that, but I was so drained it was easy. Just like when you've had a panic attack, and then you come down, and the unreal tiredness feels so sheltering to sink into. (Yes, I just compared consensually making out for the first time—to say nothing of receiving confirmation that I was, at very least, not totally straight—to symptoms of an anxiety disorder. Welcome to Lesleyville.)

Come morning, I woke and sat up to find Clare still dozing, her duvet tucked tight round her ruddied face, her hair even wilder now. The sight of her curled up there was so delicious I could barely stand it, but I made myself get dressed before creeping over to sit on the bed next to her.

When I ran my hand lightly over her hair and back in echo of the night before, Clare let out a groany mumble and lifted her head. "Wha—"

"Wake-up call," I said, and kissed the edge of her ear.

She kept her hands over her face, ostensibly rubbing her eyes, but I could see through her fingers that she was smiling. "I missed you."

"Even in your sleep?"

"Yeah." She sat up slowly, yawning. "How long have we till breakfast?"

"Ten minutes."

I got up so she could get up. Turned my back as she went towards her dresser. Out of awkward politeness, mainly, but also 'cause I knew we had to be careful. Not like there were blinky-eyed cameras in the room, but still.

I busied myself getting my binder for groups together, straightening the top of my dresser—every twitchy, unnecessary tidy-up you could imagine. Each time I heard a drawer open or slam shut, each time I heard the rustle of stepped-out or stepped-into fabric, I felt myself jump. Bethan always told me I was "hypervigilant," but this seemed different. Nervous startly excited bracing for—

Oh, hell, I couldn't help it. I snuck a glance at her standing there barefoot in her long skirt, hair neatly braided again, one hand poised to pluck a modest blouse from inside her armoire. On her back, rising up from beneath the wide chest band of her beige bra, was a long scar. The kind you couldn't give yourself.

Later, I'd learn by feel how far the puckery line traveled in the opposite direction, curving around her side along her rib cage, terminating in a tiny shadow-slit beneath her left breast, but right then all I could see was the arch along her shoulder blade, cresting in a dense channel of tunnely tissue.

"What—what happened to your—"

Clare selected an embroidered shirt I especially liked. "They had to open up my heart. To fix it."

When she said that, I felt my own heart open. I went and stood behind her, hands on her waist. "Last thing about you needs fixing," I said, kissing the flowery skin-knot.

Clare reached back and grabbed my left hand. Drew it round her front and slid my long sleeve up to my elbow, lifting the ugly flesh-rope of my bad forearm to her own mouth, God the pinchpull of that hurt, but it was worth it. Two minutes left before breakfast door-knock, careful careful, two lips pressed to the clean edges that were miracles, two lips pressed to the jagged ones that were mistakes.

8

When I think back on those next two months, my memory has a soft-focus glow, not *boom-chicka-wow-wow* so much as that sheen scenes get in films when the director's trying to prove that the snippet of time they're showing in a flashback was simply wonderful, uncomplicatedly divine, the sort of place you'd kill to go back to.

Now there wasn't a damn thing about that situation that you could label uncomplicated, but sweet flipping hell, was it divine. Lying awake at night, whispering and kissing. Sneaking hard hand-squeezes under the table in art therapy. Writing little notes and leaving them places—folded between the pages of a book, or tucked in a dresser drawer—for each other to find. (I still have them all, stashed in the front pocket of my old groups binder. My favorite is a dialogue between us. Clare: *Want to buy short dress this weekend. After Mum & Dad leave. Bad idea?* Me: *Oh. Fuck. No. Will buy for you!!!*)

And I did, with the social services allowance Francesca made sure I still received, next chance we got to go the shops on ADL training. Fitted little cherry-colored number with black grommets, femme but punky, paired with clunky-soled Mary Janes and black patterned tights. Best purchase of my life, I'm telling you. Not just because it was hot as fucking Hades, but because of the way Clare walked—bolder and brighter and unashamed—when she had it on.

She wore it the Saturday Miss took us out to lunch on an afternoon pass. We squished into the restaurant's booth, Miss on one side, Clare and I on the other, aiming for the perfect amount of space between: not so much we looked cross, not so little we'd give it away.

While we waited for our steak plates, Miss asked us heaps of chatty questions: Were we still required to interrogate pieces of card stock? Was it still all Radio Enya, all the time? How about those A-levels, hmm?

I reached for the plate our server handed me. "No, no, and no."

She shook her head. "Les . . ."

"I'm busy, Miss," I said, picking up my knife. "This staying-sane gig is a full-time job."

A wry, conciliatory grimace. "Can't exactly argue with that."

"Well, then it's my turn for Twenty Questions," I said. "They replace me at school yet?"

"You're irreplaceable." She put up a hand. "And yes, I know what you meant, and no, they have not."

Whew. "How's your husband?"

"Busy doing ice sculptures for the Moscow-on-Thames crowd."

"And your son?" I said.

"My baby?" Her face did the melt. "He turned eighteen last week."

"Off to university soon, I reckon."

Miss beamed. "Art history at Oxford in the fall."

Of course. I stared down at the smudgy tabletop, my eyes smarting, my chest cramping with a sudden pang of yearning: to be more than a day-tripper in achievement country, to accomplish something concrete and easily validated rather than merely refrain from doing something fucked up. (Which, yes, was and is a major achievement, but at the time I didn't think of it like that. Didn't even want to. I wanted an acceptance letter I could hold up, wave under everyone's noses. Make them impressed. Bask in the congratulations. Prove intellect was as equally strong a force in my brain as unrest.)

Beneath the table, I felt Clare's hand rest soothingly on my knee, rubbing it. I looked over at her. *Watch out,* my gaze said. And then: *Thank you.*

Across from us, Miss was still smiling, but in a more subdued way now, wrapped in the shawl of her own nostalgia. "Want to see a picture?"

"Please," Clare said. Bless her, my girl, so eager.

I didn't really care to, but no way was I shooting Miss down, so I gave a polite nod and dutifully opened the small black leather folio she passed over.

"Ooh, wedding!" I shrieked in spite of myself when I spied the picture of her in her velvet dress, standing next to a tuxedoed fortyish man with hair dark as hers and a smoldery, solemn expression.

"He always this broody-looking?" I asked, holding up the photo.

Miss laughed. "Just having a Russian moment."

Clare slid closer to me. "Flip to the next one."

We paged through, weirdly giddy, hungry for glimpses of a life utterly unlike our own. Our forearms brushed. Our hands touched.

"You have dogs!" Clare squealed, pointing to a pair of long-haired dachshunds. One black, one red, curled up on a couch together, bored and languid.

"The hellhounds," Miss said. "Molly and Leopold."

On the next page, there was her boy, six feet tall and towheaded, captured in a doorway with one hand in his hair and a bottle of Guinness in the other, laughing. His ease so effortless it made me want to smack him.

"Girls completely lose the plot over him, I'll bet," Clare said.

"Oh, you have no idea," Miss said.

"Not a player, is he?" I asked.

"Would *you* be one, with me to answer to?" She laughed and reached over to take the album from Clare, her thumb brushing her son's cheek, leaving a glossy imprint. "Nah, Curran's a dream. Total sweetheart."

She redid the album's clasp and tucked it in her purse. "Will we be needing dessert, you think?"

"Just the loo right now," Clare said.

I got up to let her out of the booth, careful not to touch her, not even with a jostle. After I'd sat back down, Miss took a sip of her water, then set her glass down with a decisive thunk.

"You two," she said, "couldn't be any more adorable together if you tried."

My mouth fell open, same as it had the first time I saw
Clare in The Dress. "How did you—"

"Forty years of accrued intuition, darlin'."

Should have figured.

"I—I wasn't looking to," I said, staring down at the tabletop again. "It just . . . she just . . . happened."

"Best ones always do," Miss said.

"So no . . . no lecture?"

Miss leaned forward and put her hand over mine.

"Lesley," she said, "I'm in no position to judge anyone
else's hard-won happiness. Least of all yours."

"You won't tell, will you?"

"Why would I?"

"Because I'm—"

"Playing fast and loose with the rules? Taking some
risks? Yet another thing I've got no room to judge on." She
leaned back again, tucking her hair behind her ear. "Look,
if you were adult enough to sign yourself into the hospital,
you're adult enough to make your own decisions about how
much romantic adventure you're up for."

"Quite a lot," I said, grinning, as Clare came back towards us.

When she sat down in the booth, I slid up close and
draped my arm around her. She stiffened, glancing from me
to Miss, then back again.

Miss gave her a small smile. "No need to keep up the
charade on my account, Clare. Just promise me you'll be
careful, all right?"

• • •

In the photograph she took of us that day, Clare and I are pressed up against the side of her car, our arms wrapped round each other. Clare's grinning, bright-mouthed, facing the camera straight on, while I keep my head ducked, my own lips doing a *Mona Lisa* smile as they skim a wayward lock of her swept-up hair. The delectable flesh of her upper arm peeks out from the dress's short sleeves, squishy and soft in its reach across the plain baggy T-shirt concealing my chest. I look hardened but happy, my stance slouchy in my cargo trousers, my love-struck eyes, all shine, stuck fast upon her.

It's the only memento of us I have, save for our binder notes and the proclamations they wrote about us in my chart after. Even back then, crowded round Miss for a look, our heads bent over the teeny view screen of her phone's camera, we craved that proof, like graffiti: *Lesley and Clare were here.*

"Oh," Clare breathed. "You've got to make us a copy."

Later, Miss would get me one. Terrible print quality, even for a mobile snap, but I still keep it in a frame. I'd send a copy to Clare, too, if I knew where she was. Which of course begs the question: Does she even want to remember me? Haven't got room to ponder that one, not hardly, not now, so I content myself with remembering: her arm across my chest, my arm around her waist. Dark hair, pale cheeks, mixed-state gray sky.

• • •

Which is not to say, of course, that it was all Smartie-crapping unicorns and nibbled earlobes. 'Cause it wasn't. 'Cause it was hard.

Hard watching her parents show up and having to pretend I was the friendly roommate, nothing more, all the while wanting to throw it down, to shout: *You people are deluded asshats, and I'm madly in love with your daughter.*

Hard counting the days till May, nail-biting our way through the calendar, aching for us both to have autonomy.

Hard setting alarms on our watches at night for a quarter till midnight, reluctant and drowsy, sliding up and out into the cold air, into the empty bed opposite.

Hard (if also, let's be honest here, a little exciting) to have to press my hand over her mouth so Amal or Miranda or whoever was on night shift wouldn't hear.

And the hardest, the absolute hardest: that I wouldn't let her in.

Wasn't about wanting to be in control of her; it was just about wanting one hundred percent control over *me*. Which she always let me have.

Still, for all her acquiescence, I knew she ached for things to be different. You'd never guess it from the demure front she put on, but my Clare was fierce. "Don't knock it till you've tried it, baby," she'd murmur, her eyes all wicked-glinty behind those glasses, her mind full of naughty ideas I knew she was dying to test out on me. And I'd shake my head mournfully and slide back on my bed, watching her eyes turn plaintive, then dejected. I'd have been in heaven till 11:45 alarm call, if only I'd allowed myself to open up. But I couldn't.

"You're quite invested in avoiding feeling vulnerable, aren't you?" Bethan asked me once, crossing and uncrossing her mulberry-stockinged legs.

I thought of the wind-sharp slap of shocked embodiment that hit me each time the crotch of my knickers went damp. Of the way every muscle in me tensed, not with arousal but with greyhound alertness, whenever Clare shyly attempted to lean over me and pin my hands down or slide her knuckles inside my trousers.

"No idea what the fuck you're talking about," I said. Which, as Bethan was quick to note, proved her point precisely.

"All right, then," I said. "So I'm a closed trap, a walled fortress. Does that mean I'm never going to be able to have a proper relationship?" (Said earnestly, as if I'd never shared so much as a chaste kiss, much less a star-crossed *ELOPE-MENT RISK* love affair.)

"Not necessarily," Bethan said. "It's just going to take some time whilst you unknot all these issues."

Fuck that fuck that fucking fuck that. I didn't have time to spare, and the only things I wanted to unknot were my belt buckle and Clare's plait.

And so, the night after Miss's March visit, I decided I would give it a go.

Things started out all right, our usual tangle, mouth arms legs, me still in my yoga pajamas. When her fingers tugged cheekily against my waistband, I didn't stop them. Clare glanced at me, one eyebrow raised in an expression equal parts quizzical and sexy.

"Yeah?" she said, her mouth against my ear.

"Yeah," I said, my voice hoarse. To her it probably sounded husky with excitement, but in reality I was terrified.

She slipped her fingers into the space between the stretchy trouser fabric and my knickers. I held my breath. My hips stayed stiff.

"Kiss me," I said, hoping that would distract me from the goings-on down below.

Her mouth sank into mine, my tongue meeting hers, moving while she moved, familiar safe dance, soothing enough to let me let her stroke with her fingertips. Suffused, swollen twitch. *Just relax, love,* I told myself, as if I were one of those medics who'd picked me up off the floor of the girls' toilets and strapped me on their trolley.

"Mmm," Clare hummed in my throat, as she inched her fingers back up to my waistband and then inside my knickers. Clumsy, fumbling hand, same as mine had been the first time I'd done for her. Knuckles twining through dense fronds of hair. Ticklish.

I pulled back for air. Laughed a little. Tinny, tremory. Felt good to make noise, break the awkwardness into mosaic pieces of sound.

"Sorry," she said under her breath.

"It's cool," I said, even though I had no idea whether it was or not. My body in limbo, dangerously close to dissociation.

Clare slid her hand down farther. Jerky, inept motion. Abrasive and dry. Not like she had much to work with, though, seeing how tightly I was holding myself together.

"You know," she said, "this would work a lot better if you—"

"Okay." Still freaking big-time, but hell if I was going to let her see.

Swift and assured, her hands moved to help me out of my clothes, but I stopped them. Couldn't help it. I wanted— no, *needed*—this part on my terms.

I peeled the trousers off, leaving them in a wad close by. Snuggled up closer to her.

"Sorry I'm so slow," I said. "Assess-and-adjust period, and all that."

She laughed. Gave me a grin. Licked her index finger.

My legs shifted, their upper thighs opening just a touch. I was rocking some granny knickers, their elastic frayed enough to make them quite loose, so her hand worked its way in and down easily now.

Her voice at my ear was elated and breathy. "Oh my God, you've no idea how much I've—"

Shut up. Just kiss me.

Mmmph. The hum tinged with hard breathless swallow this time. Her moist finger finding exactly what it was looking for, tracing swirly little circles, spirals almost. Curving in on themselves, round round round, endless.

My legs fell open. My mind curled to the ceiling. Wisp of smoke, pigtail, silky nylon end of that funfair balloon. Float, bob, float.

A sucking sound, slick. Wet fingers? No, no, no. Water gurgling down a drain? Maybe. That's better. Closer. Seaside? Yeah, down Margate. Old soothing memory. Carousel, candyfloss, him carrying me on his shoulders, not holding me by the hair. Wasn't more than a few seconds before I was back on the ceiling, going round round round, riding a dark horse, licking pink nothing.

And then, jerking down to find myself sprawled on my back, my dislocated arousal making a moist sound like boots squished through mud in time to the rhythm—dive, retreat—of her fingers, Jesus flipping Christ, her beautiful broad fingers that needed to get the fuck out of me, and then I was sitting up, shaking, rocking, babbling that old litany of childlike protest: *Nonononono.*

"Lesley?" Tiny voice. Hesitant hand on my spine.

Whimper, rock, whimper.

Her tone shaky, scared now. "Honey?"

I gave Clare a skittish glance. "C-cold."

"Here. Oh, here." She gathered up my cast-off under-wear and yoga trousers. "You want me to—"

I shook my head furiously. Scrambled to put my clothes back on. Huddled with my back to her, up against the wall.

"I'm s-sorry." Even with my head turned, I could tell from the break in her syllables that she was on the verge of crying.

I rolled over to face her, my hands locked protectively between my knees as I watched her wipe her drippy nose.

"I should have known," she sniffled. "But I just thought you were spaced out from enjoying it."

"Were you?"

"Enjoying it?" She frowned. "Well, yeah, till I realized what I'd done."

"Clare," I said, freeing one hand to touch her arm. "It's not your fault."

"I know, but . . ." She looked away.

"Hey," I said softly. "Come here."

A skeptical glance. "You still want me, after that?"

"You still want *me*?"

In answer, she crawled over and drew me into her arms. "Soon as you graduate from trauma group," she murmured, "I'm rocking your world."

I cuddled my face against her chest. "Don't talk about it. Too scary."

Clare stroked the back of my neck with her damp fingers. "What shall we talk about, then?"

"What you're making for dessert next time you're on kitchen duty."

"Ohh, that's a good one." She nestled her chin atop my freshly buzzed scalp. "I was thinking some bread pudding with chocolate shavings atop it. Not just any chocolate, either."

"No?" My eyelids began to flicker, the drained post-panic sleep starting to overtake me.

She kissed the top of my head. "Nope. There's a gourmet shop I saw in town last time Mum and Dad took me out. Super posh. You can get all these exotic-flavored chocolate bars, with the craziest stuff in them."

I yawned. "Like what?"

"Chilies. Blueberries. Bacon."

"Nasty."

"Yeah, but you know which one wasn't?"

"Mmm."

"Lavender." She whispered the word into my ear. "Could you imagine that, little lavender chocolate bread pudding? Wouldn't that be ace?"

I nodded. "Or those poached pears you did last week. With the whipped cream."

"Yesss. What do you want for your birthday dinner?"

I wiggled even closer, close as I could get, my bony hips pressed against her well-padded ones, my arms nestled round her waist. "Dunno. That's like a month away."

"Right, but I need to plan. Pesto tagliatelle? Chicken korma?"

I grinned into her nightdress. "Unicorn Smartie trifle."

We both laughed. "No, really," she said. "What do you want?"

Safety? Recovery? Five A-levels? *Your mouth everywhere*, I almost said, would have said, had I not already been spirited off to the land of unconscious oblivion, sedated as if I'd been doled out ten milligrams of Valium, lulled by her breath's steady rise and fall.

9

My seventeenth birthday fell on a Saturday in April. I'd have gone out to celebrate with Clare, but of course her parents were coming up for the afternoon. That killed me. Not just because their visit would ruin any chance of our spending time together, but also because it was one more reminder of my parents' absence. (I'd yearned yet again for a card, but no such luck.)

"You'll have a brilliant time with Mrs. Kremsky," Clare said soothingly, just before she left our room for the day. "Won't you?"

"Sure I will," I said. "But that's not the p—"

Clare silenced me with a kiss on the mouth. "Your birthday will be fantastic, I promise."

After she'd gone, I sat on my bed and flipped through my soul postcards, trying to distract myself from the reunion I knew she was having.

Didn't work, so I curled up, and closed my eyes, and

chastised myself: *Her parents are homophobic arseholes. You shouldn't envy her them.*

Didn't work, either.

"Call for you, Les," I heard Nina yell down the hall.

Mum. Maybe?

I jumped up and sprinted for the phone. Grabbed its clunky black receiver.

Please, please, please. "Hello?"

"Hey, Lesley."

Any other time, I'd be thrilled to hear that voice, but just then my heart plummeted. "Hi, Miss."

"Listen, sweetie, the traffic is completely ridiculous, but I'll be there soon as I can."

I went back to my room. Sat slumped against the wall on Clare's bed. Hugged one of her pillows. Drifted to the ceiling.

Next I knew, there came a knock at the door.

"Come—come in," I said, startled.

Miss peeked her head around the corner. "Better late than never, right?"

I grinned despite myself. "Flippin' yeah."

She hurried over to sit next to me. "I am *so* sorry, birthday girl."

When we pulled back from our long hug, I was struck by how feminine she looked in her linen dress and matching jacket, her hair pulled back demurely, her earrings delicate dangles.

For a second I was afraid she'd lost her edge, but then she licked her thumb and reached over to wipe a smudge from the corner of my mouth. "If you want to keep covering your tracks, you'd best start wearing lipstick in earnest, kiddo."

"Not a chance," I said, and gestured towards my new boots. "How d'you like these bad boys? Scored them at a charity shop. Steel toes and everything."

Miss surveyed the scuffed leather. "Well," she said with an amused smile, "you've certainly outpunked me."

Sweet. We went downstairs and headed out to her car for the unveiling of my present. "Close your eyes," she ordered, and began rummaging about in the back.

I heard a thump, and then the slightest hint of a metallic twang.

"Okay. You can look now."

I opened my eyes to see her holding out a guitar case.

My hands flew to my mouth. "No. Bloody. Way. How did you—"

"Clare," Miss said, passing it over. "We had a secret hall-phone conference plotting what to get you. Figured you could use a little music therapy."

"God, Miss." My fingers wrapped round the case's handle, squeezing it in delight. "You two are fucking ace."

She grabbed a picnic blanket and we headed for the garden, where I pulled out the guitar and commenced ineptly picking out chords.

"I wanted to bring us some sangria to celebrate with," Miss said, peeling out of her jacket and sitting down next to me. "But they apparently don't take too kindly to booze-smuggling around here."

"That's okay," I said with a laugh as I lay back on the blanket. "I'd be good with just some chocolate."

"Well, that I've got." She reached into her purse and handed me a packet. "My emergency stash."

On its wrapper, a reproduction of an old-timey oil-painted cherub stared coyly at me, plump-cheeked, its bow lips pouty. I ran my fingers over the Cyrillic letters above the baby's head. "What's it called?"

"Red October," Miss said.

I ripped the papery angel in two, straight down the middle. "Revolution-worthy, huh?"

"Nah, just my husband's childhood favorite."

Yum, more hazelnuts. "He ever take you back there to visit?"

"Not yet, but we'll be going soon." Small smile, girlish and tentative as Clare's. "Hopefully."

I draped an arm over my eyes to shield them from the sunlight. "Must be a mess to sort out the visas."

"Oh, no, that part's easy. It's more an issue of whether or not we'll be able to . . ."

Her voice was matter-of-fact, but her hesitant trail-off made me both concerned and curious.

I lowered my arm onto my chest so I could see her properly. "What?"

Her shoulders hunched in a mash-up of what looked like tenderness and excitement and nerves. "My husband and I, we're . . ." Her face did the melt. "Trying to adopt a little girl from Russia."

Gobsmacked, I sat up slowly. "You're joking, right?"

She shook her head. "For the longest time, Jascha kept asking me, 'Don't you want another?' And I always said, 'No, no, one's all I can handle.' For *years*, I kept insisting!

But then, that night at the hospital, being there with you, it just . . . opened up that maternal desire again."

I wish I could say that I'd been happy for her, or at least honored, but all I felt was deserted fury.

"That's right," I said, scrambling to close the latches on the guitar case. "Make sangria off my rotten lemons. Call me an inspiration and then ditch me on my fucking birthday."

Her mouth crumpled. "Lesley, I'm not—"

"Oh, don't even. Soon as you find your new waif, that'll be the end of visiting me, won't it?" I shoved the guitar at her and stood up. "Fine. Let's just get it over with."

I stomped towards the patio where the adult patients were out having their cigarette breaks, but only got in a few huffy paces before Miss caught up and grabbed my arm.

"Les," she said, breathless, turning me round.

"Let *go* of me."

"No," she said, so sharply I stopped trying to wrench away. "I won't. Not ever."

On those last two words, her voice softened. She let go my arm, and brought her hands up to cup my face.

"I'd adopt you if I could," she said quietly. "I know you won't believe that, but it's true. Ask Francesca."

My heart just about flipping stopped. "You—you talked to her about . . . doing that?"

Miss nodded. "She said the approval process takes at least a year, at which point you'd be eighteen already, so—"

"But you—you were keen on it," I said, my voice shaking. "You wanted to."

Soon as she nodded, I burst into tears. Threw my arms around her.

"Oh, lovey," she said, kissing the top of my head. "Don't cry. Don't worry. You'll always be welcome with us."

"So your husband, your son," I said, sniffling, grinning. "They're okay with some crazy girl being an informal part of their family?"

"Why not? They've had me as a formal member for ages." She draped an arm around my shoulders and walked me back to our blanket. "Besides, Jasch isn't exactly a stranger to PTSD, either."

That rocked me back for a second. "Really?"

She nodded. "Survived a horrible car accident years ago. Bad enough to kill his first wife and daughter."

"Holy shit," I breathed. "Talk about rising from the ashes."

"We're all phoenixes in some way or another, sweetheart," Miss said, reaching across me for another piece of chocolate, her firebird ink peeking out stubbornly from the elegantly seamed confines of her sleeveless dress.

Later that afternoon, on my way back up to the third floor, I took the stairs instead of the lift, swinging my new gift around like I was flipping Julie Andrews skipping down the road with her shabby carpetbag to catch her Salzburg bus.

"Surprise!"

There they stood beneath streamers in the commons, Nina and Parvati and Chloe and Amal and Miranda and even Kath, holding a banner with my name done up all swirly in purple art workshop glitter glue.

"Sentimental fuckers," I said, shaking my head. "You'd think I was graduating or something."

"Clare's in the kitchen," Parvati said, as if anticipating my eyes' hungry scan. (Crap. Did she know?)

We all trooped in, me still clutching my new guitar *(my! new! guitar!)*, to find a massive spread on the counter: paper cups full of punch, little sandwiches, and, right in the middle, the main attraction—not simple chocolate-topped pudding, but a layer cake that looked like it ought to be on one of those reality shows where bridezillas tear up tulle dresses in fits of rage.

"Told you it'd be fantastic," Clare said.

"You sneaky thing," I said. "Your mum and dad never even came, did they?"

"Nope." She gave me one of her wicked glances.

Of course I went over to hug her, every muscle in me tight with propriety, so guarded I was sure everyone could see what a giant faker I was.

We took our plates to the table, me in the place of honor at the head, Clare next to me. The room truly festive: our usually sullen crowd full of laughter, forks clinking, the anorexics actually eating without protest. Closest we ever got—ever will get—to a wedding reception. No brides from hell, just my own teenage transparency, burning bright and simple as striped candles.

Someone—Nina?—had bought trick ones to stick in the cake. Clare was vexed, but I just kept blowing. Take that, and that, and that, like the first delicate pricks of my blade. Put that light out. Right out. Applause. My invincibility so fragile in retrospect that I long to reach over, and touch my former self's sharp shoulder, and whisper in warning short-hand: *pride, fall, can't, won't, last.*

Pointless. After all, what need was there for her to listen? She had a guitar, and a family waiting for her back in London, and a birthday cake to put the food hall at Harrods to shame, and a mood good enough to ensure that later that evening—to cap off the best bloody day of her short, histrionic life—she would let her girlfriend really, truly, properly fuck her.

It starts with a lavender candle atop my dresser in a silver metal tin. Soothing flicker. Clare's face, shining but shadowed, in the mirror. She turns round in a short new nightdress, sleeveless and silky purple, another birthday surprise for me. Her hair loose, a dark smoky silhouette.

I am burrowed beneath blankets, curled up in just my T-shirt and knickers. The press of my bare legs against the sheet, against each other, cool and satisfying.

Her sock feet shuffle across the linoleum. She sits down on my bed next to me, the mattress sighing with her weight, her bum nudged up against my thigh. She jostles my hip with her hand. "Not falling asleep on me, are you?"

Half-smile. I look up, mellow enough for a ceiling hover, but this time, I'm right here. Right *here*.

I curl in closer, savoring it. Roll onto my back as she strokes first my hair and then the side of my face, the whispery trail of her fingers slow and deliberate.

When she bends to kiss me on the forehead, first thing

I think is *No, not like that.* I lift my head, the muscles in my neck hardening as I struggle to meet her mouth.

"Let me do it," she murmurs, cradling my skull in her palms like I'm my own daughter, the one she'll never meet. My shoulders fall back, obedient and grateful, as she lowers me, her hair falling round the pillow, a coarse corkscrew waterfall. Her breath, seconds from breathing into mine, smells of buttercream and vanilla.

And then she kisses me. Not lets me kiss her, not kisses me back, but kisses *me*, opening my mouth up, taking my tongue over, so self-assured I ought to be scared, so gentle I'm not at all. When she lies down atop me, the ample-fleshed press of her makes my hips arch.

Clare props up on her elbows as she draws back for air. Her hair still all around me. Haloed. Her lips crooked, smiling.

I smile back at her, amazement-drunk.

"You okay?" she asks.

I nod. Shift a little, wriggling my knees open so she can get more comfortable. As she settles into me, her thighs push mine apart, anchoring her in me, me to her. Grounded. I think of flowering trees, of the earthy flourish of roots' gradual tangle, and then she scoots down, and loosens the blanket, and kisses me all over through my T-shirt, rolling the shirt's fabric up, revealing me in flickery half-light, pale nipples and prominent ribs, so embarrassing I shiver.

The covers bunch at my waist now. Clare smooths my T-shirt back into place. Lets her hand rest, palm flat, fingers spread, along the upper hem of the blanket. Not at my knickers, but close. Her body poised to slide down farther or sit up fast. Her eyes blinking in silent query.

I want to close my own eyes, but I force them to stay open. Sink fully into the feel of her palm's light but sweaty pressure atop my lower belly. *Breathe*, I tell myself, and I do, so deeply her hand rises.

"Les," she says, her voice hoarse. "If I'm . . . if we're . . ."

Her throat catches. Shit, it hurts to watch her like this.

"You—" Trembly lip. Oh, sweetheart. "You're gonna need to stay here, okay?"

No way I can promise and not mean it. No chance I can just think, *All right, sure, we'll give that a go*, and keep the ceiling backup plan handy. So I look straight into her lush, sorrowful face and—

"Yes," I say. Not quite Molly Bloom, but hardly closet Lesley, either.

Clare hears the difference in my voice, I can tell. Her expression too guarded to be pleased. Hopeful? Can't let her down. No, can't let *me* down.

My gaze swings wildly towards the dresser-top candle and its equally unbridled flame. Something about the warm flutter gives me a sudden burst of clarity, of calm. I lift my knees just enough to slip my knickers off. Hand them to her, our fingers brushing.

When I look down, she's nestled between my legs, balanced on her elbows again, her face upturned towards mine. Her tongue darts out, moistens her lower lip in a quick flicker.

"Close your eyes," she says.

Of course I do it. Not out of fear, not out of nerves, but

because I trust her, so completely my shoulders melt into the mattress, so fully the muscles in my neck yield.

And then, soft as you can imagine, there it is, the warm-wetdelicate bath of the one thing he'd not ever done to me. Her tongue taking over again, twirling lush swirls, leaving me awash in swollen sensation, head tipped back, I start to grin but then I'm stopped by the slow, relentless rhythm of being sucked at, holy fucking sodding shit, how did I live on the ceiling for so long and not know that bodies, *my* body, could do this, spun round in a tide pool of pleasure, deep inside itself yet floating, whirling in such dervish delight that—

Short, sharp nibble of teeth. Ow. Urgh.

I wince. Turn my head. Press a hand across my eyes.

"Too much?"

I nod. Let out a deep, slow breath.

"Sorry, sorry, sorry." Clare leans up to give me a quick apology of a kiss, like the pressing of a flower, on my hip bone. Her gaze flickers to meet mine, alarmed and alert.

"Come here, you." I motion her up to me, pull her close in reassurance. The taste of her mouth is weird and swampy, but not in a bad way. In fact, it's super exciting—not just because of where it's been but because I'm still here. *Still!* We've just had a little *thanks but no thanks* moment, nothing crisis-worthy, right back in the game like a normal person, few seconds of commercial break and now, check it out, I'm nudging Clare back down.

She moves so slowly, taking her time, relishing this, I can tell. Looking up at me, giving her right thumb a brief lick, then sucking long and hard on her fingers, two at a time, all the way up to the second knuckle.

Every muscle in me clenches, not with panic but with anticipation. I breathe, and breathe, and breathe.

Without taking her eyes off mine, Clare presses her thumb to me, circling more lightly than before. I start to drift, I start to float again, back to the place where she took me before her teeth broke the spell. I feel the slip of one finger, careful and tentative, her slowness welcome now. I watch the candle, its blurry, burnished smear of light dancing in time to languid entrance, drawn-out retreat.

When the second slide comes, it's a touch harder, but I breathe through it, relax into the slight twist. My boots tramping through more mud, soft squashy footprints.

She sits up gradually, raising her right arm as little as possible, until she's crouched on her knees between mine. Gaze questioning, she crooks her ring finger.

I nod. Breathe. There's a juicy push, a demi-stretch.

Her wrist turns. "Too—"

I shake my head. Her fingers shift, triangulating, making room for her pinkie. Tiny stub, snuck in, but I still flinch, my body fighting the fullness.

Clare's face cramps. "Should I stop?"

"No," I say, and grab her free hand. Squeeze it tight as I will Gloria's and Imogen's five years later, bent double in the grip of labor, leaning into the pain like a strong shoulder, pushing out then, taking in now.

"Can I try something?" Clare whispers.

"Sure," I mumble, lost in the whirlpool.

I feel her fingers shift and compact into a dense cluster, making way for the awkward worm-wedge of her thumb. I bite my lip. Scrunch my eyes closed tight. Her hand curves, her fingers' last set of knuckles poised.

I open my eyes. "Do it fast," I tell her.

Rough, inept shove, so hard I want to scream, so hard it will bruise, so hard I have to breathe breathe breathe, candle candle candle, stare stare stare at her beautiful haloed face, tender and grave.

The fingers of her left hand caress-coax mine to loosen. The fingers of her right hand fold into her palm. Clench. Fly. Clench. Fly.

I prop up on my elbows. Stare down at the sight of her buried in me, up to her wrist. For a moment, I feel a bizarre, clinical detachment, like I'm looking at my bad arm transformed into a gaping-mouthed red change purse, but then I'm overtaken with awe: that she can go so deep, that I can let her and not die.

A grin spreads across my face. Clare reaches up, rests her left hand against my cheek. Her right fist's rhythm lunging, almost a punch, her jutting knuckles nudged far as they can go. With every list forward, there's a twinge high up in my belly, a stinging shard of pleasure.

Clare clenches her fist one last time. Slides her hand and her fingers almost all the way out, the expanse and release so huge it's almost enough to set me off and finish me up, but then—incorrigible thing, paying no mind to my tetchy little groan, her eyes warning *just you wait*—she dives back in, turning me inside out with just the barest tilt of her fingers, and then I'm gone, Margate tide rolling in, salty gush on a ragged shoreline, Howth Head flower of the mountain, yes

I'm romanticizing but I can't help it, my eyes full of tears then and now, Clare stroke-stroke-stroking my cheekbone with her thumb, whispering "There's my girl, there's my girl," as I come so hard I fear I might splinter, sounds tumbling from my mouth that drone and wail, an ambulance siren of screamsobs, so loud and unbridled I miss the alarm on my watch, miss the knock on the door, miss the "Bed check, ladies" call, miss every last reminder of where we are and how bold and sloppy with desire we've become, until I open my eyes and see no-excuses-entertained Amal, framed by the spiky jumps of the candle in ominous silhouette, standing at the end of my mattress.

10

After that came a string of moments I'd rather not remember, hard and jagged as chain-link fence in a prison yard:

The 12:01 march down the hall, strong-armed by Amal and Miranda into separate rooms.

The treatment meeting the next morning, during which Kath informed me that I had "broken the therapeutic alliance" and would have to be discharged.

The shame of being sat down outside her office, head in my hands, listening in to fragments of conversation on the other side of the door.

"Your staff promised us . . . safe from negative influences."

"But, Mummy, I told you, it wasn't—"

"Clare, please. There's no excuse for . . . godless whore."

"Mr. and Mrs. Manning, you need to understand . . . chronic history of sexual abuse . . . learned patterns of . . ."

Right. Just the latest pathological model, fresh off the factory line. Living proof the exploited will exploit.

I wanted to vomit. I wanted to bash their self-righteous heads in. I wanted to grab Clare by the hand and whisper *Let's take that elopement risk,* sprint past the phoenix mural, down the lifts, and out the front doors.

Instead I watched as, flanked by her mum and dad, Clare came out into the corridor wearing The Dress, her reddened eyes wide and damp, her tear-stained face numb. When she turned her chin to meet my gaze, just for a second, I stared back, stricken and helpless, my own face melty as Miss's, my lower lip trembling.

"So immodest," Clare's mum *tsk*ed, shaking her head as she tugged at Clare's grommety claret-colored sleeve. Hurrying her along, while her dad carried the suitcases.

And that was it. No surreptitious farewell kiss, no secret slipping of phone numbers into pockets. Inert with disbelief, still smarting with soreness from what she'd done the night before, I watched her meek retreat and thought: *Bitch. Coward.*

Years later, my heart aches not for my own day-past-seventeen devastation, but for month-from-sixteen Clare's. I imagine her now at twenty-one, with a soft butch girlfriend and a smashing job mentoring LGBT teens or managing the office of some chillaxed progressive Christian church, greeting new visitors in a Bettie Page hairdo and a vintage dress. I try not to picture her lying on a morgue slab, cold and yellowy-eyed.

But despite my reflexive habit of obituary scanning, you've got to figure: if I've been all over the telly and in the national newspapers and she's not come forward to contact me, she's probably dead. Maybe I'm flattering myself, or maybe she's brilliantly sorted out and just wants to put the crazy days behind her, but either way, I don't hold out much hope. It's in short supply right now, and I have to triage it like a casualty nurse, ration it like wartime silk.

While I waited in the hall with more than just my pride unbearably tender, Kath was on the phone to Francesca, giving her the Lesley-as-seductress rundown. After a few minutes, she ushered me in to talk with Francesca myself.

"Please," I whispered, soon as I got on the line, "you have to understand, we were properly in love, Francesca, I swear it wasn't—"

"Lesley," she said, "I want you to know two things: One, that I believe you. And two, that Clare's family plans to . . ." Her voice broke. "To report this to police."

What? "I—I don't . . . Why?"

"Under age of consent law, you're automatically considered an assault perpetrator."

Oh, shit. Jesus fucking fucking Christ.

"Just because she was—even though it was—"

"Consensual? I'm afraid so."

My shoulders shook. My hands trembled. I put my palm to my mouth. Let out a whimper.

"Listen to me," Francesca said, her voice both hypnotic and firm. "This is not the end of the road for you."

Tears and snot and sobs of disbelief. Everything running, slipping through my fingers. The cored apple of my insides dissolving into frantic mush.

"Here's what I want you to do," Francesca went on. "Take a taxi to the train station, and get the first express back to London that you can."

"But I—I haven't any money." My words were a choked gulp.

"Kath will give you some."

Anything to get rid of me, right? "And then, when—"

"I'll meet you at St. Pancras."

"With a bunch of police?"

"No. Just me."

I wiped my nose with the side of my hand. "Promise?"

"Promise."

I shuffled through the ticket hall at Nottingham station in a sluggish haze, guitar case in one hand, bin bag full of clothes in the other. My shoulders hunched with the weight of my rucksack; my mind flitted to the apex of the room's high ceiling, then crawled back down the face of its giant clock like a groggy spider.

Each time I bumped into someone with a startled, mumbly "Pardon," they stepped back so sharply I was sure they thought me a precociously afflicted version of One of "Those" People. I would have been affronted, were it not for the knowledge that they were absolutely correct. I was One of "Those," and then some: psych ward reject, alleged sex abuser, southbound for—what? Another bare-bulbed hostel? Court-mandated lockdown in a young offender institution?

In my head, I could hear Francesca and Miss giving me

pep talks filled with complete-and-utter-bollocks buzzwords like *potential* and *hope* and *resilience*. As I passed a phone box, I thought about ringing them, but then I pictured myself getting all choked up and changing my mind, and knew I couldn't take the chance. Wasn't like they'd answer, anyway; Miss was probably rushing round to get all her adoption paperwork ready, and Francesca was no doubt preparing similar documentation in order to prove I'd not coerced anyone into fucking me or being fucked.

I wended my way past benches to the ladies' room, which was almost empty, thanks to the midafternoon lull. No commuters cramming the stalls. Good.

I edged past a young mum with a posh nappy bag—pretty Asian brocade, chocolate and teal—balanced on one shoulder, and a dark-haired moppet in pink corduroy dungarees perched on her hip. She gave me a quick, polite smile as she hurried past, but the baby girl full-on grinned, flashing two top teeth, pert and pearly, so embracing of my grungy strangeness that, for a second, she convinced me I wasn't too far gone.

But then *they* were gone, with a cheerful "Let's go find your daddy, shall we?" and a thunk of the door, leaving me alone yet again before my self-hatred and a smudgy mirror.

Sharp hair spikes. Swollen eyes. Set jaw. I imagined my mug shot, all defiant chin and vacant stare, posed just above the white-on-black letters spelling out the surname of the one who had supposedly made me this way. A legacy you could legally clear, but never erase.

Soon as I pictured that, I knew the baby's smile had been a mirage, knew I had to do it. I hefted my guitar and bin bag into the largest stall I could find, farthest from the toilets' entrance, and locked the door. Placed the guitar lovingly on its side. Punched the bag into a makeshift pillow, and arranged it atop the guitar's case, in that little culvert between its neck and body. Nestled my rucksack close by and sat down cross-legged to rummage through it.

Ulysses, no. Soul cards, not under the circumstances, haha. Phoenix binder with Clare's notes, oh, no, no.

One by one, I pulled out the trifecta:

My CD player and headphones.

A bottle of water from the vending machine across the hall.

An economy-sized bottle of aspirin tablets, bought from the Boots up the road while my cabdriver waited, meter running.

I put in my headphones. Soundless, for now. Plugging my senses up. The yielding pop of the water bottle's cap strangely satisfying.

Tablet bottle wasn't messing about, though. Sticky as hell, like it was testing me, like it was channeling him back in the days of the hall closet: *You really want this? Hmm? I know you do. Show me you do.* Faking to avoid the choke hold.

Not bloody faking *now*. I wrenched that fucker open, scraping free its papery seal. Stared down into the bottle at the round white arsenal. It sounds demented now, but seeing all those pills gave me a sudden burst of strength, a quick surge of power. I wasn't sticking around to be lied about, or to be made an object lesson, or to crawl raw-kneed down that road Francesca claimed wasn't necessarily ending in a jail cell. Oh, no, I was spiriting away on a white (tablet) horse and sticking it to them. I was going to make them *sorry*.

Soon as I shook a handful of pills into my palm, though, I started to panic. What if I vomited them all up and they didn't take and I wound up in an ambulance like Clare had once, with one of those medics lubing up a big plastic tube to snake down my nose into my throat?

The thought of Clare made me shake out even more tablets. *There's my girl,* I told myself, like an encouraging lover. A waterfall of tablets cascaded into my lap. Couple bounced off my knee, landed on the dirty floor. I plucked one of them between my thumb and forefinger and placed it cautiously on my tongue, letting it disintegrate a little, all grungy chemical tang.

I longed to spit, but stood firm. Chased it down with a chug of water. Pinched a second pill from the floor and popped it firmly into my mouth, following it immediately with a throaty swallow.

Two down, one hundred eighteen to go.

First tablet past the bottle-instructed maximum dose was the hardest. I stared that little bugger down for nigh on five minutes, statue-still, while an old lady clomped in on orthopedic soles. Once she'd made her exit, I sat up straighter, and channeled him again, and ordered myself: *Swallow, bitch.*

Little by little, like Clare's knuckles, I worked my way up to three, then four, then five. Got easier, then. Scoop, toss, gulp. Scoop, toss, gulp. Automatic pilot. Head buzzing like the wonky fluorescents above me. My hand molded into a pill-catching cup. Outside, a rumbly announcement of the imminent departure of the train I'd been supposed to catch.

On the next round, I tasted salt. Reached my free hand up to my face to feel the wetness. First thought I had was: *The ceiling's leaking.* Then: My *ceiling's leaking.* And then, detached as a severed limb: *Oh. Crying.*

I looked down into the half-empty bottle. Pressed the handcup—no, say it right, *my hand*—to my mouth to stop myself from sobbing in earnest, but my body fought back. Lips curved. Eyes screwed shut. Shoulders arms fingers face quaking.

Stop. Stop it. I'll buy you a Cadbury Flake if you'll just fucking shut up. Or even, if you're really good, some Russian revolution chocolate. Hazelnuts and a little cherub, ripped in half, I know, but still, but . . . Shh, Lesley-lovely. Here.

Swig. Swallow. Swig. Swallow. By the time I'd worked my way to the bottom, the announcer had called three more trains.

One last glug. I pushed myself to my feet to unlock the door and walked out to the sinks like it was nothing. Tossed the bottle in the bin and covered it with handfuls of paper towel.

I took off my jacket. Sat on the stall floor and dug in my rucksack for the train timetable I'd plucked off the rack so I could at least impersonate a person with a plan who knew where she was going. Uncapped the plum fine-point Sharpie I'd borrowed off Chloe a few days earlier, and turned to the lightest-hued fold of the timetable.

Tell Gloria Kremsky I love her, I scrawled. *Tell Francesca Fleming-Jones thank you.*

Then I tucked the instructions at my elbow, lay back on my plasticky pillow, and draped my jacket over myself. No blood, this time. Just me and my headphones, still lifesavers. I hit PLAY.

"Little light, shining . . ." Kate Bush and her piano, out there on the waves. I knew it was a song about a disoriented woman drowning, but all I could think of was that baby's spit-drenched grin as I let the nausea lap over me like an incoming tide, then push me back out again, buoy-less, lifeboat-less, my eyelids flickering until they closed.

11

Groggy head-shake, chin-jerk, wrist-throb. Off in the distance, a beepthumphiss. Like an old radiator, only more machine-y.

My crusty eyes scraped open. Tape on my hands. Tape over my mouth. What the—?

Just swallow. Try to swallow. Can't swallow. Oh my God, there's something down my throat, get it out, fucking get it—

"Stop. *Stop.*" Steady, forceful male voice, Eastern European accent. His firm hands prying mine away from the plastic piping that protruded from my swollen lips.

I scratched at him, scratched at the drip lines, scratched at the bedclothes, scratched at the (fuck oh fuck oh fuck) catheter shoved up me and snaking out of my knickers, everything I could reach, it all had to tear.

"Lesley. Don't."

At the sound of my name, I startled. Glanced to the right. Realized it was Miss's Russian husband leaning over me. Mr.

Broodyface. I could see why she'd fancied him. All that dark smolder, now focused in forehead-furrowed concern, on me.

"Please, try to—"

What? Relax, love? I ripped my hands out of his. Slammed my fists against the bed's guardrails.

"Look," he said. "I know the last thing you want right now is some strange man trying to keep you from finishing what you started."

With my least-taped hand, I flipped him off.

Not so much as a frown. "And you're no doubt thinking, *Fucking wanker, don't give me that empathetic crap, 'cause you haven't got a clue what this is like.*"

I shook my head.

"No?"

I shook my head again. Gestured towards my gagged-and-bound mouth.

"Here," he said quickly, grabbing a pen and paper from a nearby nightstand and placing the pad gently atop my blanketed right knee.

My fingers fumbled with the pen, the top of my hand smarting from the tilt and pull of the surgical tape, my scratchy handwriting befitting the sociopath I still believed myself to be.

Reading mind. U = me? After yr accident?

He swallowed. "Yes," he said. "When I woke up, I tried to punch the nurses. Scrawled notes to my doctors that they should have let me die."

TRUE, I wrote.

"What?" he said. "That you should have died?"

I nodded. *U going 2 try 2 convince me that's rubbish?*

A quiet, world-weary sigh. "No."

Thx.

"I do, however," he said, punching the call button above my bed, "need to let the staff know you've woken up."

How long? I wrote.

"You were in a coma for two days."

Two whole days, spent pissing myself and being breathed for by a machine. God. How disgusting.

Miss send u here?

He shook his head. "I sent *her* downstairs to eat. She's not moved from your room the whole time."

Took off school?

"Soon as she heard."

I closed my eyes. Told myself to feel touched, but all I felt was the weight of obligation: to thank her for her wasted effort; to rise from my bed like one of those bloody phoenixes who, at that point, felt more like albatrosses.

Bless him, Mr. Miss (I knew he had a name she'd mentioned before, but I was blanking on it then) kept her waiting in the café while the nurses came round and checked my vital signs (status: infuriatingly vital) and my throat plug and my drip tubes and my heart-monitoring stickypads and (fuck oh fuck oh fuck) the placement of my catheter—that last procedure so terrifying I buried my face in Mr. Miss's shirt the whole time. Never thought I'd willingly seek comfort from a man my dad's age, but there I was, comforted by the warmth of his chest and the cradle of his hand against my head.

After that, I was so exhausted and shaky I sank back on the pillow. Beepy heart thingamajig slowed to a measured pace, the ceiling said, *Oh hello dearie, you've been gone too long, come sit up here with me, let it go for a while,* and then—

Hurried door swing. Urgent squeak of shoes across tile. "Oh my God, why didn't you come down and tell me she'd—"

I opened my eyes to see Miss—her eyes rimmed with such bad circles she looked like she'd been beaten up, her hair a loose, messy tangle—hovering over me on the bed's left side, stroking my closest hand, murmuring to me in a voice that sounded both despairing and elated.

"Oh, love. Sweet girl. You scared the hell out of us."

Sloppy, flustered, her fingers hit the drip line's bandage, sent a sharp twinge through my bad arm. I yanked away.

"Shit. I'm sorry." Her hand flew back up to her mouth. Her face flushed. "I'm just so—" Now her lips were trembling. "We thought you'd . . ."

Yeah, well, that was the plan, I would have snapped, had the damn breathing tube not been in the way. I hated myself for my spiteful urges, but I just couldn't stand to watch her— to *feel* her—act like a distraught mother, her vulnerability threatening to pry my own apart. Like veins, like mouths, like thighs. All those things they'd opened to take charge of me, to force me to stay.

I reached for my notepad. *Not angry?* I wrote.

Her face did the melt. Her hand moved up to stroke my hair, and then my cheek. "No," she whispered. "No, baby. Oh, God, no."

Should have made me happy, that. Or at very least relieved. But somehow it felt worse than if she'd stormed in vexed, shouting me down.

I pulled away from her and rolled over onto my right side, best I could without dislodging all the medical junk. From behind me, I heard a breathy protest of a gasp.

"Lesley, please. Don't—"

I propped my notepad against the metal rail. Printed, in inept capitals, the words I'm still ashamed to have written: *FUCK OFF.*

Her gasp turned into a sob. For a horrible minute, I lay there unmoving, trying to convince myself I was unmoved. But then I saw the pained, trapped-in-the-middle look on Mr. Miss's face, and heard the low keen of Miss weeping in earnest, and rolled back over.

She stood there with a palm to her forehead, her eyes moist little slits, her cheeks red and glistening and splotchy.

I grabbed the guardrails on each side and hoisted myself till I was properly sat up. Heart monitor commenced blipping like mad, but I didn't care. I reached out one arm to her—beckoning, conciliatory.

She shuffled towards me, uncertain. Her fingers fumbled with the top of the bed rail, her eyes questioning. I nodded. Sank back. Waited for the clicky sound of the pull-release, just as I had the autumn before at Accident and Emergency. Felt the comfort of her slow lower onto the mattress next to me.

I reached up, my hospital gown slipping off one shoulder, and pressed my palm to her damp cheek. Her lashes blinked faster. The muscles in my neck tightened, aching to lift my head back up. The muscles in my throat fought, desperate to let me speak.

With my free hand, I grabbed the notepad again and

crossed out the insult. Wrote beneath it, *Train schedule = true*. Scrawled a childish heart.

"I know you do," she whispered.

Don't deserve u. Or yr nice husband.

At that, a sighing, exasperated reach for nightstand tissues.

But I'm like yr dad. I'm mine now.

Miss dabbed daintily at her eyes. Leaned down, till she was inches from my face. "Knock that shit off."

I heard the scrape-squeal of Mr. Miss's chair shoved back. "Gloriochka—"

She put up a hand to silence him, then turned back to me. "Lesley," she said, "do you have any idea what I've been doing for the last forty-eight goddamn hours?"

Sitting here? I wrote.

"Yes," she said. "Singing you 'Best of the Screaming Women' and sponging the vomit out of your hair."

Eww, manky. Poor Miss.

"Now do you really think I'd do that for someone I thought was undeserving, much less a sexual predator?"

No, but the police . . .

She ran a hand through her hair. Bit her lip.

Mr. Miss came over and stood by the bed to read my last written line. "Lesley," he said softly, "don't give them the ammunition of your shame."

When the constable finally came round, I'd just gotten my throat tube out and was sitting up delicately sipping ginger ale from a straw with my posse clustered round me—Miss and her husband (Jascha, that was his name, I finally remembered) and Francesca, who'd driven up from London to oversee the occasion.

They'd sent a woman, thankfully, who looked even more butch than me (yet another good omen?). I'd feared it would be a giant interrogation, but she just asked a few questions, carefully phrased basics, like how old we'd been and whether everyone had been agreeable to what she termed "the acts," at which point I started spluttering my drink everywhere and croaking plaintively about love, and then Miss and Jascha were rubbing my back, and the nurse appeared with a Valium, and Francesca jumped up and said in her bureaucratic hostess voice, "Constable Vickers, my client is still quite ill and obviously stressed, so perhaps that's enough for now?"

Next morning, my guardian angels went back down to London, which would have been cause for yet another tachycardia-inducing freak-out, if not for the fact that Jascha— being the artiste with the flexible schedule and all—was able to stay up there with me.

He never asked me about what I'd done, or about Clare; he didn't even try to keep tabs on whether I was "having any suicidal thoughts" (unlike the nurses, who inquired every fifteen minutes). He just kept it simple and kind: Did I want more ice cream from the freezer down the hall? Would I like a magazine? It was rather like having a personal assistant who just happened to understand the desire to put "make it all end" on your to-do list.

I was a pretty boring boss, I'm sure, since most of the time I just licked chocolate-vanilla swirl off plastic spoons, and tried not to scratch at my drip line, and avoided thinking about anything by floating up to the ceiling or, better yet, sleeping.

Every so often, though, when the afternoon started slouching towards dusk, in that little pocket of time between three o'clock shift change and dinner, I'd feel a sudden desire to speak. No catalyst, just random blurtings.

"Sorry I was such a bitch to your wife." (My first statement, to which he replied, "It's all right; she's got bitchy moments in spades herself.")

"You probably think I'm a melodramatic teenage twat, OD-ing over someone who isn't even *dead*."

And then, after he'd assured me he didn't: "Come on, you at least think it was a stupid hookup that only happened 'cause we were in the loony bin together, right?"

He set his own magazine down and leaned forward, forearms on his knees. "You've heard the story of how Gloria and I got together, haven't you?"

I nodded.

"I sat on my hands for a year," he said. "Telling myself it wouldn't work, that a bond predicated on us both having lost spouses was a disaster in the making. When she decided to move back to America, I loaded her suitcases in my car, drove her to Heathrow, watched her walk down a Jetway."

"Stoic, aren't ya?"

He laughed a little. "Most of the time. But that night . . ." He shook his head. "*Boshe moi*, I was a mess."

"You get drunk to forget her?"

"Stopped myself just before I dialed her mobile."

I snorted. "Right, 'cause telling her you loved her a year later while she was at a psych eval was so much more classy."

He waved his magazine at me in chastisement. "Mock not your ice cream fetcher, *molodaya devushka*."

"Sorry. Go on. Moral of your story was . . . ?"

"That if I had it to do over, I'd not spend so much time debating whether our connection was just misery loving company or legit. Because that's wasted energy. That's cowardice."

I glanced over at him. "So you think Clare and I were real."

"Real, and brave."

"As fuck?"

A small smile. "Absolutely."

With the following weekend came two pieces of news, courtesy of Constable Vickers and the hospital lab: I was not going to be prosecuted, and my liver was not going to be permanently ruined.

The second announcement was a relief, but the first still begged a question: What would happen to me now? Wasn't like I had many choices to pick from. The Phoenix wouldn't take me back. Hawthorn Hill, no matter how much Miss might lobby, couldn't give me a second chance. And Clare? Constable V. had warned me, in diplomatic Francesca style, that trying to contact her would be a "quite unwise idea."

By the time Saturday suppertime rolled round, doctors were signing off on my discharge summary. Nurses busied themselves removing the last of my drip lines. Jascha made one last ice cream run while Miss helped me into my clothes: big old hoodie and tracksuit bottoms, super cozy. Scissor pop of the plastic bracelet, gathering up of the bin bag and guitar case, and then we were off to a private waiting room to meet Francesca for the post-release brainstorm.

I figured she'd have a decent plan in place, but as we all sat down, me in the middle between Miss and Jascha, Francesca across the coffee table, I could feel my anxiety rising.

You won't be homeless, I told myself. *They've all still got your back.*

"Been a rough week for everyone, hasn't it?" Francesca said.

Um, yeah, the three of us nodded.

"I've been thinking about our options, Lesley," she continued, "and I'm afraid there's only one appropriate placement left."

My hands gripped the rounded-off wooden trim of my chair's arms. "Which is . . . what?"

"A secure unit."

ELOPEMENT RISK. Darting eyes. *Hey, baby.*

"Secure?" I repeated. "You mean, like they have for criminals?"

"Well, some patients are on forensic status, yes, but—"

"How long?"

"Several months, depending on—"

"Several *months*? Locked up? With felons?" I sputtered. "No." I stood up. "No."

Miss grabbed my arm. "Les, sit down. Let Francesca ex—"

I spun around to face her. "Don't tell me you're in on this, too."

"I'm not 'in' on anything, honey," she said quietly. "I just think you should—"

"What? Sign up to get groped and accused of shit again?" I thrust my hands in my hoodie pockets. Strode towards the room's closed door. "Fuck that. I'm not doing it."

As I slunk past Francesca, she touched my elbow, so gently I stopped. "Lesley," she said, "you know how this works."

Shit. Shit.

"Come on, Francesca," I whispered. "I'm not a flipping grapefruit. Don't section me."

She ran her fingers over the bridge of her nose. Picked up a sheet of paper and handed it to me. I took one look at the pair of doctors' signatures, and tossed it back at her. Ran over to Miss and Jascha and knelt down before them, clutching both their hands.

"Please," I whimpered. "Let me stay with you. I'll be good. I promise."

Miss bit her lip. Shook her head.

"But you *told* me," I said, my eyes burning with tears. "You said I was always welcome."

"And you are," she whispered. "We just . . ." Her eyes welled up. "You need to be safe, Lesley."

"I'll be safer with you than I will in that place. Please." I buried my face in her lap.

She bent down and pressed her lips to my hair. When she spoke, her voice was so husky I could barely hear her. "I'm sorry."

I jerked away and turned to Jascha. "You get it," I said. "Tell them they're wrong."

His face stayed steady but mournful. When he leaned forward this time, there was no Russian-studded teasing. His eyes were grave.

"Lesley," he said, "if we took you home tonight, could you guarantee us you'd not open up the medicine cabinet and pinch another bottle of pills?"

"You—you could hide them," I stammered.

"What about when we're at work?"

Fuck, I knew where he was going. "I can't . . . I don't . . . I wouldn't."

"Bullshit," Miss said. "You'd be turning the house upside down the second we left."

I lowered my face onto my knees. My shoulders quaked. My breath shook.

"Gloriochka, back off her."

"No," I said, lifting my head. "She's right." The tears dripped from my chin. Once I started, wasn't any way I could stop. "I've been thinking about it all week. I thought I'd feel better once the police crap got sorted, but it's not . . . I don't . . ."

And then I dissolved into a heap of rocking and babbling, and Francesca came over and knelt behind me and draped her arm round my shoulders, and Miss wiped the corners of my eyes, and Jascha pulled me up gently by my hands, and somehow the three of them got me out of the room and down the lift and across the car park and into the backseat of Miss's Volkswagen, bound for the Midlands and the Zen rubbish that would save my life.

12

Claymoor Lodge. The name sounds like it ought to belong to a distinguished estate or a stately hotel, but in reality it was a flat-roofed concrete compound whose amenities included barbed wire fences and air-locked front doors.

For my first few weeks there, I was totally out of control, and not just by normal-people standards, either: slamming myself into walls, banging my skull on my bed's headboard, trying to disassemble the classroom pencil sharpener in an attempt to retrieve its blade and reopen my forearm.

Part of my acting out was just pure unbridled fury at being stuck there, but I was also testing the staff, pushing their buttons like a tantrumming two-year-old, pleading for reassurance that, no matter what I did, they'd let me stay.

Which of course they would, seeing as how Claymoor Lodge was the final stop on the national treatment train. Most of us, they knew, would otherwise end up dead or in jail or down at King's Cross selling ourselves, so our chances of being sent packing were pretty much nil.

What they did do, though, was put me on complete lock-down. No guitar, no garden access, no cigarettes (which, to my current nursing-mum disgust, I took up smoking while there), no phone calls, no visits. Only places I could go were the dining hall or the dayroom (which wasn't cozy at all, just a track-lit cluster of hard couches), and even there a staffer sat constantly at my elbow, ready to head off a self-flagellating fit.

At first when they held me back or took me down to keep me from harming myself, I screamed and struggled, hurling epithets and spit, but eventually I quit fighting—not because I wanted to but because I had no energy left. Just lay in my room, listless, silent. When they dragged me out of bed for breakfast, I'd hunch over the table, my head bowed like a catatonic ragdoll's.

Then they started piling on my privileges, like Christmas morning, in the hopes that I'd snap out of my torpor. Guitar? Never so much as opened the case. Phone card? Nary a dip in its balance. Cigarette break? I went, but hunkered down in the garden as far away as I could get from the other girls, staring numbly into the curlicues of smoke my lips huffed.

Come June, after school let out, Miss and Jascha drove up to visit. Last trick in the bag, sure to delight me, right, but all I did—all I could do—was slump into their open arms. Soon as she saw the state I was in, Miss went into über-Miss mode, marching over to grill the unit director: "What's going on here? Are you overmedicating her?"

I sat on the dayroom couch with Jascha, my cheek leaned into his shoulder, his arm draped behind me. "Just wait," he whispered into the top of my head. "She'll be on him about why this place doesn't offer A-levels next."

Sure enough, a few seconds later, there she went, lecturing him about not letting my keen intelligence go to waste, while he fought for an edgewise defense. "Madam, most of our residents don't possess even the most basic literacy and numeracy skills, so we've got to—"

"What? Cater to the lowest common denominator, and let this extraordinary girl languish?"

"*Boshe moi*, Gloriochka," Jascha murmured. "Give it a rest already."

For the first time since my birthday two months earlier, I let out a little laugh. Hoarse, muted, but a laugh nonetheless.

He smiled down at me. "Let me go talk to her."

I gave him a grateful nod and lay down, curled on my side with my fists tucked beneath my chin. The track-lit ceiling twinkled, called out *Come on up*, its promises so tantalizing I couldn't help but close my eyes and ascend.

At the touch of Miss's hand on my shoulder, indeterminable minutes later, I swooped back down in shaky flight. Opened my eyes again to see her and Jascha on the floor beside me, knelt down the same way I'd done in desperate supplication in the hospital waiting room.

"Save your speech, Miss," I muttered. "I'm not doing your precious A-levels."

I expected her shoulders to drop or her throat to loosen with a rueful sigh, but they didn't.

"So you're not vexed?" I asked, sitting up slowly.

When she shook her head, I gave her a disbelieving glare.

"Look," Jascha said, "I know they're keen to draw you out here, get you to participate, stop being . . . what was that term the program director used?" He glanced at Miss.

"'Treatment resistant,'" Miss replied, in her best dryly scoffing *Last time I checked that wasn't part of the National Curriculum* voice.

"Right. And we're not saying you shouldn't try. We just . . . want you to know that there's no pressure."

I shot Miss another skeptical look. She lowered her chin, then raised it again.

"Okay," she said, "I'm not going to lie. Part of me does want to haul you up and shake you by the shoulders till you rejoin the land of the living."

"Why?" I asked. "To make *you* feel better?"

I could tell from her nascent lip-chew and her cheeks' flush that I'd called her out.

"No," she said.

"Tell me the real reason, then."

"I don't have it."

Oh, hell. "Let me guess," I said, snickering. "I've got to search within myself to find the answer."

"Maybe," she said. "Or it might find you."

"Like a stalker?"

She laughed. "Not exactly."

"I know you think that's bollocks," Jascha said. "And I don't blame you."

"Did *you* think it was bollocks, after your acci—"

"Are you joking? I threw get-well bouquets at people who so much as suggested my life could still have purpose."

"Fucking ace." I turned to Miss. "What about you?"

"Well," she said, "I did struggle, you know that. But I was lucky in that Curran gave me a built-in reason to—"

"So you're saying I should have a kid?"

Now I got the vexed sigh. "For the love of God, Lesley, stop mouthing off and just listen."

I sat up straighter. Tucked my hands in my lap like it was finally storytime.

"Here's the bottom line, smart-ass," Miss said. "You don't have to do A-levels. You don't have to soul-search. You don't even have to want to live."

Whew. Awesome. I leaned back against the couch, ready to check out of the reality hostel again.

"Oh, no, you don't." She shook my knee. "Get back here. We're not finished yet."

I sat up reluctantly, leaning forward to keep my attention steady. My eyes watered.

"I—I do want to," I whispered. "I mean, I want to *want* to live. Does that make sense?"

Jascha nodded. "Completely."

"But how do I get there? Do I have to believe in a higher power? Give it up to Jesus? I really hope not, 'cause I'm tired of giving it up to omnipotent guys." I heard Miss chuckle. "And it's tempting to think that if I found a way to believe in *something*, I could . . ." I covered my face with my hands. "But . . ." Jittery exhale. "I don't know how."

From both the left and right, I felt Miss and Jascha draw my hands down gently and enfold them in theirs.

"Just stay alive and show up, angel," Miss said. "We'll do the believing for you."

Stay alive and show up. That mandate took the Easier Said Than Done Prize, but goddamn if I didn't get on it.

Baby steps, mind you, like answering the check-in question *(Hi my name is Lesley, yes I want to gnaw my own arm off, no I'm not going to do it, scale of one to ten my mood is a fat fucking zeee-ro)* during morning group, or standing next to the other girls during our cigarette break.

I rang the Kremskys every night. Mostly I'd talk to Jascha, mainly because he was the mellower one, but also because it was such fun to listen to Miss's background commentary and domestic grumblings (my favorite, even though it reminded me of Clare, being "Jesus H., Nigella, why do your recipes have to be so freaking complicated?"). Another time I told him they were going to start us on some "innovative and pioneering" new therapy from America, to which he dryly responded, "Best watch out for those transatlantic imports."

Miss muttered something I reckoned was a Russian obscenity, and then called out, "Put her on speakerphone. I want to hear all about this divine intervention."

"It's called DBT," I said.

"Which stands for what, darlin'?"

"Dialectical behavior therapy," I parroted from the information leaflet they'd given us, just as the line broke up.

"*Diabolical* behavior therapy?" she repeated.

"That, too, I suppose," I said, laughing.

"Doesn't involve more soul postcards, does it?"

"Nope. It's some Buddhist crap."

"And Francesca's on board with this?"

"Thrilled. Says the woman who's gonna run it is re-vo-lu-tion-ary."

"Speaking of revolution, how's your chocolate stash?"

"Almost gone."

"I'll send you some more tomorrow if you promise you'll get out of bed in time for the first Zen garden walk."

"Deal."

Francesca's diabolical revolutionary was actually a petite Anglo-Indian woman clad in a floral blouse and khaki trousers, her gray-tipped black hair gathered back in a ponytail (to prevent one of us from tearing it out in rage, I surmised). Her name was Dr. Patel, but she asked us to call her by the less formal "Dr. P." since she considered us her partners in therapy. When I heard that I immediately thought of smarmy Kath, but then Dr. P. followed her statement with a startling confession: "Therapists can fail."

At this, a bunch of us started nodding, like *fuck yeah, you can*. Still, she made a brilliant impression, owning up that way.

In fact, the more she talked, the more validated I felt. I mean, here she was telling *us*, a bunch of adolescent arsonists and junkies and runaways and psych ward frequent fliers, that given the tremendous amount of pain represented both in our life circumstances and our feelings, we were—get this—*doing the best we could*.

In the words of Carina, who'd drunk drain cleaner and hammered nails into her arms before she'd arrived at the Lodge: "Motherfucking *what?*"

Sure, the handful of us who were lucky enough to have people like Miss or Francesca in our lives had heard that in some form or fashion, but from a mental health professional, the person who wrote the illegible-but-damning proclamations in our charts? Nobody, never.

We looked around at each other, giving *Did she just say what I think she just said?* glances, trying to camouflage them as contemptuous, bored eye-rolls, but inside I knew we were all delirious with glee. I wanted to cartwheel down the corridor, run screaming through the high-walled garden, get the benediction tattooed on my forehead.

I'd barely had time to bask in that affirming glow when Dr. P. moved straightaway to her next allegation: that we needed to change. "But you just said we're doing the best we can," I protested.

"Ah, that's where the dialectic comes in," Dr. P. said. "Because those two things can be true at once, even if they seem contradictory."

"So you're going to compliment us and kick our arses at the same time," Carina said.

Dr. P. smiled. "In a manner of speaking."

"You're not going to make us do trauma work, are you?" I asked.

"Oh, no," she said. "Our first goal is to help you get the behaviors that are threatening your life under control."

Yeah, I'd heard that one before.

"Doesn't that mean talking about childhood rubbish?" Janine, this time, who'd no doubt heard it, too.

"Actually," Dr. P. said, "no. If you dive into those memories before you're stable enough, it can hurt rather than help. So, to start out, we'll focus on learning to manage your emotions and giving you skills to help you deal with your self-harm urges."

Managing. Dealing. Skills. The words were practical and prosaic, not nearly as sexy and quasi-inspiring as the Phoenix's promises of transformation, but the thought of embodying them gave me a quiet, unexpected thrill—at least until Dr. P. started handing out rectangular pieces of heavy paper way too reminiscent of soul cards for comfort.

Once I saw one up close, though, I realized it was the diametrical (dialectical?) opposite of Lora's art workshop creations. The flipping thing was a Monday-through-Sunday chore chart, crammed full of boxes to tick and numbers to record: cumulative daily amounts of anger and sadness and shame and happiness, assigned ratings from one to ten; impulses and attempts to self-harm and commit suicide, similarly tallied and quantified. Like morning check-in on steroids, or a time sheet for kamikaze pilots.

"Your weekly homework," Dr. P. said.

All the other girls were moaning about how this was bullshit and turning them into lab rats and they weren't having any of it, but I was so relieved to be let off the trauma hook that I could have kissed Dr. P. in gratitude (totally platonically, Phoenix staff, I swear!). No talking about feelings, just identifying them, giving them nice safe numerical values. Now that I could *manage*. That I could *handle*.

"I'll warn you," Dr. P. said, "this will be quite challenging stuff. Hardest work of your lives, perhaps. But you'll not be doing it alone."

We turned the scorecards over to find her pager number printed on the opposite side. "You're always welcome to phone me whenever you need coaching."

"During office hours, you mean?" Janine asked.

"No. Anytime."

Of course none of us believed that, so we had to interrogate her, in true Miss-telling-off-the-unit-head style:

"Will you really ring us back?"

"Within the hour."

"Even on weekends?"

"Yes."

"Even in the middle of the night?"

"Yes."

I put my hand up. "Dr. P., are you currently in treatment for your masochism diagnosis?"

She laughed. "I'm not a masochist, Lesley," she said. "Just a recovery tour guide."

At the first group session, I sat munching my hard-earned revolution chocolate, watching Dr. P. draw two intersecting circles on a whiteboard.

She turned around to face us, tapping the marker in her palm. "Everything you're going to learn here," she said, "is built around the idea of mindfulness."

Uh-oh. Zen alert.

Carina yawned and leaned her head on her arms. "Hate to break it to you," she said, "but I lost my mind ages ago."

"Don't worry," Dr. P. said. "You've actually got three."

We all frowned at her, wary and befuddled, thinking, *What dodgy school you take your medical degree from, "Dr." P.?*

"Now," Dr. P. said, "I realize this sounds utterly ridiculous. But here, let me show you."

She drew a line radiating out from the right half-moon

on the board, and wrote *RATIONAL MIND* beside it. This part of you, she said, was the detached one — not dissociative so much as all about the facts, like a police reporter *(Perpetrator X forced lewd act Y upon victim Z)* or a medical textbook *(Consumption of one hundred and twenty aspirin tablets will likely induce coma and hepatic toxicity)*.

Next, Dr. P. added a line for the left half-moon and wrote *EMOTION MIND*. No trouble grasping that one: intense, overblown, mercurial. "Any guesses as to whether the R or the E gives you the most trouble?"

"E always gives me trouble," quipped Michaela, who'd been a raver before she'd become a last-resort resident.

We all laughed, but then Janine put up her hand and said, "Dr. P., are you saying we should just be zombies?"

"Certainly not," Dr. P. said. "Your emotion mind is just as vital and essential as your rational one. It just needs to be kept in check so you don't act in ways you'll regret later."

"Is that where the third mind comes in?" I asked.

"Bingo." She shaded in the intersected parts of the circle, then wrote *WISE MIND* above them.

"This," she said, jabbing at the dark spots, "is the part of you that you'll learn to access, the part that will keep you in balance."

Oh, please. "I don't think that part came factory-installed in my brain," I said.

Dr. P. laughed. "May not seem so, Lesley, but it's there. And together we'll find ways to strengthen it, so that you can be the boss of your emotions and thoughts, instead of the other way round."

"That's bullshit," Carina said. "You can't control those things. They just pop up. They just happen."

"Again, it might seem that way. But the truth is you can, with heaps of practice, retrain your brain. It's like a naughty puppy who doesn't know any better than to chew up shoes or tip over the dustbin."

I pictured my greyhound as a lanky little thing, playful but a touch feral, its narrow, sliver-nailed feet sliding on a slick floor, its energy boundless and hyperkinetic. Not a manipulative monster or a stupid fuckup, just a tenacious four-legged fumbler.

Aww, bless. My poor houndie. I wanted to hug its neck, stroke its head, offer it little treats from my palm.

"We're not going to have to smack its bottom with rolled-up newspaper, are we?" I asked.

"Oh, no. We'll be gentle but firm with it, same as you would with a young child."

I tried to picture myself back in the day, riding on his shoulders and the carousel at Margate, no closets or choke holds, my chatter bright, my knickers clean. The very thought made my eyelashes flutter and my hands curl and my fingernails stab my palms.

I think Dr. P. could sense she was losing me, because right after that she said, "Let's move on to our first skill, shall we?"

I waited for some mystical consciousness-expanding practice or ten-step checklist, but her directive was so simple I couldn't believe my ears:

"Breathe."

Yep. Apparently I'd not received the memo that breathing—hell, even being *aware* of your breath—was an art. Most people, Dr. P. told us, breathed super shallow in their throats, all constricted, which only made them tenser, but if you breathed in deep, just like in the Kate Bush song about nuclear war, and sent the air down to your belly, all that delicious oxygen would get to your tissues faster and you'd feel more centered and calm.

Of course she made us give it a go. My initial attempts felt like inhaling my first cigarette, weird and awkward and dizzy-making, but after a few more I felt rather relaxed. Not Valium- or ceiling-level relaxed, but still.

"What you've just done," Dr. P. said, "is the quickest, easiest way to get in touch with your Wise Mind. Practice it this week."

After that, DBT and our trio of minds became a standing joke round the unit. We'd pretend we were rappers, swaggering about going "D to the B to the T, yo," or if someone jumped the dinner queue or took too long on the phone, we'd put her in her place with a crisp "Hey, quit using your Twat Mind, would you?"

Par for the course, that snark (I mean, God forbid we actually allowed ourselves some optimism, right?). But then Janine reported back that she had paged Dr. P. at three in the morning (not for a prank, but with a real panic attack), and not only had Dr. P. rung her back, she'd actually been kind and helpful, so much so that Janine fell back asleep without meds.

Well. Dr. P. was our heroine after that. We devoured her suggestions, taking notes during group and practicing meditation in the garden on break, fixing our lazy gazes on clouds, attempting to, in mindfulness-speak, "observe without judgment."

Easy to do when I was lounging about looking at the sky, but when I was losing it? Ha. When a girl on telly reminded me of Clare or I started thinking about what a disappointment I was compared to Miss's off-to-Oxford son, I went right from zero to ten on the shame-anger-sadness scale.

"Your Buddhist mind game doesn't work," I announced to Dr. P. when I sat down in her office for our first individual session. "I tried it, and I still felt like shit."

"Did you harm yourself less, though?"

I handed my diary card over to her. She scanned it, then nodded approvingly. "Wow, quite the drop since last week."

"Big flipping deal," I said, crossing my arms.

"Yes." Her voice was sharp, almost Miss-like. "It is."

"But I still feel like shit," I repeated, my voice rising into petulance.

"Lesley," Dr. P. said quietly, leaning back in her chair, "these skills aren't like an inoculation that guarantees protection from illness. They don't even guarantee you positive emotions."

"Then what's the point of all this form filling and deep breathing?"

"To make bad situations bearable."

I let out a sound partway between a scoff and a laugh. "Seriously? That's the goal?"

She nodded. "Sometimes, that's all we can do."

I shook my head. "You're a bloody fraud. Getting paid two hundred an hour to tell me I just have to *put up with*" — here I pounded the arm of my chair with my fist — "the fact that I lost my scholarship, and my girlfriend, and my freedom, and my thirteen-year-old *virginity* to my own *dad*?"

"Not put up with. Not condone. Just accept."

"Fucking cow." I leaned over to her nearby bookshelf, grabbed a paperback, and flung it at her. "What part of 'horrid injustice' don't you get?"

Dr. P. caught the book with one hand. "Oh, I grasp the concept of unfair treatment quite well," she said. "Particularly when I'm on the receiving end."

My greyhound tucked its skinny tail beneath its legs. "Sorry," I mumbled.

"It's all right," she said, handing the book back to me. "I'd be tempted to hurl things too if I were in your position."

I leaned over to tuck the slim volume into place next to a giant red-and-white hardcover. "Then why are you asking me to accept it?"

"Because radical acceptance beats choosing to be permanently miserable."

"Hey, now," I said, my fingers skimming along the spine of the big book like a threat. "I didn't choose for any of this to happen to me."

"Of course not. But that doesn't change the fact that it happened."

I snorted. "Thanks for the news flash, Dr. Pea-Brain."

Dr. P. looked away for a moment, the fingers of one hand tapping her chin. Then she turned back to me.

"All right," she said. "If we're both in agreement, the

question I have for you is: What do you want to happen *now*?" A sly smile. "Other than me getting a concussion, I mean."

Scrambly with desire, my Emotion Mind ran down the inner wish list:

Clare slipping into my bed.

The Kremskys adopting me and only me.

My father hanging from a rope in his prison cell.

"I want to be the one who makes things happen," I said.

I expected Dr. P. to cheer me on or at least look pleased, but instead she peered at me, perplexed. "And you don't think you already are?"

I shrugged. "Not like I've much room to decide anything while I'm stuck here."

"Oh," Dr. P. said, "I'd be inclined to disagree."

Now it was my turn to give her the quizzical stare.

"Lesley, I know you feel trapped and powerless," she went on, "but even from this brief time we've spent together, I can tell you're a young woman with heaps of drive and energy."

Oh, please, I thought. *You're talking to the girl who wore the same tracksuit bottoms and hoodie for weeks, who up until recently defined a decent day as one in which she never had to speak.*

"The decision is all yours, my dear," Dr. P. said. "You can either continue to pour that energy into putting out cigarettes on your arms, or harness it to build a life worth living."

13

And so I became a concrete mixer, pouring the foundation of a new life down. I'd much rather have promoted myself to architect and sketched turrets and skylights, but Dr. P. insisted that I not go in for flourishes and grand plans till I'd gone off the self-harm for good.

All told, it took four months, and I worked my arse off to get there:

Pacing the floor.

Drawing mock cuts in red marker on my arms.

Telling myself to wait just five more minutes, and then, if I still felt that awful, I could do it.

Playing guitar, both to distract myself and (yes, I'll admit it) relish the brutal-but-productive press of metal into my fingertips.

Analyzing my choices ad nauseam on Dr. P.'s whiteboard, drilling down with her dry-erase marker, my sloppy arrows delineating what she called a "behavior chain": This is what made me vulnerable in the situation, this is what I thought, this is what the thought made me feel, this is how the feeling made me act, this was the short-term payoff, this was the long-term consequence.

Kickboxing in the Lodge's gym, sweat in my eyes, my wrapped knuckles poised, my punches sloppy with fury.

Splashing handful after handful of water on my face, shuddering, reset by the bracing slapshock.

Paging Dr. P. at midnight, screaming "I can't make it better!" (To which she replied dryly, "Well, then, don't make it worse.")

Bellowing entire albums worth of songs, paying no mind to Carina pounding on my bedroom door and bellowing back, "What the fuck you think this place is, the *Nutter Idol* stage?"

Fifth of November. That's my version of a clean-and-sober date. Every year since, I've gone down the florist's and bought myself a bouquet of Bouvardias and baby's breath. Used to put it in an antique fluted vase I got at Camden Passage, but this autumn I reckon it'll just be a few sad daisies in a chipped mug.

Bonfire Night. I lay on my back on my bed, fresh off a gym session, my freshly washed hair trickling droplets down the back of my neck. With calloused fingers, I traced the glued outlines of the magazine photos Miss had clipped for her soul postcard: guitar, spoon, book, lover's shoulder, blossoming belly.

I closed my eyes. Held the card to my chest. Got up, shuffled over to my desk, and propped the card back up against my copy of *Ulysses*. Gave its outline a loving stroke, like it was the narrow face of my greyhoundie, then padded down the hall in my sock feet.

In the kitchen, a bunch of the younger girls were dipping apples into a vat of melted toffee, staff stationed round them in a protective huddle. I sat atop the table and watched them shove each other as they speared the fruit. "Want one, Les?"

"Yeah, please," I said, and reached over for a lopsided apple.

When I bit in, my mouth filled with richness, my lips smarted with sugarburn. Sticky slither down my chin. Tart crunch in my teeth. Fingers tipped with drippy melt. I sucked them clean, clear to the second knuckle. Passed an imaginary apple slice to Clare off my tongue. Silently told her: *Blow it all to bits. I'll watch the sky for the smoke.*

I slid down from the table. Wiped my mouth with the side of my hand, turned to the staff, and asked, in my best *I'm so not messing around* voice, "There somebody I can talk to about getting started on my A-levels?"

Once again, Francesca came to the rescue and got me booked in distance learning courses for English and Psychology (no, I didn't get an automatic pass) and, thrillingly, studio time at a local school's recording workshop for Music Technology.

Granted, that last one was outside of normal class times, with a Claymoor Lodge staffer parked at the door in case I'd a mind to asphyxiate myself with electrical cords, but still. Total paradise, that place: big mixing board, racks full of effects processors. I holed up in there for hours, singing from under the console, hidden beneath the table with a mike trailing down so I could burrow inside my little sonic cave. I drummed on the floor and tabletop till my palms smarted. Drank three glasses of milk and crunched half a bar of revolution chocolate so my voice got ragged and phlegmy. Flanged the bejesus out of my guitar so it sounded like a buzz saw.

The first demos sounded like a knockoff mash-up of Kate Bush and Björk, but I was so pleased with myself I didn't care. After that I went all experimental and borrowed Dr. P.'s copy of the *DSM* to troll for spoken-word bits. For my composition submission, I mixed six tracks of me reading the diagnostic criteria for borderline personality disorder, distorted until the entire list became a choral blur over a synthesized siren wail.

And I did it all without Miss hurrying me along. We kept in touch regularly on the phone, of course, but between sending her son off to the hallowed halls of you-know-where and her adoption homestudy, she visited me far less often that autumn—which actually didn't bother me. I was always glad to see her, but it was also a relief to get some space, figure out my future on my own terms.

She came up at Christmas bearing an armful of gifts wrapped in holly-and-ivy paper, her other arm reaching out to hug me with a fierceness that felt almost needy. "I've missed you, darlin'."

We went to my room and sat cross-legged on my bed, her pile of presents between us. "Where's Jascha?" I asked.

"Doing more ice topiaries for the Russian oligarchs," she said. "Hedonistic holiday bash in South Ken."

I frowned. "So he didn't want to c—"

"Oh, he did, honey, he did." She put her hand on my arm for a second, then drew back. "We just . . ." She raised the same hand to her face, rubbing her forehead. "This homestudy, it's costing us . . . Well, you don't want to know how much it's costing." She patted the duvet and its bevy of packages, putting on an overdone smile. "Come on. Open them."

Not until you stop acting all weird, I wanted to say, but her expression was so pleading I couldn't refuse. One by one, I picked at the gifts' taped seams, ripping them to find guitar tab books, a Björk T-shirt that said *Sod Off,* and a music download gift card attached to a little white box with a picture of an iPod on the front.

"Oh my God!" I squealed, so girly it was mortifying.

Miss smiled wanly. "You like?"

"Flipping love it."

"Good." She stared down at the crumpled wrapping paper, tracing its trail of vines with one finger.

"Something's wrong, though," I said.

Her gaze flickered up. "There is?"

"Don't bullshit me. I mean with *you.*"

My voice sounded so much like hers—well, at least her old one—that it shocked us both.

"The caseworkers are putting us through hell," she said hoarsely. "They pulled my decade-old therapy records from America, and now they're making Jasch undergo some—some sort of psychological profile, to prove he's not . . ." She trailed off, her lips turning down in anguished affront.

"Like my dad?" I whispered.

She gave a strangled nod.

Jesus. Those fuckers. My fists clenched. My mind scrambled—not with thoughts of what this might herald for me years later, but for solutions. Dr. P. was big on "solution thinking." Tough situations aren't threats, just challenges, she always liked to remind.

"Talk to Francesca," I said. "You know how good she is at sorting stuff out."

"But these are her colleagues," Miss said, so quietly I could barely hear her. "I can't ask her to risk her job, not after all she's done for y—"

"Then . . . then . . ." I paused, not sure whether I should say it. "If that's not working out, couldn't you just have another baby?"

Soon as the suggestion tumbled out, I knew it'd been an awful idea.

"Lesley, I'm forty-one. Those aren't betting odds." She spooled a strand of loose ribbon around her thumb, so tightly it reddened. "And besides, I just want to give . . . give . . ."

When her voice cracked and her eyes welled up, something broke open, rose up, inside me, too. Not discomfort at her display of emotion, not bristle at her vulnerability, not satisfaction that her despair proved her affection for me, but a stab of pure sorrow, rammed between my ribs, a longing to make things better, pounding in my chest.

I slid closer on the duvet just as she bowed her head and lowered her face into her palms. Her hands slid up, nails digging into her temples, same way Clare's had right before the first time I'd kissed her. Her sobs came soft and shuddery with what sounded like embarrassment. She peered at me through her fingers, her eyes darting, her hands quaking.

I rested my own palms on either side of her face. "It'll be okay," I whispered. "Promise. Curran and I, we'll write letters, tell those dickwads how amazing you are."

At that, she trembled even harder, the tears dripping down her cheeks now. "Oh, my naïve-bold dialectical Les. If only it were that easy to—"

"Shh," I said, and tipped her face down so I could press my mouth to the top of her dark, silky head, tenderly and carefully as you would a child's just before bedtime.

In that moment, I felt the dense fog of my self-absorption begin to lift, the constrained circle of my insular world widen. My breath plummeted into its rightful place. My hands brought hers down, same as Clare's yet not, love revealing itself in a shape other than a red grommeted dress, speaking from that untapped well of Wise Mind, not quite mother, not quite daughter, but sacred still.

I squeezed both her hands tight. Caught her bewildered gaze in mine. "My turn to do the believing, okay?"

14

Come January, they let me out on an afternoon pass to take my exams. First time on a high street in nine months. Strolling along with a Claymoor Lodge staff member, I stared dazedly at cars and storefronts and cash machines. My scores came back all A's.

I wasn't sure what I would even do with them, but then Francesca sent me a list of universities that had received good marks in helping formerly fostered students adjust, with a sticky note atop it that read: *Apply. We'll work out the finances later.*

In between kickboxing and therapy sessions, I sat at a table in the dining hall, chewing nicotine gum to wean myself off cigarettes while I filled out the forms. Once I'd grown tired of that, I'd ask for supervised kitchen time and work on dinner for the whole unit, in silent paean to Clare: chickpea curry, poached pears, you name it. Taught myself from scratch, the combination of renewed energy and need for distraction transforming me into a relentless autodidact.

My urges, of course, were still there, the sneaky little bastards: murmuring to me that there was no need for all that hard work, singing the praises of opioid release. At first their lingering presence terrified me, made me convinced of my eternal inability to put things right, but Dr. P. told me that was bollocks. Urges weren't anything to fear, she said; they were just signs, albeit disturbing ones, that you needed to step back and take stock of what was stressing you out. Could be something as simple as lack of sleep, or something as complicated as wondering whether you could ever let someone love you again, but either way, it all came down not to whether you felt like popping the cap on a blade but to whether you actually dragged it along your skin.

Eventually, in the Gospel According to Dr. P., if you worked your skills and trained your greyhound well enough, you might even reach a point where you didn't get urges at all. Nutter nirvana. I wasn't holding my breath (pun not intended) for that one, but it was still a smashing possibility to imagine.

May burst on the scene with torrential rains, both of droplets and dazzling news:

Six months spent injury-free.

Miss and Jascha getting approved to adopt.

My acceptance at three universities.

That last one I kept a secret from everyone except Francesca, along with my discharge date. All the way down on the train to London that June, I sat with my bin bag and rucksack and guitar case squashed in the seat next to me, staring at the notices with a huge grin on my face, shuffling them with haughty discernment. *Hmm, this one? Or perhaps that?* I felt like the posh old lady we'd wound up next to in a restaurant once for my dad's birthday, who kept crisply sighing about how she "just didn't know whether to do voluntary work or to travel." Boo-bloody-hoo, right?

But now we were like chalk and cheese, that biddy and I, 'cause for the first time in eighteen years I had *options*. Real ones, not just "Hostel or psych ward, what'll it be, love?" *I'll take the tattooed waitress and an honors degree with a side of lavender chocolate pudding, thanks.*

I'd gleaned Miss's address from her care packages, so I decided to surprise her and pop round to her place on Theberton Street. Seriously gorgeous building, set in a row of Georgian terraces with big arched windows and painted flower boxes.

She answered the door barefoot in a black tank top and denim capris, her hair pulled back with a mismatched array of silver combs.

"Oh, Les," she said, her voice rising in flustered pleasure. "You never told me they were letting you down on a weekend pass."

"They didn't," I said. "I'm out."

"*Nooo.*" Her voice was a sotto voce gasp. "Well, then, get in here, darlin'."

Soon as I stepped inside, her sausage dogs rushed towards me, their nails clicking on the hardwood floor, their throats releasing barks deep enough to befit a Rottweiler.

I set my bin bag and guitar down for them to sniff and

pulled the university acceptances from my rucksack. "Ready for another shocker?"

Miss leaned in to peer at the letterheads. Her brows furrowed for a second, and then she let out a giddy shriek, her hands flying to her mouth in excitement. "Holy shit. You *rockstar*!"

It wasn't until she'd shouted up the staircase to Jascha ("Hey, honey, come see what I found on our doorstep!") that I realized she owned the whole house. Apparently, she'd been promoted to full-on head at the Hill thanks to Headmistress Fallon's retirement, and Jascha had just won some prestigious award for a sculpture made of scrap metal, so they'd taken over all three floors — "reverse colonialism," she explained cheerfully, as we headed down the hall.

The lounge she ushered me into was delightfully lived-in, even a little messy: stacks of books for end tables, laundry baskets, dog toys, piles of unread newspapers by the fireplace. On a red tapestry-print couch, a squat elderly woman sat before a big flat-screen TV watching a football match in a pink floral housedress, her slippered feet propped on the coffee table, a plate of pastries propped on her ample bosom beneath a necklace of cast-off oxygen tubing.

"Vera," Miss said, "this is Lesley."

In response, the woman gave an inscrutable mumble, her words obscured by both her full mouth and her thick Russian accent.

"*Lesley*," Miss said, louder this time. "The girl I told you about. My former student."

Brushing crumbs from her top, Vera kept her eyes on the screen. "You mean the lunatic?"

I looked away just as Liverpool scored a goal. Felt my face go hot.

"For the *love* of God, Vera," Miss muttered. "Could you, just once, show some—"

"No, no," I said, my voice trembly. "It's all right. If I'm that much of a joke around here, I'll go."

I skulked towards the doorway, but didn't get one foot into the corridor before Miss clamped a hand on my shoulder and turned me around to face her.

"Les, listen," she said. "My mother-in-law has pulmonary failure and diabetes and dementia. Every word out of her mouth is poor oxygenation and unstable blood sugar and cognitive impairment talking, okay?"

My mouth crumpled. "Yeah, but it's—"

"A horrible welcome back to civilian life, I know." She rubbed my shoulder gently. "What do you say we escape out to the patio?"

She opened a pair of French doors, and motioned for me to step down into a small fenced garden and sit beneath a hunter-green umbrella.

"Sangria?" she said, gesturing towards the glass pitcher on the round wrought-iron table. "Made with fresh lemons untouched by your misery, I might add."

I laughed. "Yeah. Let's."

She poured a glass heavy on the fruit for me, and one heavy on the alcohol for herself, then sat down. "Aren't you warm?"

I gave the cuff of my long button-down men's shirt a tug. Felt the pull of its damp underarm seam. "Eh, I'm okay."

She took a sharp sip of her drink. Raised one eyebrow.

"Which is Lesley-speak for, let me guess, 'I'm practicing my camouflage 'cause I'm scared as hell the real world will mock me ten times worse than that barmy old Russian bag'?"

"Goddamn," I said, tipping my head back, swallowing a mouthful of kiwi. "You ever think about running a psychic hotline, Miss?"

She chuckled. "You know, Lesley," she said, "if you're old enough to get legally buzzed with me, I think we can safely be on a first name basis from here on out."

Of course she was right, but I still hesitated, struggling to wrap both my brain and my mouth around the idea. Part of me felt disappointed she hadn't asked me to call her Mum, but another was relieved she didn't want me to. I mean, I'd had a shit excuse for a biological mother, but I'd been with her for sixteen years; even with one hell of a surrogate upgrade, you can't just transfer the name over easily as you'd do for a car registration.

Didn't have too much time to reflect on that, though, 'cause right then Jascha came out into the garden, and I jumped up to hug him, and he lifted me off the ground, like I was all of three, and said, "Best doorstep parcel ever, our Leslyochka," bestowing me with a Russian diminutive clumsy as his wife's, so tender I thought my tears might well again, so full of delight I knew I was home.

I can't possibly imagine a better launch into a new life than that summer I spent living with them. Those three months, reviewed retroactively, shimmer with the same golden gleam as the beginning between me and Clare, only with one key difference: Nothing was in danger. Nothing could get taken away.

Each morning at ten, I'd roll languidly out of bed (in Curran's room, left empty while he was backpacking through Europe) to walk the dogs down Islington Green, then come home and watch Arsenal matches on the satellite sports channel with Vera. Despite all her tetchy tactlessness, she was actually super-grateful for a daytime companion, and sweet in her own way—bossing me around to eat more, calling me pet names like *krasavitsa* even though I knew that, in her eyes, my "beauty" was potential at best.

In the afternoons, I'd go out on the patio and peel out of my long shirt, knotting it around my waist and stripping down to my camisole before perching on the chaise longue to strum my guitar. Eventually, I'd drift towards half-sleep again with it draped across my chest, my good arm steadying its neck, my bad arm turned up towards the healing heat of the sun.

Round five-ish I'd startle awake to the growly *rawr rawr rawr* of Molly and Leopold rolling on their backs in the grass, and lean over to scritch at their soft-haired bellies and ruffly necks, talking to them in a mumsy chirp I'd never expected to fall from my own mouth: "Who's a good girl? Who wants his dinner, hmm?"

Once I'd got them settled with their food bowls (equally filled down to the morsel, so as to deter dissent), I'd give Vera her insulin ("How are you so good with those sharp needles, Leslyochka?" she'd always ask, to which I'd shrug and think, *You don't want to know*) and then get to work on the evening's two-legged supper in the Kremskys' brilliant kitchen, which was fitted out with jewel-toned tiles and granite counters and a stainless steel hob, all those things Clare would have killed for.

Still keen on honoring her, I worked my way through Nigella Lawson's whole repertoire, even the "instant" chocolate mousse that was complete crap. Set the dining table with Provençal linens. Arranged flowers in vases. Watched as—amused, appreciative, even a little stunned—Gloria and Jascha arrived home together, their hands loosely laced, to find the elegant spread. Every time, they'd murmur that I didn't have to; every time, I'd shake my head and protest that it was the least I could offer.

Most evenings I hung out with them after dinner, not only for the company but also because I loved witnessing their dry banter and easy affection. Everything about how they related to each other was so natural and transparent: her feet draped in his lap as they read on the couch; his hand sneakily swatting her arse with a dish towel as they did the washing-up. Total opposite of my mum and dad. Even their arguments were refreshing—no heavy sighs or passive-aggressive glances, just a straight-up shower of f-bombs, followed by a sheepish, apologetic embrace.

When the fights got really heated from the stress of their adoption's red tape, or I sensed they needed some privacy, I'd head down the road to N1 Centre to mess around, either window shopping or seeing a film at the cinema. Sometimes, alone with my toffee popcorn, I'd get the ghost-urge to reach for Clare's hand in the next theatre seat, and then I'd rush home to curl up on my boy-loaner bed, a sausage dog on either side of me, and have a good cry. Nothing too long or too intense, just enough to let the excess spill out the cup of my feelings.

Once I'd pulled myself together and was lying there tired but calm, Gloria would come in (always after a polite knock, bless her, though I'm sure there were plenty of times she got worried enough to contemplate busting down the door) and sit on the edge of the mattress. Moonlight edged sideways through the thin curtains, turning her darkbright as her mum's cello sonatas. She'd tuck the covers round my shoulders just a touch tighter, like Clare but not Clare. Brush a tilted hand against my temple, lightly, as if checking me for some fretful, brewing fever.

"Everything all right?" she'd ask, her tone both casual and solemn, and I'd sleepily nod, because it was.

In July, the prodigal son arrived home from his back-packing adventure just as I was putting the finishing touches on a raspberry trifle for his mum's birthday. As the devil dogs sprinted forward and the front door's antique handle squeaked, I licked the cream-spattered edge of my thumb and braced myself for awkwardness.

He came in the kitchen with his rucksack slung over one shoulder and his fair hair rumpled, his eyes weary but bright as he peered into the mixing bowl. "That looks ace."

Hadn't expected to blush, but I did. Wasn't like I actually fancied him, but I could certainly see why girls lost the plot.

"Thanks," I said, wiping my damp hands on the back pockets of my jeans. "You're . . ." It took all my brainpower to remember his name. Blocked it out to save myself from endless self-comparisons, I guess. "Curran, right?"

"Yeah."

Whew. "I'm —"

"Lesley," he said straightaway, confident as if he'd known me forever. "I know."

My face flushed again. "Infamous around these parts, am I?"

"Are you joking? You're bloody *revered*."

"Really," I said, giving the trifle a final stir.

He nodded. "Every week I've rung home and heard a new report." He put on Gloria's accent, nailing the Anglo-American nuances dead perfect. "'Lesley got Vera to keep her oxygen on for an entire afternoon! Lesley transposed "Human Behavior" for acoustic guitar! Lesley made us Toblerone fondue!'"

"Oh, like that's anywhere near an Oxford degree," I said. "Double cream, double boiler, couple sticks, and Bob's your uncle."

You'd expect us to have said all this cruelly, right, like we were jockeying for position in the maternal-regard league standings, hungry to one-up each other, but in reality the whole conversation was chill. No *How many girls you get it on with from Amsterdam to Zurich, pretty boy?* or *Sure you're not going to stab me with that berry-hulling knife, wackjob?* digs, just sly grins and teasing laughter.

I was just about to ask him whether he knew of any good clubs in town when, from upstairs, we heard a gleeful scream, followed by the jostle of descending footsteps. Quizzical, we glanced at each other, then turned towards the doorway just in time to see Gloria barreling at us, breathily crying out, "We got it! We got it!" as Jascha followed behind her, more sedate but still shining-faced, a sheet of paper in his quaking hands.

"Got what, Mum?" Curran asked.

"Your referral?" I said.

She nodded. "Show them, honey."

As Jascha held out the paper, translating the details on their potential new daughter—*Svetlana, aged 5, no known health issues*—Gloria extended an arm to each of us, pulled both Curran and I close.

"Best birthday present ever," she sighed, with such rapturous relief neither one of us thought to mourn our trifle-making efforts or arduous pilgrimages home.

"Look at her," Jascha whispered.

We looked. A little girl—and I do mean *little*, small enough for five that, even with an untrained eye, I could tell she'd need a whole lot of Nigella's child-friendly pasta with peas to get back on the growth charts—peered into the camera with a gaze both wary and inquisitive, her dark, chin-length hair tucked rakishly behind her ears, her expression somewhere between a somber smile and a cheeky smirk.

"Aww, bless," Curran said. "Looks like trouble."

"Nah," I said. "She looks like one of us."

I'd figured they'd want Curran to accompany them on the big Russia trip, but a day later I was down at the passport office, getting ushered through the queue by Gloria so I could have my own picture taken.

You'd think I'd have been a liability rather than an asset, but she and Jascha were keen on my going, and Curran wasn't bothered in the least—said he was tired from all that Eurail-ing, and would be perfectly happy to house-sit and keep an eye on Vera.

When I heard that, I felt a little less guilty about taking his rightful place, but I still had no idea why I'd been handed it. At least not until the night before we flew out, when I popped into his parents' bedroom to ask if it'd be all right for me to take my guitar along, and found Gloria sitting slumped on the duvet, sorting through a pile of books with titles like *Attachment After International Adoption* and *Post-Institutionalized Children and Trauma*.

She looked up, her expression startled at first, then growing more relaxed, as if she'd been calmed out of a dark reverie by my sudden appearance.

"Les," she said, "tell me honestly: How worried do you think I need to be about this stuff?" She gestured towards the fanned spread of paperbacks.

I shrugged. "I'm not really the person to ask. I mean, it's not like I'm an expert on—"

Wait. Yes, I was. Maybe not in the same way as a child psychologist or an orphanage director, but still. Soon as I realized that, it was easy to guess the real reason I'd been bought a tourist visa and a plane ticket: not so I could take the photos and make the scrapbook, not in order to embark on a belated, much abbreviated version of a globe-trotting gap year, but because they wanted—no, needed—my support.

But what exactly could I give? What could I say? I

chewed my lip in inadvertent mimicry of Gloria, then slid the tomes aside so I could move closer to her.

"You know," I said, "I think it's really smart of you to be doing your homework. Proper research and all, not just reading rubbish on the Internet."

Her mouth turned downwards in a rueful frown. "Well," she said, "I'm guilty of that, too. Been scouring the adoption forums all week."

"Find any decent advice?"

"Just stories about how bringing a child home from Eastern Europe is either a gift from heaven or an unending nightmare."

"Sounds like they could use some DBT," I said.

Gloria leaned back on the bed, rubbing her hands over the bridge of her nose. "Couldn't we all, darlin'," she said, sighing. "Couldn't we all."

15

Lesley Holloway, Live in Moscow. It sounded like the name of a concert EP, too wild a fantasy to be true, but there I was, lugging my guitar and a brand-new suitcase (no more bin bags for me, baby; my arse was moving *up*) out of a taxi and into the August heat on Ulitsa Tverskaya.

"God, I feel like such an ugly American," Gloria muttered as we stepped into the (blessedly air-conditioned) Marriott's wood-paneled lift.

I expected Jascha to squeeze her hand and murmur back *If by "ugly American" you mean "gorgeous-but-stubborn expatriate," then yes, you are,* or another of those dry, chiding-but-charming remarks he was always so good at breaking out with, but instead he stood wedged between us in the corner, his silent stillness so unnatural I knew it couldn't be explained away by stoicism. Wonder at being back in his homeland for the first time since he was Svetlana's age, perhaps?

Nope. Poor thing spent the next hour kneeling before the toilet on the posh marble floor of our suite's bathroom, sick from the combination of nerves and dodgy airline food service. I unpacked our luggage while Gloria tucked him in, and then we ordered up most-decidedly-undodgy room service and sat cross-legged with our Stroganoff and Siberian dumplings on my pulled-out sofa bed.

"You know," she said, twirling a forkful of egg noodles with one jittery hand, "I really ought to be studying my non-dirty-Russian-vocabulary flash cards right now. Or at least reviewing the warning signs of attachment disorder."

"Well, tough," I said, reaching for the remote, " 'cause what you're gonna do is sit here and watch daft telly with me to keep your mind off tomorrow."

She responded with a grumbly sigh of "Goddamn Zen distress tolerance bullshit," but I could tell she was relieved I'd cut her off at the pass.

We'd just commenced watching a local quiz program hosted by a woman with blue eyeliner and so-enormous-as-to-be-freakishly-unhot silicone breasts when, from Gloria and Jascha's king-sized bed, we heard a drowsy groan, followed by the shuffle of feet and the click of the loo door drawn closed. Even the hoots and cheers of the ebullient TV audience couldn't drown out the sounds of him retching again.

"Oh, love," Gloria murmured, and got up to check on him.

He came back out full of mumbled apologies, one hand pressed to his temple. I sat in the nearby desk's big ergonomic chair, swiveling back and forth, feeling like a voyeur as she crawled beneath the plush duvet, propped up on pillows, and coaxed him down into her arms. Wasn't a matter of minutes before he was passed out again, his own arm flung across her, his head slumped against her chest.

I watched, fascinated, as she stroked his hair, her narrow fingers trailing down the back of his neck. A soft gesture, like a reassuring whisper, but also one, I realized, you could make with far different intent, dug-in nails scratching in anger or lust or even (most frighteningly) both.

"Gloria," I said, "can I ask you a weird question?"

She glanced up at me over the top of his head. "Sure."

"What's it like to, you know . . ." I gave a shy shrug. "Sleep with a guy. On purpose."

She tipped her head back against the topmost pillow on the pile. "What's it like how, exactly?"

"Well, I'm not sure. I guess I'm just . . . wondering whether, even if you really, really fancy him, and he's really, really nice, it's still . . ." My mouth puckered in distaste. "Just lying there and—"

"Being a font of feminine receptivity while getting pounded at?"

I looked down. "Yeah."

"Sweetie, if that were the only way intimacy worked," she said, chuckling, "I'd have never gotten married once, much less twice."

"So *you* call all the shots?"

"That's not how it works, either."

My face scrunched up with confusion. "Then how does it?"

"For me and him?" She glanced down at Jascha, then back up at me, blushing a little. "Umm, well . . ."

"I don't mean to be nosy," I said. "Really. I'm just trying

to sort out who I . . ." I swallowed. Looked away. "Who I am when I'm not the girl in the hall closet."

She let out a slow sigh. "Ahh."

"I mean, I know I'm not completely straight," I said. "And as far as boys go, I can look at them and think, 'Oh, yeah, he's good-looking,' in an abstract kinda way, but soon as I picture myself having sex with a guy, I start freaking out. Shit, most of the time I can't even picture it, 'cause it's all mixed up with . . ."

"He who must not be mentioned?"

I nodded. "I just wish I could push past the panic and test myself. See if I'm put off 'cause I'm full-on gay, or because my only reference point is fucking nasty."

She sat up and slowly extricated herself from Jascha, then scuffed barefoot across the carpet to perch on the edge of the desk next to me.

"Be gentle with yourself, sweetheart," she said, reaching over to brush my awkwardly-growing-out hair back from my forehead. "You've got plenty of time."

The adoption facilitator who met us in the lobby the next morning was called Tatiana, and she was hot as the street's swelter. Cheekbones higher than what I knew to be Gloria and Jascha's hopes, hair an elegant upswept tangle highlighted gold and auburn. The guy driving us, Vitaly, wasn't half-bad either, all smoke-tipped fingers and fitted T-shirt.

My head swirled with a host of polymorphous backseat

scenarios, my imaginings going places simultaneously dodgy and delicious. Never played them out with either party, but damn if it wasn't brilliant to actually have imaginings for once.

Meanwhile, Jascha and Gloria sat squashed next to me in said backseat, its space so cramped she had to crouch on his lap.

"Goddamn it," she sighed. "We forgot the camera."

"No, we didn't," I said, taking it out of my rucksack as, with a sputter of its muffler, the beat-up sedan lurched through the orphanage's gates under Vitaly's firm hand.

It was a good thing I did remember the camera, because Svetlana—whom her caretakers all called Sveta—charmed the bejesus out of us on that first visit: bounding over in her sock feet, chattering in Russian so rapid-fire Jascha could barely keep up, leaning over my shoulder to poke inquisitively at the camera's buttons while she sang along with the screechy, sugarcoated pop song playing on the radio in the next room.

"Flipping whirlwind, you are," I said, laughing, as I lifted the camera above my head so she couldn't delete all the photos I'd just taken of her.

"Wearing me out already," Gloria said, but her face was so melty I could tell she'd fallen hard for the mad little moppet.

And Jascha? He actually teared up when, at the end of our allotted hour, Sveta's white-smocked minder returned to escort her off for her nap.

I followed behind her parents-to-be as they shuffled

reluctantly towards the front door, their arms slung round each other's waists, as if their joy had bowled them over so much they had to hold each other up.

Back in the car, Vitaly was reclining with a cigarette, while Tatiana sat primly filing her plum-colored nails. As the three of us slid into the back, she gave Gloria and Jascha a curious, appraising glance.

"So," she said, "now that you have met Svetlana, you are still wishing to continue?"

"*Boshe moi,*" Jascha murmured. "How can you even ask such a—"

"Yes," Gloria said firmly. "Absolutely. Yes."

That afternoon, while Jascha (who'd begun to flag after a malaise-free morning) took his own nap, Gloria persuaded me to go with her to a ginormous children's department store fitted with soaring ceilings and chandeliers and a working carousel.

"You've lost your flipping head," I told her as she raced breathlessly from rack to rack and floor to floor, dragging me along while she loaded up on dresses and leggings and shoes and hairbands.

"Oh, you say that now," Gloria said, plucking a fuzzy cardigan appliquéd with dragonflies from a shelf, "but just wait till you're in thrall to the nesting instinct."

Her offhand comment stopped me in my tracks.

"So you actually think I'm stable enough—I'd be decent enough as—"

"A mother?"

"Eventually," I added. "Not now."

She turned over a price tag, contemplating it for a minute before looking up at me. "Not just decent enough," she said. "Tremendous."

At their adoption hearing the next morning, I sat in the hallway with Tatiana, letting her paint my nails fuchsia in a gesture of cultural goodwill while we waited for a verdict.

The polish had barely begun to dry when Jascha and Gloria burst out the courtroom's heavy paneled doors. "Ten-day waiting period before we can leave Moscow," she said, elatedly clacking over to me in her heels, "but we've got her!"

Squeals and hugs all around, and then off they went, rushing to settle up Sveta's birth certificate and passport while my guitar and I descended into the bowels of the Metro to busk on the platform at Komsomolskaya station. I'd never performed live before, so I thought I'd try my hand at it, make this a real Russian tour.

All told I made ninety rubles, barely enough to cover a pint back in London, and Tatiana's impromptu manicure got chipped to hell, but it was worth it just for the opportunity to play the Sex Pistols and the Kooks and even (in a nod to the locale) a little Regina Spektor under yet more chandeliers and frescoes.

"God, that was ace," I said later that night, sprawled on my sofa bed, cruising the telly.

Gloria looked over at me from where she stood folding Sveta's new wardrobe into a neat stack on the desk. "You know," she said, smiling, "I wouldn't be opposed to you giving a repeat performance tomorrow after we've picked her up."

I sat up. "Seriously? You don't want me to stick round in case . . ." I trailed off, unable to envision what exact calamity I'd need to be on call for. I mean, Sveta was a little hyper, sure, but she certainly didn't seem like a mini-me.

As if confirming my assessment, Gloria's smile deepened. "Oh, I think we can handle her," she said, creasing the arms of the dragonfly cardigan, placing it lovingly on the pile.

During my next Metro set list, I decided to go for broke and trot out the Clash's greatest hits, punctuated by the kitschy intermission of a horrid, shrieky song made popular by a pair of faux-lesbian Russian teenagers a few years prior. Made a killing off that one, let me tell you. Headed back to the hotel right pleased.

Soon as I hit the lobby, though, and saw Gloria pacing back and forth before the front desk, raking her hands through her hair, I knew the party was over.

I ran over fast as I could. "Oh my God, I'm so sorry," I said, dropping my guitar case to the floor. "You weren't worried, were you?"

In answer, she flung her arms around me, the same way I'd done to her so many times, and buried her face in my shoulder, sobbing.

"Hey, shh, it's okay," I said, patting her back. "No mafia kings tried to pimp me out. I'm fine."

Overflowing eyes still scrunched shut, Gloria lifted her head. "Not you," she whispered. "Sveta."

"What about her?"

"She . . . she's . . ." Gulpy hiccup, followed by a fresh trickle of cheek-staining tears.

Aww, hell. Now what? Think fast, Leslyochka.

I picked up my guitar with one hand. Took Gloria's hand in my other.

"Come on," I said, and marched her over to one of the lobby's overstuffed chairs. "Sit down."

Sniffling but dutiful, she sat.

I squatted before her. "Just tell me what happened."

Gloria took a shuddery breath. "She was fine for most of the evening. Bouncing on the bed, playing with the television remote." Her mouth curved back in a shaky, nostalgic smile.

"She get on well with you guys?"

"Oh, yeah. Did my hair up in a million butterfly clips. Made Jascha give her pony rides till his knees gave out. And then . . ." She gave a particularly sharp sniff, fighting to suck a nascent blob of snot back into her nose. "All of a sudden, she lost it. Total meltdown."

For a minute, I was tempted to correct her, let loose with a Dr. P. lecture on how emotions and actions don't just erupt out of nowhere, but I reckoned that was a lost cause. "What did she—"

"Ran around screaming. Hid behind the curtains, under the desk. We tried to coax her out, but then . . ." Gloria put a hand to her forehead. "She jumped up and sprinted into the bathroom. Thank God she didn't know how to lock the door, because when we went in after her, she . . ."

Gloria closed her eyes. Shook her chin over and over,

like she was trying to shake the image loose from her skull. "She . . ."

I reached up. Folded both Gloria's hands in mine. Squeezed them tight until her wet eyes flickered open.

"Lesley," she said hoarsely, "she was banging her head on the wall."

Fuck oh fuck oh fuck. Now my own chin was stuttering. Poor mini-me-after-all. Poor manic sweetpea.

"We grabbed her before she could do any damage, but God did she fight." She rolled up her sleeves to reveal a quartet of short but sharp scratches on each forearm.

My stomach churned, but I willed myself not to look away. "How's she doing now?"

"No idea. I came down here half an hour ago." Her already reddened face went even ruddier with shame. "I hated to skip out on Jasch, but I felt so . . . helpless. Useless. I mean, the only Russian I know by heart is stuff you wouldn't want a five-year-old hearing, so it's not like I could—"

Now *I* felt useless for having distracted her from her index cards the other night with my existential to-boff-boys-or-not crisis.

"I figured this would be a challenge," she whispered, "but I'm out of my league here, Les. I know how to raise a mellow boy, and I guess I'm decent enough at mentoring troubled teenage girls—"

"Not decent enough," I corrected. "Tremendous."

Her mouth curved into another halfhearted smile. "Don't happen to have any advice to go with that flattery, do you, darlin'?"

I sat back on my heels, thinking it over. "Maybe she's just tired."

"Tired," Gloria repeated.

"Yeah," I said. "When you're knackered, you're vulnerable, and when you're vulnerable, it increases your chances of acting out. I mean, that's the Dr. P. theory, anyway."

Her face went stricken. "So she might have an attachment disorder after all?"

"What the hell you think I am," I said wearily, "the bloody *DSM*?"

She looked away, one hand up again. "Sorry, sorry, sorry."

"Look," I said, "here's the deal. You and Jascha are over the moon, 'cause she's a dream come true and he's back in the motherland and you've got the pictures to prove it, right?"

She nodded.

"And on top of that, you've read heaps of books that say that you absolutely must bond the very first day or else she's going to hate you and be damaged for life, yeah?"

Gloria sighed. "More or less."

"Okay, well," I said, "think about it from her perspective. Sure, her new dad speaks Russian, which helps, but she's just left the only home she's ever known, and now she's in a big fancy hotel with clothes she's never worn and food she's never tasted. Fun for a couple hours, right, but then it gets towards evening and she starts missing her bed at the orphanage—"

"And her little friend in the next one over whom she always says good night to, and her white-smocked surrogate babushkas, who would never bail out and go downstairs to contemplate a bottle of Stoli from the lobby bar, unlike me, who did because, God forbid, my new daughter turned out to be more than a grateful tabula rasa." She shook her head. "Jesus fucking Christ."

At first I thought she was giving me a telling-off for making her feel guilty, but then I realized her growly huff was directed inward.

One last rueful chin-jerk, and then Gloria leaned down, took my face in her hands, and kissed me on the forehead.

"Thank you," she said. "From the bottom of my unrealistic-expectation-filled, idealistic heart, *thank* you."

When we got back to the room, we found Jascha sitting on the end of their mattress, bent double with his hands laced between his knees, his face numb.

"Still can't get her out from under the desk," he said hoarsely.

Gloria's lower lip trembled. She went over and huddled on the bed behind him. Draped her arms around his neck.

"You'd think I'd know exactly what to do," he said, his voice quaking as, stroking his wife's wrists, he looked up at me. "I speak her language, I'm a former child émigré, but I just can't . . ."

Gloria pressed her cheek to his. "Hush," she said. "Don't beat yourself up, love. It's not the same."

He plucked a still-clinging plastic butterfly from the lock of her hair that brushed his chin. "But I just want to—"

"Let me try," I said.

They watched as I set down my guitar case, knelt on

the floor, and crawled over towards the desk. From where I crouched behind the chair, I could see Sveta rocking back and forth in her cherrywood-walled hideout, her glossy head bowed, her knees drawn up, her arms loosely circled round them. Put a pair of headphones in her elfin ears, and she'd have been a dead ringer for me my first night at the hostel.

"Hey, Sveta," I said softly.

Quick upwards glint of her almond-shaped eyes, too wary to even be called a gaze, followed by a scoot farther back inside her refuge.

"*Nyet*, it's okay," I said, putting a hand up. "You don't have to come out until you're ready."

As I spoke to her and slid closer, I kept my voice low and steady and even, same as Dr. P. had when I'd paged her during my three a.m. freak-outs. No pleading, no over-the-top attempts to soothe, just matter-of-fact calm. Wasn't like Sveta understood my actual words, of course, but I figured she could get the gist from my tone.

"I bet you're pretty overwhelmed, huh? Everybody up in your business, giving you presents and wanting you to call them Mum and Dad. Which you'll want to later on, believe me, 'cause they're brilliant people. The best."

From behind me, I heard Gloria let out a touched whimper.

"But right now," I said, "you don't have to worry about any of that, because we've plenty of time to hang out and get used to each other, and I'll make your mum and dad take it slow. Promise."

Sveta raised her head again, slower this time, her stare at me less guarded, more constant.

"I'm sure you don't know what to make of me, either," I said. "I mean, I'm just some weird-looking person along for the ride. But guess what? I'm also like you."

Curious now, Sveta stopped rocking and wriggled her bum forward till she was midway between the back of the desk and its opening.

I could have taken that positive response as my cue to elaborate about how I'd once been scared and overwhelmed and at the mercy of well-intentioned strangers, or make grand, sweeping statements about the simpatico bond that would deepen between us.

But she was five, and we were both exhausted, and her shattered parents were hanging by a thread whose opposite end I clutched in my tentative hands (no pressure there!), and I was almost out of words, so, right quick, on the fly, I pulled the one phrase I remembered seeing on Gloria's flash cards from my brain like a stubborn splinter.

"*Ja znaiyu.*" I know.

Sveta hunched in on herself so tightly I thought for sure she was going to rock again, but then she curled down onto her knees, her narrow little shoulders bunched all the way to her chin, her palms flat on the carpet.

"If you come out with us," I said, "I bet we can ask the front desk people to bring you up a cot. Nice and cozy, just like the ones at the *dyetski dom.*"

At the sound of the Russian phrase, she raised her head, suddenly emboldened and alert.

I held out one arm. "What do you think? Should we give it a go?"

Silence. Her eyes darted from the floor, to me, to Gloria and Jascha on the bed, then back to the floor.

"You don't have to," I said gently. "I can always give you my blanket if you'd rather sleep in there."

Tucking her chin down, Sveta walked her hands forward. Dragged her knees, scuff by inexorable scuff, across the inches between us. Collapsed onto her elbows and into my lap.

My held breath released with a sigh so deep I could feel the rush of air into my belly. "Oh, there's a girl," I said—both in praise of her and with amazement at the fact that, yes, of her own brave volition, there she was.

When she sat up, I gathered her into my arms. Drained, she leaned against me, her face cuddled into the space between my unbuttoned shirt and my tank top, her warm cheek and sharp chin pressed against my breasts.

Caressing her tangled, sweaty hair, I rocked her with a rhythm so instinctual it came as both a shock and a delight. Lean forward, draw back, so smooth and serene I could have done it forever.

16

The minute we got home, Francesca hit the ground running: lining up therapy for Sveta, ringing every week to check on how her adjustment was going. (Perennial answer from Gloria: "Fabulously, thanks to you.") Don't get me wrong, Sveta was still a spunky whirlwind, just a far less destructive and disregulated one. Doing her Auntie Lesley proud.

I was proud of Gloria, too. Once she got over the initial shock, she embraced her second go-round at motherhood with her usual ferocity and warmth. You should have seen her when the headmaster of Sveta's school was being a dick about her special needs. ("I've seen Russian orphanages with better person-centered planning. You *will not* treat my daughter like a second-class citizen. Are we clear?") She came home that night fuming, but I went upstairs after dinner to find her and Sveta curled up together on Sveta's bed with a pile of picture books, their dark-haired heads nestled against each other, her formerly enraged face tranquil as she helped Sveta sound out words, pausing every few pages to lavish her with encouraging kisses.

And as for me? My own adjustment period at university was easy-peasy. The college was in South London, so I stayed in student housing to avoid a nasty commute from the Kremskys' place. All the "Welcome to Higher Education" leaflets cautioned about how this might be a "challenging life transition," but I just sat back and watched, amused, as my residence hallmates accidentally shrank their clothes in the launderette's washers, and phoned their parents weeping with homesickness, and struggled to remember which class met where and what day such-and-such essay was due, and got shit-faced all weekend.

Not saying I was a perfect angel, mind you, 'cause I failed a few exams and drank so much vodka one night that I got sick all over my shoes, but generally I had a damn good handle on things—after all, I'd been living in quasi-dorms for years.

I wasn't the only one in that streetwise position, either. The school I'd accepted a place at was on Francesca's "We Heart Former Fostered Kids" list, and they were keen to get us together for study sessions and social dos.

It was at one of those orientation picnics that I met my best friend, Imogen. Straightest girl I've ever met, and an über-femme fashion design student to boot, but we got on smashingly right from that first moment when, bored in the sandwich queue, we commenced composing mock football anthems for Team Six Percent (named after the percentage of foster care leavers who go on to university). Best one went like this: "We're the ones who saw it through, hell and back, badass and true, so sod off, you posh entitled fuckers, 'cause Team Six Percent's gonna bury you!"

(Yeah, I know, hardly as iconic as "England Till I Die." But when you've been beaten down for as long as Immi and I have, you'll take all the cheeky morale-building you can get.)

The next three years were briskbusy fun: commandeering the mixing board at school concerts, taking the train to visit Curran at Oxford, pushing Sveta on park swings. I developed a serious following as a DJ, too. Standing gig every Friday at a club in Hoxton called the Bin.

Immi swore the whole dance floor was crushing on me. Whenever she said that, I'd blush and brush it off with a snort—"Ha bloody ha, you just want me to hook you up." But then I'd program a long set, go into the ladies' toilets, and check myself in the mirror: new turquoise Asian brocade dress, old shit-kicker boots, now-chin-length cute choppy hair.

Not bad, Leslyochka, I'd think. *Not bad at all.*

Then I'd fetch my free drink from the bartender, knock it back, and disappear into the crowd, twirling like a dervish in the heat, beneath the lights.

Every so often, I'd wind up making out with some guy or girl, the two of us pressed against the wall, my palms in his pockets, my hands in her hair. Their mouths tasted delicious; their fingers' trailing stroke down my spine made my body half-sigh, half-shiver.

And every so often, one of them would murmur in my ear an equally delicious proposition for a private gig up in the booth or back at their flat. I'd lift my head from a warm shoulder, pull my mouth away from a warm neck. Mumble

an excuse about being too tipsy, too tired. Whatever it took
to dodge.

I didn't mean to play anyone. I just wasn't ready. Well,
mentally, anyway. I'd go home frustrated as hell—at the fact
that I wasn't getting any, sure, but also at the pitiful person
whom my smack-talking brain whispered I was: a former
psych ward seductress turned cowardly tease.

Fucking freak, I'd think, lying in bed at two a.m., fighting
the old urge to bloodlet my self-deprecating vitriol. Eventually I'd page Dr. P., and we'd talk it out, and I'd curl up
tight in my blankets and wrap my arms around myself and
whisper, "There now, Lesley-lovely," soothing myself to sleep
without a single pop of a blade cap.

When I graduated with honors in sound recording (on
time, and as the first in my family to earn a degree), it was
with a whole entourage in the audience: not just the Kremskys but also Francesca, who'd even brought a professional
photographer along. "Come on, let's get a picture for the
Children's Services website," she said, motioning me in front
of a banner at the official university reception.

"Only if you're in on it, too," I said, slinging an arm
around her shoulder to hug her as the camera's flash popped,
bewildering and sharp.

The after-party came later that night, at a big house
in Greenwich some of Team Six Percent were renting. We
all put in money for drinks, but made the mistake of sending
Immi out for them. She came back with "wine" (ish), cheap-
est plonkiest of the cheap plonk, so nasty we were all *Jesus*,

Im, what off-license you get this from? But it was sweet and plentiful, and by the second jug we were all dancing in the living room like fools, and then suddenly I was sitting down, catching my breath with this adorable Irish guy I'd never seen before, one of the housemates' (Moira's?) cousins, only in town for the week. Scruffy sort of cute. Goateed and all that.

Just then someone put Coldplay on the stereo, which made me snort. "What?" dear scruffy boy, whose name was Declan, said to me. "You don't like them?"

"Oh, come on," I said, leaning back on the couch and taking a messy swig from a can of draft Guinness I'd managed to scare up from the fridge. "Every goddamn melody line of theirs sounds the same, like you could flipping meow it."

He gave me a skeptical, amused grin, then tilted his head to listen. Wasn't more than two seconds before he commenced snickering. "Holy fuck, you're right."

So we sat there and did the chorus for "In My Place" like plaintive kitties wanting to be let back in—"meow meow, meow meow meow meow, MEOW meow"—and soon my legs were draped over his knees, and I was going on about how I was a better guitarist than Chris Martin (not that that was saying much, but still, I was buzzed and full of bravura). Dec looking all impressed. "You play?" (To which Imogen, overhearing, shouted over: "She's a woman of many talents, our Lesley.")

He let his fingers play along my ankle. "Are you, now?"

I shifted a little closer. Like I was just doing a stretch. "Maybe," I said, smiling.

By the time Moira switched the CD over to the Killers,

I was settled backwards in his lap with my legs round his waist, having another fierce, giddy make-out: nibbled lower lip, licked-at ear, the works.

"Your friend . . . wasn't . . . joking," Declan gasped.

I slid a hand down to his hard-on. "Neither am I," I said.

Once I'd slid off his knees and taken him by the hand and led him past the drinks table, though, I started to second-guess. Then, out the corner of my eye, I saw Immi give me a thumbs-up, and thought, *Why the hell not?* I was twenty-one. A university graduate. A survivor. Not a terrified child. Not a prim PTSD victim. Might as well let it go and celebrate.

In the corridor, we slammed against the wall, my hands mauling at his belt buckle, his hands twisting in my hair. For a second, I startled, but only at the sound of a toilet's flush, followed by a creak and then footsteps.

"Jesus, you two, get a room already."

Declan flipped the naysayer off, and I reached behind him for the nearest door handle. It opened into a closet, but I didn't flinch. I was ready to reclaim that claustrophobic space, to turn it into a den of hot dirty awesome.

I dragged Declan inside. Slammed the door closed.

With one hand, he pushed aside a row full of wool coats and leather jackets; with the other, he pushed open the buttons on my blouse. My tongue worked its way into his mouth again as my fingers undid his belt in earnest. I heard him moan, felt his hand fly up to flip the light switch.

Bare bulb. Again: not a flinch.

Instead, I waved Dec's belt above my head in a teasing, snakelike waggle.

"You're insane," he said, grinning. The accusation finally a compliment.

I grinned back. Dropped the belt to the floor. Flipped the light switch back down. Pressed him up against the wall.

"Aren't you hot in that?" he muttered against my neck, pushing my long sleeves off my shoulders and down my arms.

I shrugged the shirt back up. "You asking me or telling me?" I said, laughing under my breath.

Unzip, untie, step out. Post-ceremony jeans and baggy shorts mingled at our ankles as, Declan's hands on my hips, I jumped and grabbed the closet rail with both palms, hoisting myself up to knot my legs round his waist again. From out in the living room came the dim thrum-thump of a cranked-up bass as, haloed by Moira's chenille scarf, I tipped my head back and—careless, drunk, delighted—came.

That summer I got a job working as a receptionist for a recording studio in Shoreditch. Nothing sexy, just phones and tea, but, coupled with DJ gigs and my final social services grant, it earned me the deposit on a tiny flat over by King's Cross, with a kitchenette and (sigh) its own bath.

The day after I settled up the letting paperwork, Gloria dropped off me and Immi (who'd scored her own studio flat and tea-pouring job at a style mag the week before) at the IKEA in Croydon for a household smash-and-grab. Giddy at the prospect of picking out our own dish towels and draperies, we careened trolleys through the marketplace and tested every piece of furniture in the showroom.

"Would it be horrible," Imogen said, sprawled out on a big round mattress dressed in satiny red linens, "if I spent my grant on this pimp bed?"

"Im, think about it," I said, flopping down next to her. "It'd take up your whole flat. You'll bring some guy in after a date and stumble over the edge and fall right onto . . ." I paused, recalling her university track record. "Wait. Never mind. That's how all your dates go."

She smacked me with a beaded pillow. "Which is more skanky than sneaking off into closets *how*?"

I rolled onto my stomach. Rested my chin on my arms. Glanced over towards the children's area, with its fairyland bedrooms and toy bins and nightlights shaped like stars.

"Les, come on." Immi shook my shoulder. "I didn't mean to give you shit, I was just—"

I let my cheek slump against the slippery fabric of the duvet. Watched as a woman about Francesca's age sprinted after a toddler along the laminate floor's guide arrows, her hair flying loose from its ponytail, her backpack-style nappy bag bouncing on her weary shoulders.

"No," I said softly. "It's not that."

Imogen's eyes followed mine, then widened. "Fuck. You're not pregnant, are you?"

I sat up slowly. "I don't *think* so."

"But you're late."

I nodded. "Couple days."

"Eh, that's flat-hunting stress," Immi said cheerily, patting me on the shoulder with one hand as she gave the pimp bed a final smooth with the other.

•   •   •

For the rest of that afternoon, I figured Im was right, but come dinnertime back in Islington, the lazily rotating plates at Yo! Sushi convinced me otherwise. One look at the gaily colored platters of tuna and eel, one whiff of hairy prawn and salmon, and it was all I could do to keep myself from spewing onto the conveyor belt before sprinting to the ladies'.

"Steady on, there, volcano roll," Imogen said, entering the loo with a perky door swing just as I leaned over the basin to retch.

"Very . . . funny," I gasped, swiping at my mouth with the paper towels she handed me.

"So, umm, okay," she said after about the fifth rip from the dispenser. "You fancy a bowl of stomach-calming miso, or a trip to the chemist's?"

"Yes."

An hour later, I found myself stationed yet again in a disabled stall, this time fighting the urge to drum a pissed-on plastic stick against my palm while listening to Immi's heels click-pace outside.

"What's it say?" she demanded.

"Same thing it said fifteen seconds ago," I said.

"Which is what?"

"That you're still a twatwaffle."

"Jesus, Les. How you can even joke right now is beyond . . ." Quick pause (clock-checking on her phone's screen, I knew), followed by a pound on the door. "All right. It's been three minutes. Check."

I took a deep-belly breath. Looked down.

Mere icy-white, or was it . . . *Was* it?

Two. Blue. Crosshairs.

"Well?"

I leaned my head back. Closed my eyes.

"Come on, Les, spill. Good news, or—"

Muted but insistent smile, tugging at the corners of my mouth no matter how hard I told it—told myself—to stop.

"Yeah," I said. "Oh, yeah."

Now I'm not saying that desire wasn't a surprise. Even before my dad got his hands on me, even before he made damn sure I felt like damaged goods, I never pictured myself as a mum-in-training. Never cooed at the snot-nosed sprogs in the checkstand queue, never jumped at the chance to mind the neighbors' kids for pocket money growing up.

And later on, it wasn't like all of a sudden, once I met Gloria and her family, or fell in love with Clare, or commenced work on my Emotion Mind with Dr. P., some giant lightbulb got turned on and illuminated all that yummy-mummy potential inside me, either. It came to me in soft shadows, occasional dapples: my momentary wonderment in the face of despair, kindled at the Nottingham train station by that baby's drooly smile; the halting question I asked Gloria in the Moscow department store; the peaceful motion of rocking Sveta back and forth, lulling us both into stillness. Each of those small moments was a puff of air blowing a slammed-shut door back open, creating a crack into which, sideways, I could slip; into which, sideways, a pinhead-sized possibility could shimmy.

And once we were both standing inside that wide-open space together, my little crosshair good news and me? Sure, it was a shock, but also a deep, visceral satisfaction, a laughing, unexpected outcry of surprise: *Oh hello, little lovely thing I didn't know I wanted*. Like realizing how famished you are only after you've eaten your fill, or how bone-cold you've been only after rubbing your hands before the fire.

I rubbed my hands before the fire (hand dryer in the Boots toilets, but never mind the details). I ate my fill (of miso soup and digestive biscuits, but still). I chuckled in dismissal of Imogen's shrieks of disbelief ("Les, are you on *crack*? *Tell* me you're not serious about doing this"). Skimmed my hand along the subtle bloat as I zipped back up, and adjusted my waistband, and thought: *Yes, hello, my little lovely thing*.

Thankfully, nobody else accused me of being on crack for signing up for motherhood. I was worried Gloria might give me a disappointed telling-off, but all she did was warn me that single parenting would kick my arse super hard. And Dr. P. of course gently advised me to cultivate as much support as I could, but it wasn't like they were all "*Nooo!* You must not procreate!"

I thought about telling Declan, too, but decided against it for several reasons. First of all, I didn't even know his contact details. Could have asked Moira, sure, but how awkward would that have been? *Oh hi, cute boy whose surname and mobile number I've just learned months after we had sex in a closet. Remember me? Sorta? Well, guess what . . .*

No. No flipping way. Besides, I wasn't craving a Relationship with a capital *R*. Someday down the road, with the right person, sure, but for the time being I was all about doing it DIY, thanks.

And I took the whole pregnancy gig dead seriously. Stopped eating dodgy takeaway and started buying organic fruit. Got myself a big bottle of vitamins so loaded with iron I couldn't shit for days. Cut back on my DJ bookings so I could get more sleep (which, dear God, did I ever need— who knew growing a creature the size of a sand grain could be so bloody exhausting?) and avoid the clubs' smoke. Researched midwives and hospital birth units.

At my first appointment with the one I'd chosen, I sat on the edge of a plastic chair in the clinic, staring straight ahead, bracing myself for the required blood test, de rigueur long sleeve rolled up past my left elbow. Should have been terrified, but those first eight gestational weeks had made me bold and pragmatic: swallowing down nerves, emanating matter-of-fact calm. I was someone's mother now; I would do what needed to be done.

My new midwife, Tasmin, tore the corner of an antiseptic packet. Swiped a cold, damp swab across my vein. "What happened here?" she asked, her voice guarded but curious as her gloved fingers probed the old ropy raised knot.

For a moment, I was tempted to lie, to make up a glib, reassuring story—about a childhood bicycle accident, perhaps, or a clumsy fall involving broken glass.

Anything, really, to avoid the grotesque awkwardness of the truth.

I had just cleared my throat, rallying myself to put forth the bicycle explanation, when, in a moment of what can only be described after the fact as heartbreakingly good intent and maddeningly stubborn pride, I thought, *Fuck that, I'm not ashamed*. And so I made the bold declaration, equal parts laudable and idiotic, biggest mistake of my mistake-strewn life:

"I'm a recovered self-harmer."

To her credit, Tasmin didn't flinch or make a face or scoff that, like an alcoholic, I had no way of being fully recovered. Instead, she simply reached for my fresh chart and made a small notation. "How long has it been since your last incident?" she asked, crisply but not unkindly.

Much easier answer, that one.

"Three years, nine months, and three days," I said, smiling.

Quick, perfunctory smile back. "Good on you," she murmured, reaching for the needle. "Make a fist for me, please?"

My fingers curled up tight. Squeezed hard.

"Mmm. That vein's not going to cooperate for us, I'm afraid."

I unbuttoned my opposite sleeve's cuff and pushed it up so that Tasmin could survey my alternate forearm, free of major souvenirs but still sporting several delicate, whitish lines.

"Well, we'll make this one work," she said, sighing a little.

Another swiping sting, another tight fist, followed by

a pinprick. "You wouldn't be opposed to a referral, would you?"

I turned my head away from the sight of the vial rapidly filling with my own blood. "Referral to where?"

"Just to social services for a needs assessment," Tasmin said quickly, putting up her free hand. "To make certain you've all the support you're entitled to, of course, not—"

"Sure," I said. "I'll speak with them."

Tasmin looked relieved and more than a little surprised, as if she wasn't used to hormonal preggos acting so nonchalant about the prospect of being scrutinized. Couldn't say I blamed her, given that her usual clientele was comprised of thirtysomething professional women, already wedded both to affluent husbands and their own bespoke birth plans. As for me, the scruffy exception whose arse social services had saved multiple times over? Least I could do was grant them a reassuring afternoon chat in return.

"Thank you," Tasmin said, giving me another tight little smile as she capped the vial with a red lid. "These situations are so much less awkward when we're straightforward with each other, don't you think?"

I nodded. Felt my arm begin to throb as she pressed a piece of gauze to the wound, then secured it with a bandage. "You can let go the fist now, dear," she said, all gentle suggestion, but my fingers wouldn't unclench.

All that autumn, I strolled blissfully along the raised walkway on Upper Street, and sucked at nasty crystallized ginger while praying I wouldn't get sick all over my work desk, and bought used copies of pregnancy books with bland drawings of dowdy, rotund women on the front. I marveled at the illustrations of my little sand grain as it grew, all the while wondering who the baby might look like (would it have Dec's blue eyes, or my pixie face?). No matter what, I knew that it would be its own person, free from those old perverse legacies, and that healing thought thrilled me.

I kept expecting social services to ring, but heard nothing. Until the first week of November, when I came back from lunch to find the voicemail indicator on my phone blinking madly.

"Miss Holloway, your home visit is scheduled for this Saturday at noon. Please ring back to confirm."

For a moment I balked, contemplating a cheeky answer: *Sorry, can't make it, I've a long-awaited engagement involving Nigella Lawson, a kitchen floor, and a mixing bowl full of caramel sauce.* But then I caught myself, brought myself back with that mantra-mix of pragmatism and transparency: *Nothing to hide, plus I owe them one.*

I picked up the phone. Dialed the office back. "Yes," I said, when the receptionist on the other end answered, "Saturday at noon will be just fine."

17

Soon as she heard I was letting a social worker up in my business, Imogen commenced calling me "daft and naïve," but I didn't pay her any mind. Her head had been full of nanny-state contempt ever since she'd shagged a *Daily Mail* intern, and besides, wasn't any reason to get freaked out over a simple visit.

When the knock at the door came, I was hoovering my striped IKEA rug and singing Amy Winehouse. Nothing like bellowing "Tell your boyfriend, next time he around, to buy his own weed and don't wear my shit *down*!" as a preassessment warm-up, is there?

The gods must have been smiling upon me (at least temporarily), though, because when I opened the door, who did I see on the landing but good old Francesca. Hugs and apologies ("Sorry to keep you hanging on for months; we've had a massive case backlog") and mugs of tea and a cozy sit-down on my bed-slash-futon, so much relief and serendipity that my thick skull still didn't get it—at least not until I asked her how she'd wound up transferring over to the adult mental health team.

"Lesley, I'm . . ." Francesca's slender throat worked hard, gulping some words down, pushing others out. "I'm still in child protection."

By reflex, my palm pressed to my bump, guarding it. I slid back on the bed, as far away from her as I could get, leaning into the stack of pillows I kept handy to prop up on when my heartburn drove me mad. "So you're... you're *investigating* me?"

"Of course not, Lesley."

I hugged one of the pillows to my chest. "Just covering your arse?"

Of course she couldn't own up to that, but I detected a sly admission in her careful reply. "Well, I do take concerns raised in referrals quite seriously. But in your case?" She smiled. "I'm not overly concerned."

I leaned my head back against the wall. Gazed at my harm-free fourth anniversary bouquet on the kitchenette counter. Let out a long puff of breath.

"Now," she continued, "I do think it's a good idea to book some extra sessions with the health visitor. Assuming that's all right with you?"

"Course it is," I said. And there wasn't any reason for it not to be. Gloria had already explained to me that health visitors were nice ladies who popped round in the early weeks after the baby was born, to make sure everything was going well with the breastfeeding and that you weren't batty from lack of sleep. She said they'd helped her loads with Curran back in the day, so I figured it couldn't hurt to take them up on the offer. Besides, I was so grateful not to be facing a tribunal that Francesca could have told me, *We'd like you to spend the rest of your pregnancy standing naked on your head,* and I'd have replied, *Sure, no problem, just give me an hour to get my swollen feet in the air.*

"And if you ever feel like you're on the verge of a relapse," she continued, "I want you to ring me or Dr. P. immediately."

I nodded. "Got you both on speed dial, still."

"Good." Her own mobile jangled, and she reached into her skirt pocket to retrieve it. "Francesca Fleming-Jones." Her face went stark. "We do? . . . With a police escort? . . . Right. Be there soon as I can." She hung up the phone with an efficient snap and stood. "Sorry to dash, Lesley, but I've an urgent situation with another client."

She didn't elaborate further, but I could tell from the furrowy, uncomfortable look on her face, and the way her hand jittered as it hoisted her folio bag from the floor, that she was on her way to take a child into emergency custody.

When I walked her to the door, she gave me a hurried squeeze. "You needn't fret over this, love," she said. "I'll vouch for you."

That night, Imogen and I went up to Alexandra Palace for Bonfire Night. We were too old for winning giant hammers and goldfish at the funfair, and I didn't plan to partake in the beer garden on account of my "condition," but you can't really call yourself a North Londoner unless you go for the fireworks. I've been every year of my life that I can remember, save for the two I spent in hospital.

When I was tiny, I'd walk around the stalls with Mum and Dad, tucked snugly between, each of them holding one of my mittened hands. Every few feet they'd swing me up off the ground, and I'd giggle. Later on, I'd go with my school friends, compulsively checking my watch to keep an eye on curfew, knowing I'd have closet hell to pay if I got home late.

My baby wouldn't get to experience that first kind of Bonfire Night, but it wouldn't have to experience the second, either. A more-than-decent trade-off, I thought, now that the long-memorized date of my father's release from prison had just passed.

I listened to Imogen crunch a toffee apple now as we watched little boys slam their motorized cars into each other on the dodgems.

"Look at that one," Im said, pointing to a gap-toothed redhead. "On a flipping mission, he is."

I waggled my finger sternly at the bulge under my hoodie. "You," I said, "are never getting a driving license, ever."

"Oh my God," Immi said, "you're talking to it already."

"Of course I am," I said. "My book says it's good for them. Prebirth bonding and all that."

"More like bondage." She licked her fingers with a satisfied smack. "Know what you're having yet?"

"A giant squid."

Imogen whacked me on the arm. "I meant the baby's *gender*, stupid."

"Not yet," I said.

"Well, have you a preference?"

"Girl," I said without hesitation, taking a sip of my cocoa.

"That'll be cute for a few years," Imogen said. "Until she hits the teen stage."

"Yeah," I said, "let's hope the trouble's not hereditary."

Soon as I spoke the words, I felt my chest constrict with a tightness far worse than the usual heartburn, its grip so relentless that, no matter how many times I tried to calm myself by envisioning this scene the same time next year, strolling through the games stalls with a squirmy eight-month-old cuddled up against my chest in a front pack, it wouldn't let go.

When I didn't hear back from Francesca for a week, I figured no news was good news, but then I got a letter in the post with social services' hunter-green-and-lime logo on its envelope. *Dear Miss Holloway,* it read, *we are writing to inform you that your new assigned worker in our ongoing child protection enquiry is Ms Sophie Burnham.*

New worker? Ongoing enquiry? Now I was starting to wonder if Immi was on to something. I rang Francesca countless times, but her mobile went straight to voicemail, so I phoned her office's main line.

"Ms. Fleming-Jones is on medical leave at the moment," the tired-sounding man on the other end said.

What the fuck? She'd seemed totally healthy. Didn't look pregnant like me, either. "Any idea when she'll be back?"

His voice went downright shaky. "I'm . . . I'm honestly not sure."

I looked up her home number, but it was unlisted, no doubt to protect her from stalkers like myself. Found her email on the Children's Services website (just below the photo of her and me at my graduation, with its caption of *Client success story: Lesley Holloway, aged 21, earns degree after an extraordinary journey to recovery*), and dashed off a quick *Hi, hope you're feeling better, please ring when you get a sec* note. No response.

And then, just when I was about to give up and leave myself at the mercy of Sophie Burnham, I got a phone call from Francesca's husband.

The emergency case she ran off to the day she met with me, he said, had gone without a hitch, but two nights later, after a long day spent working well past suppertime, Francesca was unlocking her door in a near-empty car park when the father of the little girl she'd taken into care—big burly guy with an assault record—came up behind her, grabbed her around the neck, and slammed her head multiple times into a nearby concrete pillar.

Francesca's husband relayed all these details in a monotone so numb I knew he was at least halfway up to his own ceiling, but as he went on his voice began to crack. In the ambulance, he said, she'd come to screaming and disoriented, with no idea of who she was or where she was, thrashing so hard the medics had to restrain her.

At that point, I had to bow my head and press a hand to my mouth so as not to cry.

"I don't mean to distress you with all this," he told me, as if sensing my silent anguish. "I just want you to know that, during her lucid moments in hospital, she talks about you constantly. Can't even print her own name, my girl, but she's drawing page after page of scribbles, desperate to finish your assessment."

Soon as I heard that, it was all over, my shoulders quaking with quiet sobs.

"Can—can I visit her?" I whispered.

"I'd happily let you," he said, "but she's so . . . so combative right now, they're trying to keep the stimulation to a minimum."

I thought of her firm arms holding me fast through the years.

"Then keep her safe, and give her my love," I said.

A few days later, he rang me again with an update. She'd stabilized enough, he said, to be transferred to a rehabilitation center for people with traumatic brain injuries out in Kent. No visitors other than immediate family till she'd settled in and stopped throwing things, but he'd let me know soon as I'd been issued clearance.

"Oh, and one other thing," he said. "For what it's worth, given her state, Fran told me to tell you you're in excellent hands with Sophie Burnham."

18

"Eww, that looks like it should be on the conveyor belt at Yo! Sushi," Imogen whispered to me the following Tuesday, as my sonogram technician—a stocky, cheerful-faced woman whose name tag read *Monica*—turned a squirt bottle upside down and squeezed out orange-hued jelly onto my bump.

"Some moral support you are," I said, shuddering, as the cold goop hit my bare skin.

"Sorry," Monica said. "Always comes out chilly."

"No worries," I said, more than willing to take a little discomfort if it meant getting to see the tiny being whom Immi and I now referred to as Squidlet, if it meant proving that everything really was growing—and going—right.

"Do you care to know the sex?" Monica asked.

"Yes, please," I said.

"She'll take all the sex she can get, our Lesley," Imogen said.

"Shut it, twatwaffle," I said, and punched her on the arm.

"Now, now, girls," Monica said, her voice light but tart, like lemonade without enough sugar. She pulled her cart closer to the padded exam table on which I lounged and snaked a squat plastic wand out from its holder.

On my other side, Imogen snickered.

"Oh, save your dirty mind for Mr. *Daily Mail*," I muttered, but I couldn't help giggling with nerves as Monica turned on her little TV-screen-with-superpowers and began tilting the wand to and fro on my belly.

The screen flickered with dense gray shadows.

"Arm!" Imogen squealed. "See it, Lesley?"

"Where?" I asked, squinting, as I lifted my head from the paper-cased pillow to get a better look.

Monica slid an experienced finger across the screen. "Right there."

At first I couldn't see it, but then, like one of those drawings of faces and vases melded together, the contours of Squidlet's wiggly limbs dawned on me.

"Aww, bless," I said. "Look at that."

"She's waving at you," Monica said.

I was about to coo again when I realized which pronoun the tech had just used.

"She?" I asked. "You said *she*?"

Monica nodded.

"You got your girl!" Imogen said, grinning.

I eased back onto the pillow. Pressed my quaking palms to my face. Tasted the wet warmth of my own elated tears spilling down my cheeks and past my curved-back lips.

"I can't finish my scan unless you stop crying, love," Monica said, patting my shoulder.

"You're dripping snot, Les," Imogen said. "Here."

I wiped my nose with the tissue Immi handed me, and watched as Monica skimmed the wand over my bump again.

"Is that her face?" I asked, pointing to a hollow-cheeked, angular shape that looked freakishly like a UFO abductee's sketch of an alien head.

Monica nodded. "I know it looks peculiar to you, but to my eye everything appears just fine," she said. "Well done, Mum."

"Hear that?" Imogen said. "No more crap high-risk status."

"Well, that's up to your midwife," Monica said. She punched a button on her console, and it spat out a glossy scrap of paper. "One for your memory book."

I lunged greedily for the printout. It was a terrible image, with Squidlet's body a lit-up blur and her head turned in creepy profile, all bony skull, but to me it was the dearest thing I had ever seen. *My little alien,* I thought, pressing the photo to my chest as if wrapping my arms around her. *My girl.*

All the rest of that afternoon, I answered phones with a giddy "Shoresound Studios, how may I direct you?" and emailed back and forth with Immi, debating the merits and flaws of a gendered layette. *(Come on, Les, pink is flippin' adorable!)*

When my mobile rang at three, I assumed it was her calling to entice me out for a shopping spree after work. Still cradling my ultrasound photo in one hand, I reached for my phone with the other and scanned the name on the caller ID.

S Burnham.

Once I saw that, I got so nervous all I could do was sit there, dumbfounded and cowardly, waiting for the message. When I checked it, the voice I heard was low and husky, a bit older sounding than Francesca's. "Miss Holloway, could you please stop by my office to sign a few release forms? I'll be here till six."

The forty-ish woman who met me in the lobby was tall and thin and angular, her dark hair cut short in a style equal parts gamine and spiky, her suit jacket host to an array of extraneous zips. Sounds imposing, that Sophie, but I had to say, there was something refreshing about the efficient way she handed me her card, then hustled me up the lift and into her office.

"Rather awkward being the hand-me-down client, isn't it?" she said as we sat down.

"Little bit, yeah," I said.

"Well, if it helps, Francesca spoke quite highly of you." Her face darkened. "Before the, ah . . . Her injury." She looked down, flipping through a manila folder. "Of course, she never submitted a recommendation, so I'm afraid we're going to have to play catch-up."

"Which means what?" I said slowly.

"A records review, first off. Both our internal files from when you were in care, and your psychiatrist's case notes." She slid a stack of forms across to me. "Which I'll need your permission to access."

Part of me was impressed that she'd actually asked

instead of just faxing Dr. P. for the goods, but another wanted to say, *Come on, let's not make this so complicated, just set me up with those extra health visitor drop-ins.*

Of course I never suggested that. Not only because there was no holy grail of documentation that could prove Francesca's prior confidence in me, but also because, after an adolescence spent banging my head against walls and limitations, I was hungry to be recognized for more than my sullen fury, keen to represent: as a grown-up, humbly collaborative, *Show me where the sticky labels are and I'll sign.*

Waterbirth can be a secure, relaxing way in which to deliver, chirped the leaflet I'd chosen for my waiting area reading at my midwife appointment the following afternoon. Given the hours I'd recently spent soaking my achy back and throbbing feet in my own lavender-bath-salt-scented tub, I didn't doubt it; in fact, I'd a mind to ask Tasmin if, now that my scan had come back normal, I could add a nice big soaking pool in my (as-of-yet-undrawn-up) birth plan. The dowdy-covered pregnancy handbook had made it sound like perilous hippie nonsense, but I reckoned it'd be far better for Squidlet to go from moist warmth to moist warmth rather than to be stuck under bright lights and poked at.

In what I took to be a harbinger of approval, Tasmin entered the exam room all bustly-brisk-bright. "First off," she said, opening my chart, "I'd like to thank you for cooperating with the social services referral."

"Sure, of course," I said. "I just want the best for her."

"Ah, that's right," Tasmin said, with the slightest of smiles. "You're having a daughter." She glanced down at what I assumed to be my ultrasound results. "Quite healthy, too, from the looks of your scan."

I couldn't help beaming, but I still aimed to phrase my next question as meekly as I could. "Reckon that might mean I'm low-risk now, yeah?"

Tasmin chewed her bare lip for a moment before she spoke. "I'm afraid not, Lesley."

What the hell? "Wait, but . . . You said at my last visit I was . . ." Eye-water. Lash-blink. Fuck. Don't even. "Taking excellent care of myself."

"Yes, and that's certainly true, but—"

"Please," I said, rubbing a hand over my damp eyes under the guise of pushing my hair back. "I don't mean to be difficult. I'm just trying to understand how, if she's healthy and I'm doing all the right things, I can still be—"

"Lesley, look," Tasmin said, so patronizingly gentle I itched to slap her, "the status isn't some horrid stigma. Plenty of women are high-risk, for a variety of reasons. They might have diabetes, or high blood pressure, or—"

A serious case of ex-nutterhood? I wanted to snap, but, true to team-player form, I refrained.

"Okay," I said softly, "so what does it mean?"

"In most situations," Tasmin said, leaning back in her rolling chair, "high-risk status simply involves keeping certain safeguards in place."

Jesus, enough white-paper speak already. "Like what?"

Lo and behold, I thought I'd stumped her. She tilted her head. Blew out her breath. "Well, in your case," she said, "I'll want you closely monitored on the labor ward rather than in our birthing center."

"So . . . so no waterbirth option?"

She shook her head. "I'm afraid not."

Fucking cow. What was she so afraid of? Me drowning Squidlet? Fists balled, shoulders clenched, I had a mind to jump up and stomp out, shouting tirades about patient rights, but my body spoke for me, all snuffles and hiccups.

Tasmin leaned forward, elbows on her knees, gaze locked on mine as she handed me a tissue.

"Lesley," she said, her voice somber, "our goal here is a thriving child and a stable mother. Not some idealized notion of the perfect birth."

Soon as she said that, I felt like a selfish, deluded teenager. Just who did I think I was, stupidly chasing candlelit, lavender-scented bliss? Only candles I ought to have been lighting were ones of gratitude that Tasmin was still willing to manage me instead of passing me off to some male obstetrician who'd have got his hands up my lady bits fast as you could say *perinatology consult*.

"You're right," I said, nodding vigorously, dabbing my eyes.

By the time I got home, my forcibly-simmered-down indignation had risen to a roiling boil. What the hell did a psychiatric "history" have to do with the kind of birth I could be "allowed"? And what right did she have to talk down to me like that?

I paced the paltry width of my studio's floor: three steps

one way, then the other. I hadn't felt this agitated in years, and the freshness of the returned feeling gave it a frightening edge. *You are not in crisis,* I told myself, looking to the willowy grandeur of my anniversary bouquet as proof, but neither the reminder nor the lush blossoms quelled my jittery compulsion to tread and retread. I tried all my old mindfulness tricks—cataloging every blue object in the room (*duvet, dish towel*), then every green one (*jacket, teacup*) to distract myself; inhaling and exhaling slowly—but nothing worked. The angry thrum of pressure built in my veins. I needed to open, scratch, break.

In one swift move, I flung the fluted vase across the room. It slammed into my wardrobe and crashed onto the laminate floor, shattering into dozens of shards that looked like chunkier versions of Gloria's earring collection. Subdued yet shocked, I hugged myself until the thrumming stopped, then grabbed the blue dish towel and a dustpan and shuffled over, dazed, to kneel before the mess of bruised petals and broken glass.

With shaky hands, I swept all the splinters I could find into the pan and sopped up the puddle of water with the towel. When I leaned back on my heels and wadded the soaked cotton up in a ball to squeeze it out, a needle of pain shot into my right hand. I dropped the towel by reflex, and spied a few tiny studs of glass stuck in it.

I knew it'd do me in to look, but I had to. I took several deep breaths. Forced my gaze to shift to my hand.

At first, it was like looking at a medical drawing of an injury, clinical and disembodied. I turned my hand to and fro, observing it from all angles: the tiny droplets of red like inkblots on my palm, the thin diagonal slash across the top. Then, like air rushing into a bottle as its cork pops, the pain whooshed back into me, began to pulse with a childlike rhythm: *Hand. Bleeding. Hurts.*

"Oh my God," I whimpered. "Oh my God."

I told myself that the cuts were shallow; I reminded myself that they were accidental. Still the panic drenched me like a somatic wave.

I crawled back to the kitchenette. Reached up to yank open a drawer. Pulled out a new towel. It was white and soft and clean, and streaked pink when I wrapped it around my hand.

Pink. See? Little streaks. That's all.

Eyes screwed shut, I rocked back and forth, fighting to ground myself in the motion, my free hand resting against my belly, my lips silently babbling the old familiar string: *nonononononono, don't, scared.*

And then, beneath my undamaged hand, a burble, a jump.

My eyes flew open. Surely I was just imagining, but—

No. There it came a second time. Flutter-flicker. Not weird and sinister, like I'd expected it to feel, but gentle and delicate and sweet.

"Oh my God," I said again, my voice lilting in wonder.

According to my *Your Miraculous Pregnancy, Week by Week* book, such gymnastics wouldn't happen for another month, but my girl was obviously a prodigy. Either that or horribly stressed. After all, if adrenaline was pounding throughout me, then it was surely surging doubly so through such a little bean of a thing.

"Shh, shh," I murmured, stroking the contours of my bump. "I'm right here, lovey. Don't be afraid."

Minor though my wound had been, its gappy edges refused to close, so off I went to Accident and Emergency — reluctantly, and with Gloria in tow for moral support — to see about a glue-up. This time, the doctor assigned to my cubicle was a young, amiable trainee who made sympathetic noises and offered me anesthetic without my even having to ask. (Of course, I kept silent about my infamous "history," so he hadn't any reason to doubt me or refuse to make with the painkiller.)

Figured I was scot-free, and was just about to apologize to Gloria for interrupting her dinner with my drama, when a nurse with an *I'm so not messing* look on her face came in to give me my (preggo-safe; I checked) tetanus booster jab.

"Roll up your sleeve to the shoulder for me, love?" she asked.

By instinct I reached for my right cuff, just above my bandaged hand, but the nurse stopped me.

"Sorry, left side."

I swallowed. Gave her a questioning glance.

"Your right's had enough trauma for tonight, don't you think?"

Now, in hindsight, I can concoct a million deflecting responses to give her. *Got my sleeve turned up already, I'm not keen on needles. Please, let's just do it before I faint.* But back then? I was tongue-tied and defaulting to dutiful, offering up my flesh-knot like a scrabbled-for sacrifice, making my second biggest life mistake.

"Oh, my," the nurse said, soon as she saw. "How'd you manage *this*?"

Think fast. Think fast. Broken glass? No, won't work, already here for that.

"When I was younger," I said, slow and halting, "I had a . . ."

Bicycle accident. Come on, you stupid shit. Just say it.

My voice broke. "A really hard time," I said.

Gloria leaned over and draped her arm around me.

"Lesley used to self-harm as a teenager," she said, hugging my shoulders, "but she hasn't done it in—God, how many years has it been, sweetie?"

"Four years and five days," I whispered.

No *Good on you*, no hurried half-smile. Just a muted sigh, a skeptical glance at my bandage, and then: "Who's your midwife, dear?"

I stared down at the cover of the parenting magazine I'd been reading during the long wait, reaching out my good hand to stroke the cheek of a hazel-eyed baby sporting a lacy headband on her fuzzy head.

"Tasmin O'Shea," I said softly, my ears ringing with the *tap, tap, tap* of a thousand cascading dominoes knocking my pride all the way down.

19

Once the fax detailing my hospital visit landed on Tasmin and Sophie's desks, it was all over. No more coy mentions of extra health visitor appointments; now my case was a "Section 47" investigation — Section 47 being the (sorry, it's about to get technical) paragraph of the Children Act of 1989, which sets forth social services' right and duty to ascertain whether or not "there is reasonable cause to suspect that a child is suffering, or likely to suffer, significant harm."

Sophie never told me this straight-up, of course, but it wasn't hard to figure out once she started interviewing the Kremskys and Dr. P. and Immi. I mean, sure, she *could* have been sitting down with them over a cup of tea chatting about how fabulous I was, but let's face it: fairly or unfairly, I'd, by virtue of an impulsive, furious vase-fling, given the child protection powers-that-be the impression that I'd already dove off the deep end and wasn't coming up for air any time soon.

Still, I clung doggedly to the belief that I could prove myself. After all, I had stellar references: Gloria said in her interview that she trusted me completely with Sveta, and Dr. P. referred to me as the "most successfully recovered patient she'd ever treated."

Looking back, I'm tempted to chalk up my denial to hubris or complacency, but honestly I think it was a survival mechanism, same as escaping to the ceiling or self-harming had once been. I didn't know anything about how the Section 47 machinations worked, but I bloody well knew I had to hold myself together, even if it meant locking up every last vague but ominous possibility inside my PTSD containment safe.

And please understand: My stubborn refusal to entertain the thought of any outcome except triumph, my fragile-but-not-unfounded confidence, didn't mean I acted like a defensive, intractable adolescent in front of Sophie or anyone else from Children's Services. If anything, I went overboard trying to appease them.

They asked me to:

Book appointments with the mental health consultant who worked with Tasmin. (Done, regardless of the fact that Dr. P. could have served the same role much more efficiently.)

Go on anxiety medication, as per the consultant's recommendation. (Done, even though I was scared to death of how it might affect Squidlet.)

Attend expectant mums' groups. (Done, despite the fact that nibbling at lemon cake while listening to magazine editors twice my age complain about their stretch marks felt like hell on earth.)

Agree to the prospect of going inpatient on a mother-baby

psychiatric ward after the birth. (Done—and I even gave them the contact details of a unit one floor down from the Phoenix.)

This eager-retriever action didn't go unnoticed, either. All through the rest of November and into December, Sophie talked up how well we'd forged a "productive alliance" (shades of Kath and her lofty visions of the therapeutic milieu, not that I noticed, or wanted to notice, then). There were still "concerns," of course, but she was certain we could work out a "solution" that was "mutually agreeable"—and quick to reassure me that, despite the tabloids' alarmist squawkings, the "vast, vast majority" of investigations never resulted in losing custody of your kid. Worst case, I'd do the mother-baby unit to get over the six-week postnatal hump, then stay on my meds and check in regularly.

Immi said that was firm evidence of socialism gone awry, but it seemed fair enough to me. After a two-year stint in hospital, six weeks sounded like a flipping spa day. Nothing we couldn't breeze through, Squidlet and I. Little bit of mandala coloring, couple support groups, stroll in the garden (far away from the smoke, of course), cozy curl-up together on that hard single bed. Hell, even the thought of a blinky eye in the ceiling corner didn't faze me. I'd show *it* what resilient motherhood looked like.

That Christmas was the best ever. I made Mum's epic pudding from memory and took it to the Kremskys' (along with Imogen, who'd over the years grown to be an honorary member of their family, too). No silent, awkward dinners there; the place was all riotous laughter as Sveta careened through the kitchen on her new roller skates, and Gloria collapsed with delight into Jascha's lap after opening the rare edition of *Finnegans Wake* he'd bought her. (Immi's verdict upon viewing her reaction: "Mr. K.'s getting some tonight, for sure!")

All day long the doorbell kept ringing with visitors: Curran's girlfriend, ladies from Vera's bingo hall, neighbors from across the road. Everyone raved about the pudding and cooed over my heftier-by-the-minute bump, which Sveta had insisted upon decorating with a red bow and tinsel.

By midafternoon, I was crashed out on the couch from food coma and third-trimester aches. I woke from my nap to the sounds of a crackling fire and holiday specials on the telly. Next to me, Vera sat polishing off the last of the pudding.

"Here, Leslyochka," she said, and passed me the plate. "Is one last token inside, I think."

I'd stirred them all into the mixing bowl three weeks earlier, but there was no telling which one I'd get now. I forced down the first bite, then eagerly took another. *Damn, I'm good,* I thought, just as my teeth hit metal.

This time, I got the ship's anchor. A symbol of safe harbor.

I felt my eyes well up. In the other room, I could hear Gloria on the phone with her mum in America. "I miss you, too, Mom. Next year for sure, okay?"

Next year. I pictured Squidlet crawling around wearing the tinsel, pulling the dogs' tails, charming the entire room just like Sveta had that first day at the orphanage. She'd never know her real granddad and nan, my girl, but she'd have a whole chosen family adoring her, surrounding her.

Safe harbor, I thought. *For both of us.*

The grateful tears started trickling.

"Oh, *krasavitsa,*" Vera said, and draped her arm around me, gathering me against her bosom. "Hush. Don't cry."

"It's okay," I said, grinning. "I'm good."

She patted my hair. "Wish I could say same for her." She gestured towards the pop star on the screen. "Needs less plastic surgery, more singing lessons, *да?*"

There was even more celebrating a week later when the Kremskys held their annual New Year's Eve party—though "party" seems like much too mannered a word to describe the cumulative impact of the entire Soviet diaspora crammed into one dining room with enough Stoli on the sideboard to stock an entire off-license.

By one a.m., the place was a wreck of "Happy 2010" streamers and salad plates. Vera had taken up my snoring post on the couch, and Imogen looked ready to repeat my university vodka-spewing stunt.

"Come on, girlie," Gloria said, draping an arm around Im's shoulder to steady her. "I'm taking you home."

After they'd left, I went to check on Sveta, who'd been feeling poorly thanks to Vera's geriatric posse incessantly plying her with sweets. She lay curled up in her blankets now, long eyelashes fluttering in fitful sleep, both fists tucked under her chin. I bent down, best as I could, and kissed her on the forehead. As I stood back up, Squidlet gave me a nudge.

When I returned to the dining room, I found Jascha sitting at the table before a small rectangular box wrapped in Christmas paper.

He slid it across to me. My brows furrowed. "What—"

"Russian moment," he said, giving me a small smile.

"Aww, bless," I said, fingering the ribbon. "You guys were generous enough to me last week. Really."

His smile deepened. "It's . . . it's not for you."

I peeked at the attached tag. *To Squidlet*, it read, in his angular print.

"Didn't want to jinx it," he said. "You know, buying her anything before she's born. But—"

"No, no, that's great," I said, tearing open the wrapping.

When I glimpsed brown cardboard printed with the black-and-yellow Doc Martens logo, my face broke into a grin. I undid the top of the box to find a tiny pair of hot-pink lace-up boots.

"Oh," I breathed, entranced as I'd been when I'd gotten the guitar for my seventeenth birthday. "Too awesome." I caressed the shiny leather, the miniature laces. "Gloria pick them out?"

Jascha's smile went sheepish. He shook his head. "All me."

I pictured Squidlet stomping her clumsy-footed, brazen way along Upper Street like a member of Enya's cinematic dwarf army, her little hand in his big one.

My throat went lumpy. I jumped up from the table and ran round to the other side to hug him.

"Aren't too girly with the fuchsia, are they?" he whispered onto the top of my head, as I rested my cheek against his shoulder.

"Not a bit," I whispered back. "They're perfect."

When Immi rang me while I was doing the last of the party washing-up the next morning, I figured it was to moan about her hangover, but her taut, lowered voice was grave.

"Les," she said quietly. "You're in deep shit."

"Why?" I said. "Sophie's not made any plans to—"

"She will now."

"Im, please. Last way I need to start the new year is stressing out over your—"

"Ainsley MacIntyre," Imogen said firmly. "Look her up."

I knew I had to humor her, so I grabbed Gloria's laptop and sat down at the kitchen table, squinting at the screen, preparing myself for an amused head-shake.

What I found were mug shot photos of a stringy-haired, haunted-looking woman not much older than me, her exhausted eyes staring into the camera with an expression equal parts blank and feral, just below headlines howling *NEW MUM'S A MURDERER.*

Soon as she heard, Dr. P. sent Sophie a letter listing what we hoped were reassuring statistics about the rarity of postnatal psychosis, along with a statement that read: *In my opinion, Lesley is at no more risk of this disorder than any other pregnant member of the general population.*

You'd think that'd have been sufficient to smooth over any worries, but once the Ainsley MacIntyre case's details got released and the headlines switched to screams of *SOCIAL WORKER MISSED CRUCIAL WARNING SIGNS*, the slim, subtly phrased piece of paper turned worthless, and only an "independent" evaluation of my current mental state would do. So off I went to the office of some big-shot called Dr. Orton.

Must have had a full schedule of nutters, 'cause he could only spare a whopping fifteen minutes. Brusque handshake, harried sit-down. Me perched on the chair edge in my ill-fitting maternity work trousers, fingers twisted in my lap.

No messing about for Dr. O.; he went straight to the trauma work. "You're an incest victim, correct?"

"Survivor," I said. Sharper than I meant to.

"How many times have you attempted suicide?"

I paused.

"Once," I said.

"You don't consider a severed artery indicative of a desire to end your life, then."

"I didn't sever it." Hairsplitting, but I clung to those fine threads.

"And you've been inpatient in"—swooping neck-crane at my records—"three separate hospitals?"

Nottingham ICU had to count, didn't it? Crap. "Four."

His eyes lingered on the still-healing scar atop my right hand. "I'm curious what strengths you think you bring to motherhood, given your significant mental health challenges."

Crack! went the containment safe. *Pop!* squealed its

fifteen locks. Down the cavern in your spelunking gear you go, dearie.

(Fists held fast to the hall closet's back wall. My tongue struggling to resist his. Sneer-snicker, stale breath. *Who do you think you are, little girl?*)

A woman who reclaimed that hall closet. A mother. Stable. Alive.

"Well," I said, "I'm not Mary Poppins or anything, but I certainly know what *not* to do."

I ended my answer with a small smile, trying to catch Dr. O.'s eye, keep the mood light.

Big mistake. His own lips turned down, not up. "And you're adamant about raising your daughter on your own."

"Wouldn't use those words, exactly," I said, "but yeah, I'd consider myself a pretty independent person."

"And your sexual orientation, what words would you use to describe that?"

Try *none of your flipping business*, fuckface.

"Queer," I said.

One last sentence-scrawl. "Thank you, Miss Holloway. I think I've all the information I need."

At that point, mid-January, I was seven months along. Registering for birthing classes. Phoning nurseries about child care openings.

I know it sounds mad that I managed to concentrate on such mundane details, but really, what else could I—should I—have done? Returned the fuchsia Doc Martens, canceled the nursery tour under the assumption I'd no longer need a place in the infants' room come the spring? Fuck that fuck that fucking fuck that. Innocent until proven guilty. I'd be damned if I let paranoia poison me.

So I took my heartburn pillows and waddled up the road to the hospital each Tuesday night to learn about epidurals and episiotomies ("They do *what* to *what*, now? For God's sake, Les, I'm eating!" Immi shrieked when I relayed the details of the latter to her over lunch), and made up a spreadsheet detailing my Squidlet-minder short list during a slow afternoon at work.

After two weeks of silence from social services, I reckoned I was safe enough to embark on the full antenatal shopping spree. "Told you you'd be doing this!" Gloria said, laughing, as I loaded up her arms with blankets and booties.

When I came home with my bags, I found another hunter-green-and-lime-logoed missive in the letterbox. I tried to reassure myself it was a bill, but my hands shook so badly I nicked my index finger slitting the envelope open.

Dear Miss Holloway, your final case conference is scheduled for Tuesday at 3.30 p.m. You are welcome to bring a family member, friend, or legal counsel.

The page fluttered to the floor. Squidlet did a somersault. I sucked my smarting knuckle, and prayed.

20

Tuesday, quarter past three. My hastily instructed solicitor on one side of me, Gloria on the other, the three of us parked in the corridor outside the very same conference room where, five years earlier, I'd scrawled the list of my father's transgressions.

"You'd think they could have picked a different one," Gloria murmured.

"We were lucky we got advance notice, Mrs. Kremsky."

I leaned my head back against the wall. Closed my eyes. *Please please please don't hurt us.*

This time, eight chairs crowded the table. Three of them empty, five full. Nary a warm gaze, much less a vending-machine-run offer. Straight plow into the introductions.

"Nicola Deming, independent meeting chair."

"Olivia Andrews, director of the Children's Services Team."

Looked familiar. Yes, my crisp-and-soda fetcher, back at that first meeting with Francesca. Holy—

"Paul Orton, M.D."

Christ, not him again.

"Tasmin O'Shea, primary midwife."

Tell them. Tell them I've done it all. Mums' tea and meds and every single appointment on time, iron tablets and organic fruit and plenty of sleep, double-check on the tetanus jab, yes yes yes I'll see your specialist, anything, everything you ask, just please don't—

"Les," Gloria said softly. "Your turn."

What was I supposed to say? *Hello, lovely to see you all again now that you've put your heads together and deconstructed me?*

"I'm Lesley," I said, stupidly as I had the first time I met Clare. "The . . . the, umm . . ."

Infamous one? Most Likely to Be Voted Daft and Naïve? Meeting chair (Nicole? no, Nicola) jumped to fill in. "Client."

Oh, don't even. Clients run the show, hire out minions to design their websites and file their taxes and clean their already spotless flats. Clients can boss people around or even fire them; they're not stuck in a windowless room at the mercy of some five-person jury.

"Gloria Kremsky."

Director of Children's Services perked up, leaning forward, intrigued. "You're headmistress of that school in Harrow that's won so many curriculum innovation awards, aren't you?" Smarmy as Kath, all faux camaraderie.

"I am." No flattered blush, no buy-in to the buttering-up. "And I'm here to support Lesley."

At that, the woman reared back a little, her face aiming for a neutral *Hmm, how interesting* but telegraphing a disgruntled *So much for that.*

My solicitor mumbled his obligatory firm-pimping bit, and then, last but not least, we came to the savior who—I was convinced, I was certain—held our "mutually agreeable solution" in her sensible hands.

"Sophie Burnham." Her voice sounded raspy, as if she'd just been having herself a cigarette. Or crying. "I'm the lead professional who's been working with Lesley."

With. Hear that? *With.*

I glanced over to give her an appreciative smile, but she wouldn't even make eye contact. Her fingers jittered as they pushed up the sleeves of her blouse.

"So," Nicola what's-her-name said, "several of you have met recently to discuss Miss Holloway's case. Am I correct that a strategy was agreed upon?"

Across the table, Sophie bit her lip.

"After much deliberation," she said, "yes."

Steady on, Les. Indie cool.

Nicola turned towards Directress Butter-Up. "Ms. Andrews, what was the determining factor in your team's final decision?"

Her voice was crisp. Unwavering. "The report Dr. Orton prepared."

Shit. Shit. Shit.

"Dr. Orton, could you be so kind as to summarize your findings?"

"Certainly." He scraped his chair forward. Adjusted his

glasses. "Miss Holloway's symptoms clearly mark her as meeting the criteria for borderline personality disorder."

Still? Even after half a decade? Cut me some slack, fuckface.

"These symptoms include repeated self-harm, emotional instability, chaotic relationship patterns, and unstable sexual identity."

My hands hardened into fists under the table.

"And what implications does this diagnosis have for her parenting capacity?" Nicola asked.

"Well," he said slowly, "whilst Miss Holloway is admirably high-functioning and high-achieving, she is also at grave risk of causing her child harm."

I opened my mouth to protest, but the only sound that came out was an offended, breathy sigh.

"Her risk profile particularly fits that of a condition called factitious illness. Also known as Munchausen syndrome by proxy."

"Wait," I said. "You mean like those women who poison their kids with salt, or mess around with their medications?"

"You're familiar with it, then," Fuckface said, as if I'd just proven his point.

"I'm kind of a *DSM* junkie," I said.

Nice move, Leslyochka. I looked over at Gloria, stricken.

"Look," she said, "I know you've all got legitimate concerns about Lesley. But do you really think, do you *seriously* believe, that she would make her daughter sick in order to gain attention?"

"Given the fact that, in the past, she's seriously wounded herself in order to do so," Olivia said, "yes."

"That's not why I did it," I said, my voice rising. "And besides, harming yourself isn't the same as harming someone else. I'd cut myself to bits before I hurt my girl."

The whole room frowned. My shoulders sank. "Not that I'm planning on doing it, of course."

"What about the injury that sent you to A and E?" Nicola asked.

"Accident," I whispered.

"She's telling the truth," Gloria said. "It was a dropped vase. I saw the broken glass myself."

"Which," Dr. Orton droned, "Miss Holloway very well could have used to—"

"Before this gets too heated," Nicola said, "perhaps we ought to move on to the proposal itself."

Yes. Please. Let's just get it over with.

"Ms. Burnham," Directress Butter-Up said, "would you care to read our team's recommended course of action?"

Sophie startled, her face plainly advertising the fact that she'd rather not, but she dutifully squared her shoulders and sat up straight. "We'd like to create an official child protection plan for Lesley's daughter."

Mother-baby unit. Health visitor drop-ins. More meds and supervision. All of the above. Come on, come on.

I reached for Gloria's hand. She squeezed mine back.

Nicola looked impatient. "Could you elaborate on the specifics, please?"

Sophie bowed her head. Ran her fingers over her temples.

"Yes," she said. "It would involve a custody order initiated immediately at birth."

My hand loosened from Gloria's and dropped. Rigid and heartsick, my body froze as my mind's silent wail crested and broke: *Oh my God oh my God oh my . . .*

Breathe.

Squidlet darted from left to right. Thumped my ribs.

Breathe.

I sat up straight as Sophie. Listened, half in Rational Mind, half dazed, as Tasmin went on to detail my new birth plan: fifteen minutes of "contact," followed by "removal."

Across the table, five faces watched me, confounded by my lack of skin-clawing, my paucity of screams. Emotion Mind campaigned for all those and more, but I held fast, I stayed silent, I deprived them of their satisfaction.

After the tribunal filed out, I leaned forward in my swivel chair and laid my head on the table. Bile burned in my throat.

Gloria slid her chair closer and rested her hand on my shoulder. "Les?"

"Dizzy," I mumbled. "Feel sick."

My solicitor brought me a cup of water, which I drank in tentative sips while Gloria rubbed my back and he debriefed us.

"My experience with prebirth cases is limited," he said, "but I've never seen this extreme of a decision unless the mum was abusing street drugs or had harmed a previous child."

"Then why are they doing this to me?" With every affronted word, my voice soared higher.

"Ainsley MacIntyre?" He shrugged. "That's my best guess."

Gloria gave him an *I'm so not messing* look. "What options does she have?"

"There's an appeals process, but it's conducted by social services, not an independent body."

Yeah. Like that'd work.

"We're getting you a new solicitor," Gloria said soon as he'd left. "And I'm going next door to talk with that Children's Services bigwig."

Sitting outside Olivia's office, listening to snippets of Gloria's attempt to talk sense into her, I couldn't help but think of the conference between Kath and Clare's parents.

"Listen, Ms. Andrews, from one administrator to another, I have to tell you that . . . deeply troubled by . . . awfully Draconian."

"Surely as an educational leader, Mrs. Kremsky, you recognize the importance of safeguarding youth."

"Which your team did a fantastic job of for Lesley. But now —"

"Our priority is not maternal aspiration . . . first and foremost with the vulnerable child."

"So you're going to condemn every equally vulnerable young woman who . . . What do you mean, my 'American' disdain for social welfare? I've lived here for twenty-five years. I vote Labour, for pity's . . ."

I couldn't stay for the rest, thanks to Squidlet using my bladder as a trampoline.

In the loo I found Sophie by the window with her back to me, one foot balanced on the radiator in what I guessed was an attempt to adjust her tights. Classy.

"So much for collaboration, huh?" I said.

As she whipped round in startle, a plastic syringe nose-dived out of her hands and onto the floor.

"Shit." Hurrying to smooth her skirt down, she bit her lip as she knelt to retrieve the needle. "Lesley, I—"

"Needed to shoot some smack to soothe your conscience, did you?"

"No. *No.*" She scrabbled in her purse. Held up a small case and unzipped it to reveal a bottle of liquid affixed with a prescription label. "I'm . . ." Hesitant swallow. "Doing fertility treatments."

"That why you screwed me over?"

She shoved the syringe back in its case and slammed the whole kit down on the window ledge. "I didn't screw you over. I argued for you and got outvoted."

"Even on the mother-baby placement?"

"I rang every unit in the UK and Ireland. They're all full or losing their funding."

She came over to me. Tucked a strand of hair behind my ear. Leaned in to caress my cheek, just before she turned to leave.

"I'm sorry, Lesley," she whispered. "I'm so, so sorry."

• • •

After that, I went completely numb. Didn't say a word, didn't feel a thing: not on the walk out through the automatic doors, not on the ride home in Gloria's car.

Soon as I got back to my flat, I crawled under the duvet and huddled there while she sat next to me. "Just want to sleep it off?"

I must have nodded, because she nodded back. "Okay, but don't forget your class tonight."

"Huh? What class?" And then I remembered. Pillows and *breathe breathe breathe* and embarrassed laughter.

"No bloody point now," I muttered, burying my face in the pillow.

"Yes, there is." Her voice was soft but firm as she leaned down to stroke my hair. "I know it doesn't feel like it, but —"

I swatted her away. "Stop. Just wanna sleep."

"Do you need me to stay with you? I have to go pick up Sveta from school, but I can always ask —"

"Nah. S'okay."

"So you're all right in the safety department."

"Uh-huh."

"And you'll phone me if you're not when you wake up?"

So many fucking questions. "Yeah, sure."

"Promise me."

Shut up shut up shut up. I pulled the covers over my head. Rolled over with a grunty heave. "I promise."

21

When I woke thanks to another bladder-gymnasium session, it was already past eight. Rubbing my eyes, I staggered into the bathroom and pulled down my granny knickers. Peed like a racehorse. She kept kicking.

"Stop," I whispered. "Please stop."

That morning, I'd delighted in every heel-punch and elbow-jab, but now I couldn't bear them. Too much dissonance: inside me, but no longer mine.

She'll stay yours forever, Smack-Talker Brain whispered, *if you —*

Fuck off, I told it, and got up to wash my hands.

Plunged beneath the faucet, they shook from the water-shock. Soon my whole body was quivering with an off-kilter tremble, all jangly, pained twitch.

Just relax, love. You know how.

No. Not that way. Use your skills.

I made myself a cup of tea.

I counted all the blue (not pink, no) things in the room.

I waited ten minutes.

And then, like a flipping idiot, I opened *Your Miraculous Pregnancy* and turned to Week 34.

Gas! Piles! Leaky breasts! Beneath the tick-marked tallies of annoyances, a sidebar jumped out at me. *This week might be a good one to record some pregnancy memories for posterity. Remember those cravings? That first piece of baby gear you just had to buy?*

That first strategy meeting? That last unsullied moment?

I got up again. Walk-waddled the floor till my back smarted. Rubbed my forearms briskly, as if that might suffice, but no.

They already think you're broken. Little slip won't matter.

I went back in the bathroom. Opened its cheerful turquoise shower curtain and reached inside to pluck my shaving razor from the soap ledge.

Wait. No. I still have the appeal —

Hahaha. Nice try.

I sat down on the closed toilet seat. Pushed the crisp sleeve of my work blouse up. Stared at the pale-veined, blameless skin of my less-messed-up wrist.

Two minutes, I said to myself. *Two minutes, and then if you still want to, you can —*

Out in the other room, my mobile rang.

Answer. It's Gloria. She'll come back over, hold your hands in hers until they stop shaking, talk you through it.

No, she won't. She's sick of you treating her like shit, sick of you taking her for granted, sick of you yanking her away from her real family for yet another stupid —

Four rings, followed by the bright bling of voicemail.

Get up.

I let the blade hover.

Go on, darlin'. Soon as you start, it'll be easy.

Tears welled in my eyes. I pulled back.

Idiot, I told myself. *Just do it.*

I rested the razor against my skin. Thought of the ridiculous poster on the wall of Tasmin's reception area, with its Photoshopped pictures of babies holding shot glasses and cigarettes. *Whatever You Do, She Does Too!*

Just like that, the blade sailed away from my hand, and Squidlet flickered.

I raised my hands to my face and began to rock. My mouth twisted. My lashes fluttered. I knew I should whisper to her, press my palm to her, smooth the scare over again, but all I could do was sob: "I want my mum, I want my mum, I want my mum."

The hallway of my childhood flat's floor was just as I'd remembered it: rain boots perched on wooden racks, bikes parked at odd angles. Chaotic but clean, at least on the surface.

I could tell she (please not they) still lived there because of the welcome mat's print: four little Scottish terriers dressed in polka-dot jumpers. She'd always wanted one, but my dad said no. ("Why?" I taunted once in the hall closet. "You want me as your only—" Couldn't say *dog,* much less *bitch,* 'cause next I knew I was seeing stars.)

I looked down. Traced the pert outline of the topmost Scottie tenderly with the toe of my shoe. Maybe she had one now. Maybe she fed him treats and talked to him about how someday, if they were lucky, if she came back to them, he'd meet her daughter.

Pathetic, Smack-Talker Brain snorted. *Only thing she's got is a fresh-out-of-prison husband who can't wait to get his fingers up in —*

Fuck you.

I curved my own fingers. Held them an inch from the door, poised to knock.

Forget it. Go home.

I knocked. No answer.

I knocked again. Pressed my ear to the door. Listened for shouts or strains, but all I heard was the telly.

Knock three. "Mum?"

Nothing.

"Mum, it's Lesley."

Shufflings. Mutters.

"Look, I know I screwed things up, but —"

Scuff, scuff, coming closer. I could see her now, in her pearl-buttoned wisteria cardigan, still wearing my rose pin. Framed photos of her and me — not a single one of him — arranged artfully above the same couch where we used to have our cuddles while watching Christmas specials. *Oh, Lesley-lovely,* she would say, mouth widening in amazement, arms reaching out to enfold me. *It's been so long. Too long.*

I put my hand on the doorknob, like I was reaching for her. My voice softer now. "Mum?"

Silence.

"Mummy?"

Scuff, scuff, retreat.

I pounded on the door. "Please, Mummy. Don't go, Mummy. I'm scared."

The neighbor across the hall poked his head out. "Miss, is there a problem?"

Careful. Wouldn't want to harm your precious appeal prospects, now, would you?

"No," I whispered, hand pressed to my mouth. "I was just leaving."

After that, I walked round the borough for what felt like ages, fists in my pockets, gaze dislocated and soft as it fell: on the Upper Street pedestrian walkway, full of chattering teenagers and yummy mummies; on the Spanish cantina, its fairy lights strung like luminous baby's breath.

Don't even bother turning onto Theberton, Smack-Talker Brain scoffed. *Your new family won't let you in, either.*

I thought of my mobile still at home, no doubt full of panicked voicemails.

Head back. Get cozy under the covers. You don't have to swallow the whole bottle, just enough tablets to —

Shut up shut up shut up.

They'll take you to Clare. You know they will. Picture it, Lesley-lovely: The three of you nestled in together. Her mouth on your belly, her nimble fingers . . .

Breathe.

You stay here, you lose.

I turned onto Theberton Street.

• • •

It was Curran who answered the door. "Oh, good," he said. "Mum's been ringing you for—"

He stopped. Peered into my face. "Les?"

I tried to speak, but couldn't.

He took me by the arm and led me into the foyer. "Don't move, okay? I'll go get her."

I didn't move. Well, anywhere except the ceiling.

"Lesley." Firm hands on my shoulders.

I dropped down. My lips trembled as I stared foggily into Gloria's gentle-but-alert face.

"Hey, you," she said softly.

My eyes welled up again.

"What's going on?" She tucked a strand of hair behind my ear, just as Sophie had. "Hmm?"

Rough gag. Hard swallow.

"Talk to me, honey."

Lip-purse. Breath-huff.

"Not," I managed. "Not safe."

"Okay." She stepped nearer. Held my shoulders tighter. "Did you do anything?"

Furious head-shake.

"Attagirl. Call Dr. P.?"

I shook my head again.

"Well, then, let's get on that." She put her arm around me and led me towards the kitchen. "I'm guessing you haven't eaten yet, eith—"

"Auntie Lesley, Auntie Lesley!" Sveta shrieked, tearing down the stairs in her pajamas, Jascha following behind.

"Svetlana," he said, soon as he saw me, "go finish getting ready for bed."

"But I want to —"

"Now, *pazhalsta*."

I knew I should smile at her when she stuck her tongue out at him, knew I ought to chuckle as she stomped back up, but all my emotional wires were snipped.

"Here, Leslyochka." Vera pushed a plate of leftover potato dumplings across the kitchen table to me.

I stared straight ahead. *Thank you,* I wanted to say, but my words had evaporated again.

Ungrateful bitch. Tribunal was right. You're just a —

"Yeah, hi, Dr. Patel. Lesley's in pretty rough shape at the moment, and . . ."

At my feet, Molly and Leopold whimpered for scraps and attention. I pictured them cuddled up next to me as the tablet haze took over. Silky fur, nuzzly noses. I knew where the medicine cupboard was. I could sneak a water glass. Dead doable. Dead, doable.

"Gloria," I said, my voice tinier than Squidlet's toes. "I think I need to go to A and E."

"I'm sorry," I whispered as they took my blood pressure.

"I'm sorry," I whispered as they slipped the plastic bracelet on my wrist.

"I'm sorry," I whispered as they escorted me to the stripped-down psychiatric cubicle.

"Don't be," the nurse said. "We'd much rather have you

walk in a little embarrassed than roll in a lot unconscious. Wouldn't we, Mum?"

"Damn straight," Gloria said.

After the nurse left, I turned out the lights and lay down. "You didn't correct her," I murmured to Gloria as she covered me with a stack of thin blankets.

"Would you rather I had?"

On her final tuck-in, I tunneled out of the waffle-weave pile and clasped her hand. "No."

This time on the inpatient unit, there were no strip searches, no ogling men—in fact, no men at all. Apparently staff had got the memo that female patients weren't sex toys and made the wards single-gender.

What a flipping relief. Not just to know that, but to stay there, sheltered from the twin tyrannies of *Your Miraculous Pregnancy* and hunter-green-and-lime letterhead. Sure, the blinky-eyed camera still blinked, but even that felt like a plus. If I lingered under its watch long enough, I reckoned, maybe the grainy black-and-white evidence would accrue in my favor.

Smack-Talker Brain of course snickered at such a pipe dream, but then the ward psychiatrist upped my (preggo-safe; I checked) meds dosage, and it shut its trap right quick. By the second day, I stopped pacing; by the third, I could feel Squidlet kick without the urge to slice my wrist.

I had so many visitors I filled up the dayroom. They came bearing mandala coloring books and fuzzy slippers,

Vera's pastries and my guitar. Imogen trumped me in a game of dirty Pictionary; Gloria entertained me writing snarky captions inside the unit's collection of celebrity magazines. *(Doughnuts are for eating, not regurgitating. P.S. The '80s phoned; they want your Lurex leggings back.)*

Best visit by far, though, was Sophie's. Not for the surprise factor or her touching contriteness, but because she walked in with a plan.

"Here's what I'm thinking," she said, sitting down across from Gloria and me at the dayroom's most intimate table. "The proposal calls for your daughter to be placed with an approved foster carer, but it doesn't specify whom." She gave Gloria a tiny, sly smile.

"Sophie," I whispered. "That's genius." I turned to Gloria. "I mean, assuming you're up for —"

"Jesus, how doped are you?" She leaned over, smoothed my messy hair. "Of course I am." Her voice somber now. "Of *course* I am."

She turned back to Sophie. "Give me the consent paperwork. Let's do it."

"Not that straightforward, I'm afraid."

"Even though I'm preapproved? We still have the certificate from when we adopted Sveta."

"How long has it been since your last homestudy?"

"Three . . ." She paused. "Almost four years."

Sophie grimaced. "Olivia will push for a new one, but I'll work on her."

•   •   •

Two days later, she came back with an update that was more like a litany of refusals:

We don't place newborns with couples over forty-five.

Even if we did, you've got too many caretaking responsibilities already.

Even if you didn't, the reapproval process would take longer than the five weeks your surrogate daughter has left.

Therefore, it is with great regret, Mr. and Mrs. Kremsky, that we inform you that you are not an appropriate fostering placement.

"How?" I sobbed. "How can the people who love me and put up with me and stick with me when no one else gives a fuck, how can they possibly be ina—"

"Yeah, I see how this works," Imogen huffed. "It's okay if Mr. and Mrs. K. want some scruffy teenage girl or an orphan from Russia, but Squidlet? She's a hot commodity. Adoption fast-track."

"God," Gloria murmured. "I never should have gotten into it with the big boss. Stupid, stupid."

And Sophie, once again, all earnest cold comfort: "I tried, Lesley. I tried."

On my discharge date, she picked me up and we drove out to see Francesca, who'd finally grown stable enough for visitors.

Her rehab center looked like a dead ringer for Claymoor Lodge. Inside, we found bulletin boards proclaiming *TODAY IS SATURDAY, 3rd FEBRUARY*, and a middle-aged man in the corridor who kept asking every woman who walked by if she wanted to suck him off. ("Please don't take it personally," his nurse said. "Many of our patients have issues with impulse control.")

I felt bad for the poor guy, but was still relieved to edge past and head for the dining area where we were supposed to meet Francesca after one of her physical therapy sessions.

Her husband had warned us that the head injury had caused major changes, in both her personality and her motor skills, but actually seeing what that meant was so sobering I wanted to cry. She sat in a wheelchair, hunched over a bowl of soup, a napkin so big it was more like a bib tucked into her T-shirt. Her hands shook as she fought to bring the spoon to her mouth.

"Shit!" As the broth splashed down her front, she slammed the spoon against her bowl with an enraged clatter.

"It's all right," her nurse said. "Just give it another go when you're— Oh!" She turned to face us. "Look who's here to see you."

Francesca sat up, her mouth trembling with shame. "Les. Soph." Our names slurred into an excited blur as she reached out her better arm to receive our hugs.

"Soon," she said when my bump bumped her.

"Yeah," I said softly.

"Sorry 'bout . . . manners. Broken brain."

"Oh, please, like you need to apologize for that around me." She gave a lopsided grin. "Olivia still a bitch?"

"You didn't hear this, Lesley," Sophie said, leaning down to whisper in Francesca's ear. "Yes."

Francesca let out a phlegmy chortle, then quieted. "Lily Bridger." That was the little girl whose dad had attacked her in the car park. "Still okay?"

"Better than. Gets on smashing with her foster siblings, has good contact with her biological mum."

Francesca gave her a thumbs-up. "Sveta?"

I gave her a thumbs-up in return.

"And our Lesley, how's she?"

Soon as we told her about the case conference, she exploded. "Those fuckers!" With one fist-swipe, her soup cascaded to the floor.

"Francesca, you need to calm down." Matter-of-fact as the Claymoor Lodge staff, her nurse bent down to retrieve the bowl.

"Bullshit! Need to fight." She pointed a quaking finger at Sophie and me. "Both of you."

"I think she's reached her limit, ladies. Perhaps you can come back another—"

"Wait, not finished!" Finger-jab towards the nurse, followed by a flail back at me. "Get Brad . . . Brad . . . Bradford Kamen. Best children's law sol . . . What's the goddamn word? No, don't tell me. Solicitor. Get him. You want *him*."

We had barely pulled out the clinic drive when I turned to Sophie and said, "I want to go to Margate."

She bit her lip. "In February?"

"Yeah." Candyfloss, ridden shoulders. Don't make me explain.

We walked the boarded-up high street and pink-painted arcades till her hands froze and my back ached. Arms linked in an awkward clutch, we picked our way down the sands and up to the rock shelter where T. S. Eliot sat and connected nothing to nothing back in the day.

"There's an amusement park somewhere around here, innit?" I said.

"Used to be," Sophie said. "They closed it a few years back. Right after my husband and I last came here on holiday."

I pictured her in summer sandals, hand draped loosely in his. Fresh off a really good hotel-room shag and relishing her freedom, but still shyly eying the toddlers buckled on the carousel ponies.

"You'd think I'd remember what the place was called, wouldn't you," she went on, "but—"

The name leapt from my mouth, quicker than Squidlet's acrobatics. "Dreamland."

22

Francesca wasn't kidding about Bradford Kamen being my man. Soon as he sat me down in his glass-and-chrome office, he laid it all out. "What they're proposing to do to you and your daughter is a human rights violation. Plain and simple."

"Then how can—"

"Expert testimony holds a ridiculous amount of sway, I'm afraid. Particularly when there's been public outcry over a child's death."

"So an appeal won't help at all."

"Generally, no, because the allowable grounds for one are so limited. We can't argue, for instance, that there's zero evidence to back up their decision, because you do have a history of mental health difficulties. But what we can assert is that your case was grossly mishandled."

"Because they ignored all those statements from Dr. Patel?"

"That, and the fact that their hired gun spent a grand total of fifteen minutes assessing you."

Rational Mind for the win. "Reckon that's enough to change their minds, innit?"

"Well, we've certainly a solid argument. As well as a compelling story." He smiled at me. "I don't normally suggest this, but you might want to consider giving media interviews."

I pictured the crap headlines: *MAD MUM VERSUS THE SS; PREGNANT CUTTER PLEADS FOR A CHANCE.* My stomach turned.

"No," I said. "I've had enough scrutiny."

"Court of public opinion swings both ways." He looked down. "Sorry. Not the best choice of words."

I couldn't help but laugh. "You really think it would—"

"Lesley," he said, leaning forward, "you're the most articulate client I've worked with in twenty-five years. If there's any disenfranchised parent who can bring this travesty to light, it's you."

No pressure there. I tried to hustle myself along with tough love *(You want her that badly? Well, then, suck it up!)*, but every time I pictured myself on a chat show or in print, my panic pushed aside all I had at stake.

In the end, it was Imogen who broke through the static buzzing in my scared skull.

"Look, twatwaffle," she said. "This isn't just about you. It's about every girl who's been in care, every girl who used to harm. Think about Team Six Percent. Think of Sveta."

Remember Clare.

A week later, I was backstage getting femmed up by a TV studio makeup artist whose purple nails and chiseled face harkened back to Tatiana's. Once she'd finished inflicting mascara and eyeliner on me, a show assistant ushered me into the green room, where, to my shock, I found Sophie sitting on the guest couch.

"What—what are *you* doing here?" I spluttered.

"Speaking out."

"They're letting you?"

"I don't need anyone's permission, Lesley. I resigned."

Holy shit. I lowered myself down next to her, amazed.

"You did that," I said. "Gave up your salary, your fertility fund, because of me?"

She nodded. "Once I saw the response to Gloria's fostering application, that was just . . . That was it. I couldn't, in good conscience, work on our—their—team anymore."

I shook my head slowly. "And now, going on telly . . . You're probably killing your chances of another job in—"

"Oh, I'll find another. Maybe not in child protection, but it . . . It doesn't matter." She reached over to pour herself a cup of water from the glass pitcher on the table. "What matters is that someone in social work owns up. All these bloody campaigners and pundits keep shrieking"—she put on a hideous, grating voice—"'No worker ever comes forward!

They're all complicit!'" She took a long sip, then clinked her glass back down. "Well, not this one."

I was so staggered I could barely rasp. "Th-thank you."

"Here." She passed me another full cup. "Got to keep your voice intact."

"What, and ruin my lipstick?"

"Never thought I'd hear those words from you." She patted me on the shoulder. "Don't worry. We've got this."

Hot lights. Stupefied squint. The questions justified but intense.

"As someone who's survived abuse, how do you feel about being accused of it yourself?"

"What will you do if your appeal fails?"

"Do you think social workers are truly incompetent?"

"You recently spent time in hospital, didn't you?"

"If you had another relapse whilst you were caring for your daughter, how would you handle that?"

"What about the baby's father?"

"Is it true you were a young offender and spent time on a criminal psychiatric unit?"

"Are you still in contact with your family?"

"How are you supporting yourself financially through all this?"

"Is there anything you'd like to tell our viewers who might be skeptical about whether you're truly stable?"

Breathe. Let your gaze soften. Breathe.

"I'm not arguing that social services are evil," I said.

"And I won't claim that I've not made mistakes, 'cause I've made plenty. I'm just asking for a . . ." My voice shook. "An opportunity to prove to everyone that those mistakes aren't . . ." Spit it out. "Aren't etched on me."

After that, I had heaps of "sympathizers" ringing and emailing: Scientologists and conspiracy theorists, family rights renegades and Lib-Dem MPs. They each talked a good game, offering "connections" and outrage and well-wishes, but I knew all they were really after was an opportunity to make me their pet agendas' poster girl.

I thanked them, of course, but in the end my greyhound won out over my golden retriever. Did that stubbornness doom me? Hard to tell, and no sense guessing now, but at least I can look back and say I never sold myself out in anybody's political hall closet.

Week thirty-seven. *Your baby is now full-term,* quoth *Miraculous Pregnancy,* so unabashed in its editorial excitement I chucked the bloody thing in the bin.

At my appeal hearing, my hands stood sentry across my bump. Bradford Kamen on one side of me, Sophie on the other. Olivia glaring at her across the table.

"Given your recent mental health crisis, our decision still stands."

Now they got what they wanted. Wild-woman fingers raked through my hair. Snot slobbing down my nose. There. Confirmation. Happy now?

But this time, after the conference room exodus, Bradford was right on it.

"Lesley, this is not a given. The ultimate decision doesn't rest in their hands."

"Yes, it does," I wailed.

"No. You need to understand. Social services have to *apply* for an order once she's born. They'll request one from a family court judge, who can either approve or deny it. So there's a chance—"

"Oh, please. You know he'll rubber-stamp their paperwork." I stared down Sophie. "Right?"

Her face went all squinchy. "Well, erm . . ."

"How many of your old orders went through? Huh?"

"All . . ." Ashamed whisper. "All of them."

"So that's it," I said. "I just wait to go into labor and pray I get a sympathetic judge."

Bradford's face went still and solemn. "Ms. Burnham, may I have a word alone with my client?"

Once Sophie had ducked out, he drew his chair closer to mine. "You do realize," he said, "that whilst you're still pregnant the plan is one hundred percent unenforceable."

I nodded.

"Which means, legally speaking, you're free to go as you please."

"You mean, move to another borough where they won't mess with me?"

He nodded. "Another borough, another region. Even another country."

I bit my lip.

"Look," he said, "if your baby were already here and

subject to a child protection plan, I would be completely unethical in suggesting such a thing. In fact, we'd both be breaking the law. But now, when you have this small window . . ."

"They wouldn't come after me?"

"And waste their already-strapped resources on an international womanhunt?" He chuckled. "I believe your adoring fans' paranoia has gone to your head, my dear."

"So you think I should do it."

"I think," he said carefully, "that you should consider all your options."

"But if I were your daughter? What about then?"

I was pushing him well past his boundaries, but I had to know.

He glanced away. Rubbed his forehead. Looked back at me.

"If you were my daughter," he said, "I'd tell you to pack your bags."

You'd think, hearing that, I'd have grabbed my passport and bolted straightaway, but I spent several sleepless nights debating. Where would I go? How would I get money? What would happen if I *really* cracked up?

"Just look up Dec," Imogen said. "Take the ferry over to Ireland. Easy-peasy."

No, it wasn't. No guarantee he'd take me in. No guarantee he could deal.

"Okay, then let that Scientologist lady hook you up with her people in Sweden."

Ugh. Blech.

"What's your fucking problem, Les? You heard your solicitor. It's the best way out."

Alone on a windy upper deck in the dark, rucksack and bin bag and guitar, pulling cold and exhausted into Dún Laoghaire or Stockholm. Alone at another hostel. Alone on a foreign maternity ward.

"I don't want out," I sobbed late one night, my head on the Kremskys' kitchen table. "I don't want to have to go."

"Leslyochka." Vera reached over to rest her hand atop my hair. "*Ja znaiyu.* But you must."

I glanced up.

"You remember, when we first met, I was so rude to you about having been in hospital, *da?*"

"Yeah," I said, impressed that *she* remembered.

"I did not mean to be. It was knee-jerk reaction, from . . . From old situation. Past."

What? "You mean you were in a—"

"No, no. Thank God. Not me. But my family. They were . . ." She looked over at Jascha. "What is word *po-angliski?*"

"Dissidents," he said.

"Right. And in those days, Stalin, you disagree, you get sent to *psikhushka.* Shock treatment, all that. Horrible. Never no idea who is next."

Shit. Poor Vera.

"We were so afraid, you know, that even still, anything to do with mental problems, it . . ." She pressed a hand to her mouth. "I hate to think about."

"God," I said. "I'm so sorry. I had no—"

"*Nyet*, is okay. Am not telling you this for sympathy. Just to apologize for being idiot, and to explain why . . ."

"Why you left Russia?" I asked.

She nodded. "This one was so tiny." She gestured towards Jascha. "Couldn't take chances. So we had to take huge chance. You understand?"

"Yeah," I said softly. "I do."

Once I'd made up my mind, there remained the question of where. The EU would be easiest in terms of job prospects, but the thought of being a baby-toting backpacker with a bad case of travel fugue still didn't sit well with me.

"Just go to America, then," Curran said.

"Easy for you to say," I told him. "You've got dual citizenship; I'm just some layabout on a six-month holiday visa."

"You're not the sort of immigrant they're fired up about, Les."

"No, but what the hell would I do?"

He shrugged. "You could always stay with my gran."

Hmm. I didn't know Caroline well, but I'd met her a few times when she'd flown over for Christmas, and she'd been almost painfully nice: flipping excitedly through Imogen's design portfolio, eagerly talking shop with me about studio techniques for orchestral recordings.

Of course, she also drove Gloria round the fucking bend with her constant fussy, fastidious chatter—"Honey, are you *sure* you don't want some highlights from that new salon in Chelsea? You know, your kitchen would be just adorable if you painted it a light peach. And have you thought about putting Sveta in an organized sport? It'd be such a good way for her to burn off all that hyperactive energy . . ."—so I went to her for a second opinion.

"My mother," Gloria said, "would spoil you and Squidlet absolutely rotten."

I pictured us tucked away in her floral guest room, the darkbright strains of a cello drifting down the lush-carpeted hall.

"But," she went on, "you need to realize that my former homeland is not the land of the Smartie-crapping unicorns. Far from it."

"I won't have social services on my back. That's good enough."

"Until you need, oh, health care. Or child care. Or—"

"I don't give a fuck. I just want us to stay together."

Consent from a medical provider is required for women traveling past their 36th week of pregnancy, every international airline's website read.

Right. Like I could just ring Tasmin and ask for her blessing immortalized in written form.

I was about to say *Screw it* and click over to the Stena Line ferry schedule when Vera tapped me on the shoulder.

"Don't," she said. "I can fix this."

"How?"

"Back in Krasnoyarsk, I was midwife's apprentice. Not for long, but still."

I wanted to grin, but all I could think was worst-case scenario. "What if—"

"What if nothing. Is simple. You hand British Airways check-in person my signed letter. Take leap of faith. Get on plane."

And so I gave notice at my job, and transferred the lease on my flat to one of the Team Six Percent girls, and crammed all of Squidlet's and my clothes into one suitcase. I held Sveta on my lap as she whimpered, "Why do you have to go, Auntie Lesley?" I DJ-ed one final time, with Immi and Curran helping me up in the sound booth. I snuggled the hellhounds while watching *Match of the Day* with Vera. I visited Francesca and made fun of her nurse to make her laugh. I sent Sophie and Dr. P. thank-you letters, and slipped an impulsive, sorrowful one containing my new address in Baltimore to my mum, just for my own closure, under the jumpered-Scottie mat.

My last night in London, I went with the Kremskys to the Russian Orthodox cathedral in South Ken, where the signs read *No Stilletos* and you had to stand for the whole flipping service. My bump clenched and my back cramped and my stomach churned from the incense, but I stood strong between Gloria and Jascha, bathed in candles' flicker for the first time since Clare. When I bowed my head, I prayed with ecumenical reverence: for the dutiful daughters and the sad slumped men, the ones who pinned wrists down and the ones who stroked foreheads, the saved children and the lost workers, all of them.

23

On the way to Heathrow the next morning, Immi and I sat in the backseat of Gloria's car, lobbing one last round of gleeful epithets while clutching each other's hands.

"Twatwaffle."

"Daft-and-naïve."

"*Daily Mail*–fucker."

"Goatee-shagger."

"Christ," I whispered. "I'm going to miss you."

We made a detour for scones and lattes. Cranked "Best of the Screaming Women" loud as it would go.

By the time we pulled into the Terminal 5 car park, I had to pee so badly it hurt, so we skipped the bag check and headed straight for the ladies'. Giant queue, but bless them, everyone let me cut to the front and snag my dear friend the disabled stall.

Whew. Flipping epic. Even Squidlet did somersaults of relief.

Out by the sinks, I could hear Gloria and Imogen rallying themselves.

"We won't cry, will we, Mrs. K.?"

"No. We most certainly will not."

I grinned. Hoisted myself with the side rails and pulled
up my jeans. I was just about to rebutton them when I felt
the most massive plunge-plummet you can possibly imagine.
Waterslide, waterfall, surgebloompgush.

I widened my stance, like I did that night I had to prove I
was wearing contraband-less knickers. Glimpsed the massive
ovals of damp denim stain that wended from my thighs down
to—I'm not joking—the insides of my knees.

At first, I stood there dazed. Then I put my hands to my
mouth. Willed myself not to sway.

"Hey, Les." Jaunty knock at the door from Immi. "You
fall in, or what?"

"No," I said. "I'll—I'll be right out."

I scrambled to unbutton again. Lowered myself back
onto the toilet. Felt the insides of both my knickers and my
jeans. Sniffed my fingers.

Margate ocean, not urine.

No, I thought. *This isn't happening.*

A few stalls down, a little girl was describing in exquisite
detail the anthropomorphic characteristics of her poo—
"two snakes and a dragon, Mummy!"—while her morti-
fied mother gently chastised. "Really, Hannah, that's quite
enough."

I put my hands over my face and began to silently weep.

Meanwhile, Hannah had commenced singing "Eensy
Weensy Spider," and Imogen was trying to convince

Gloria to go shopping for "saucy boots" once they'd seen me off. "Drown our grief in retail therapy. You know what I'm saying?"

I tore off a piece of tissue and blew my nose. Pulled off another and dried my eyes. Pulled off a third. Patted it between my legs.

More damp. More salt.

Think, I told myself. *What did the birthing instructor tell you?*

("If your waters break, it does not necessarily mean you're in labor. Nor is it a cause for concern unless twenty-four hours pass.")

I rolled my suitcase closer. Unzipped it and pulled out a clean pair of underwear and cargo trousers. Nearly fell on my arse balancing, but I got them on. Quick stuff-down of some extra loo paper for insurance, hurried cram of my dirty clothes into the suitcase's outside pocket, and Bob's your uncle.

"Well hello there, fashionista," Im said when I finally came out the stall. "What'd you do, piss yourself?"

I flipped her off and handed her my guitar to carry.

Check-in queue was ginormous. We wound up behind Hannah and her mum, who made empathetic noises about how awful it was to travel while pregnant. ("Of course, you've not got *this*" — a loving hand-swipe towards her daughter — "to contend with yet, so perhaps it's easier.")

I was about to tell her I'd read a juicy magazine and take a good nap on her behalf when my bump clenched and my back twinged.

Chillax, Wise Mind said. *It's just one of those practice contrac-tions, remember?*

But a few minutes later, there it came again.

"Disney World, Disney World, Disney World," Hannah chirped.

Power of suggestion, Rational Mind scoffed.

"Earth to Les." Im nudged me.

"Ow. Stop."

Clench. Twinge.

Gloria's mobile rang. "Hi, Mom." I watched her shake her head, unable to sneak a word in.

She grinned. Passed the phone to me. "Your turn."

"Lesley, it's Caroline." Breathy, mellifluous voice. "I'm so looking forward to seeing you again. And so sorry it's under these circumstances, poor dear girl. But don't worry. About anything, all right? I'll be there extra early to meet you. Rush hour will be terrible on the Beltway, so I'm thinking we can stop to eat on the way home—you'll be famished, no doubt. Which reminds me, is there anything in particular you'd like me to stock up on? Anything making your stomach turn that I should avoid? I asked Gloria, but all she said was 'For fuck's sake, Mom, all she needs is a safe haven.'" She chuck-led. "True to form, no?"

I wanted to laugh in agreement but couldn't. My body too taut. "Yeah."

"Listen, honey, I know this is awkward. And I'm sure I'm going overboard here since I never got to experience it with Curran—awful ten-year silence, horrible, but my own idiotic fault, so I can't exactly . . ."

Blah well-intentioned blah endearing blah. Slow turn

round the corner to the next segment of the queue. I put my hand on the divider. Drew in a sharp breath.

Clench. Twinge. Clench.

"You can tell her to shut up, Lesley," Gloria said. "Really."

Her mum laughed again. "She's right. And I will."

"N-no," I managed to gasp in what I hoped sounded like shy appreciation. "It's . . . you're . . . brilliant. Thank you. So much."

"Something's wrong," I heard Imogen whisper to Gloria. "Look at her."

"I'm fine," I said, soon as I hung up. "My back's just killing me."

"Want to sit down for a little while?" Gloria asked.

"Go on," Im said. "I'll hold your place."

On the slow shuffle towards the waiting area, I felt my eyes screw shut: first in anticipation, then in actual pain.

You've been on your feet. Carrying a heavy rucksack. Not drinking enough water. Drinking too much coffee.

That's all. That's all. That's all.

I lowered myself into the rigid metal hold of a too-narrow seat. Tried to imagine myself stuck in a similar one for eight-plus hours, hunkered down on the moist bunch of my wadded-up coat, white-knuckling it all the way to Balti-more: *What if they what if she what if I what if we —*

What if nothing, Leslyochka. Stick a proper pad in your knickers, and lumber down that Jetway.

Gloria put her hand on my back. "Where does it hurt, honey?"

"Everywhere." I leaned forward into crash-landing position.

Clench. Clench. Clench.

She rubbed my shoulder blades, then down my spine. Stopped just above my hip bones, where it twinged the most. "Your water broke in the bathroom, didn't it?"

I let out a twisty-mouthed whimper. Looked up to see her pull her mobile from her coat pocket.

"Don't ring anyone," I said hoarsely. "Please."

She nodded. We stared down at her open palm, in which the phone lay cradled, its home screen lit with nothing but the time: *10:45*.

"Tell me," she said, equally hoarsely. "When the next one—"

Clench clench clench clench.

Now, I mouthed.

Screw-shut. Crash-land. Blown-out *whew.*

When it stopped, she reached over and stroked my head with her free hand. "Still all in your back?"

"Front," I huffed.

"Getting worse?"

I sat up. Pushed my hair out of my eyes. "Uh-huh."

After I breathed through that contraction, I glanced over at her. "Seven minutes apart," she said.

"I can still get on the plane," I whispered. "*Miraculous Pregnancy* says it's not active labor. Not until the pains are less than five—"

Clenchclenchclenchclench.

Now.

Hang on. Head-duck. Breathe. "How many?"

She bit her lip. "Six."

We're okay. We're okay. I'm still talking through them. There's a margin. Wiggle room through the cabin doors. I can have her on an emergency landing in fucking Greenland. Little Inuit Squidlet. Whatever it takes.

"I'm getting back in the queue," I said, grabbing my chair's leather-padded armrests for leverage.

"Lesley, maybe you should—"

"What?" I flapped a hand towards the ticket counters. "Look at Immi, how far up she is." I hefted up with a grunt. "Come on, hand me my bag."

She hesitated. Sucked her lips between her teeth so hard her mouth was one thin robot line.

"Fine, don't." I lurched forward to heave my suitcase from the floor just as a brutal cramp shoved me onto my knees.

"Ohh." Gut-punched dribble of a moan. I turned round in a slow circle and rested my head on the warm slant of the now-empty seat in front of me.

Clench. Fly. Clench. Fly.

Don't open me. Don't make me open.

Clench. Fly. Clench. Fly.

"Lesley?" Soft hand on my shoulder, shaky-gentle voice at my ear. "Talk to me."

Contractions are like waves. Picture yourself riding them.

Fuck that fuck that fucking fuck that.

I tipped my head back. Mad-wet-dog-drippy head-shake. How long ago had I prayed, in those hot droplets? How hard had I laughed, under that tingling spray?

"Imogen!" Gloria, above me, shouting out into the crowd, her hand tilting in frantic wave.

Hand them the letter, Im. Tell them I've just nipped into the toilets again. Back any minute. Passport at the ready.

"Got here fast as I could, Mrs. K. That queue is fierce.

What's . . . Why's she down on the floor like that? She's not in . . . Oh my God." Her voice rose to a shriek. "She is!"

(No. *Your Miraculous Pregnancy* says, and I quote: *Labor can take many hours in a first-time mum. Contrary to what hospital dramas and comedy films depict, there is almost never a need for panic.*)

Almost. Almost.

Not happening. Is *not*.

Luggage trolley roll-squeak. "Mummy, is that lady going to have her baby right here in the airport?"

My fists rose. My head whipped round to spy poor little Hannah in her Mickey Mouse ears.

"No," I choked out, just as the next clench hit and a security guard came walking over.

"Relax, love."

No, really. That's what he said.

And then: "Hospital's just up the road."

Breathe. Rock. Breathe.

Imogen's and Gloria's arms around my back.

"I've radioed our medics."

Ceiling ceiling ceiling.

Clenchclenchclench.

(Dr. P., back in the day, all Zen chuckle: "Don't push the river, Lesley. It flows by itself.")

Into me, out of me.

My arms wrapped around her, harder than the belt I'd teased her father with, tighter than the belt her grandfather had used to bind my wrists above my head.

Little light, shining . . .
Blue one. Atop an ambulance.

"Every five minutes. No idea on dilation."

God, that trolley mattress felt brilliant. Didn't want it to, but it did.

"Roll onto your left side for us, sweetie?" Broad-shouldered, kind-faced lady medic.

I rolled. Wrapped my fingers round the cold metal of the protective rails. Chillygood.

"Any urges to push?" This from her male partner, wheeling me from behind.

"No." Head-shake so vigorous it hurt. My free hand still guarding my bump.

Stay with me. With *me*.

Clenchclenchclench.

I closed my eyes. Deep-belly breathed.

"That's it. You're doing marvelous."

At the sound of the ambulance doors' unlatch, my eyes flickered back open. "My . . . my family. I need them. Where are they?"

"Following us straight there."

Heave-ho into the cavern. Gritting my teeth on the jostle.

"Anyone else we should contact? Your partner? Midwife?"

"Haven't one," I mumbled. "I'm moving abroad."

Will be. No, admit it: *was*.

Man slipped a pair of those oxygen prongy-bits like

Vera's into my nostrils. Lady rolled my sleeve up. The closest one. The left one.

Not a word. Not even a sigh-gasp. Just an apology. "Quick poke here. So sorry."

They don't know. They won't know. I'm marvelous. I've a chance.

Eye-squinch, followed by soft flicker, followed by eye-squinch again. Squeezing the steady fingers my guard offered me through the bars, counting down the seconds to clench clench clench clench fly.

24

Ward bustle hand-off. Flying jargon. *Primipara, precipitous labor, and* . . . "Wait. What's her name?"

Clare Manning. Molly Bloom. Kate Bush.

Lie, do it. Lie, damn it.

Pain like a wave, no choice but to ride.

"Lesley," I gasped. "Lesley . . . Holloway."

Phone calls. Whisper flurries. My trolley's wheels locked in park at the nurse's station.

"She's that one . . . From on telly . . . You know. Custody order? Harm risk?"

Unit head paged. Protocol spelled out. "Get her on a fetal monitor, and don't leave her unattended, even for a second."

I jammed my fists in my mouth. Curled up tight as I could.

"Keep away from that drip line, now." My assigned nurse

swatted lightly at my hand as they wheeled me towards my single room.

When we passed by a suite fitted out with a glossy egg of a birthing tub, my eyes welled up. Stupid sluice-tears. Wistful lavender ache.

"Here. Put these on."

Old diamond-print wisp of a gown, same gray fluff-socks.

No, I wanted to say. *If you can't treat me with dignity, you can at least let me keep my goddamn clothes on.*

But of course I balanced. Of course I scrambled, in the four (ohmygod, *four*) minutes I now had between cramped huffs.

"Lie down. It's less stress on the baby."

Not your baby. *The.*

I'd just got settled on my side—well, best I could given the pair of electronic jetpacks attached to my bump—when a white-coat manly-man came in, all "Let's see where we stand, shall we?"

"What do you mean?" I asked.

He gave me a look like *Surely you know all these procedures by heart, Miss Munchausen.* "A progress check. Of your cervix."

Nonononono.

("They do what to what now, Les?")

Imogen. I needed Imogen. Where was she?

Glove-snap. Hand-beckon. "Slide down for me, please."

Inch by inch, quaking beneath blankets, I slid.

His hand angled under. Tilted my knee open.

Every muscle in me tightened. I willed my legs not to clamp shut.

Good girl. I'm a good girl. See?

He rolled me onto my back. Reached for the waistband of my knickers. Whisked them down and off.

I grabbed fistfuls of blanket. My head rocketed off the pillow, rigid-necked, as both the gut-clench and the shove of his fingers overtook me.

"Ow. Ow. *Ow!*" My protests like empty-air punches.

"Seven centimeters." Nonchalant latex peel-off. "You're well on your—"

"What the hell?" Immi, all indignant in the doorway.

Still naked and bent-kneed, I reached out my arms for her. She ran into them and grabbed me tight, rocking me into a sitting position. "Flipping sadist," she whispered. "Next time, I'm punching him out."

I tried to smile. "Where's Gloria?"

"Still trying to find parking. This place is a pit."

"Careful you don't dislodge her monitor," my nurse called from her chair post.

Mrm-mrm-mrm-mrm-mrm-mrm-mrm, Imogen mouthed in scowly, head-cocked imitation of her. "You need anything, Les?"

"Just my knickers."

I'd barely got them back on when the next pain rammed me. Back, belly, front, bottom, everyplace. I sank forward onto my hands and knees, moaning pitiful moo-cow sounds, wracked with shakes.

"Please," Imogen said to the nurse, her voice equally shaky. "Can't you give her some drugs?"

"She's too far along for an epidural."

"Just rub my back, Im," I gasped.

She hovered over me, her hand timid.

"Not like that. Harder."

Blanket-grip. Head-lower. Door-swing. Gloria.

She hurried to the bed. I reached out for her. Fought to steady myself as the clench hit.

"I've got you," she whispered, stroking my hair as I buried my face in the warm wool of her coat. "Just lean into me, angel. I've got you."

"She really ought to lie down again." Public service announcement from my nurse.

I leaned back, turned over, closed my eyes. Immi fed me ice chips; Gloria draped a cool cloth against the back of my neck. Tranquil, almost sleepy. A blessed lull.

And then I was up again, back on my hands and knees. Sweating. Swearing. "It's too fucking hot in here! Nobody talk!" Shades of Francesca and her soup.

I puked into a basin. I bled pinkish egg white onto a crackly square of aqua-bordered padding hurriedly placed between my trembling thighs. I made guttural growls that sounded like I was rending raw flesh with my teeth. I slammed my fists down on the mattress in fury as the pressure descended and my body betrayed me with a push.

"Get on your back!"

Trifecta of round lights gleaming. My fluff-socks hoisted into stirrups. Manly-man between my splayed legs, imperious. Nurses frantically consulting. "At what point should security be dispatched?"

Never never never.

"Ring Bradford Kamen," I panted to Gloria. "Right now."

On my other side, Immi clung to my hand. "It—it'll be okay, Les." Her words an unconvincing stammer. "Really, it will."

"All right, so Lesley." Bradford, his voice thin through the stretched cord of the bedside table's landline. "I want you to listen to me, hard as you've ever done in your life."

"'Kay," I grunted.

"Don't let medical staff take her out of your sight without your explicit consent. And if a Children's Services worker from *any* borough shows up without a court-issued order in hand, send them back down the lifts."

"How . . . long . . . decide?"

"Several hours. During which you have sole custody. Do you hear me? *Complete.*"

"Six, seven, eight, nine . . ."

Stop counting. Shut up.

"Aaaand rest."

My eyeballs throbbed. My lips stung.

So much pressure, too much skin-stretch.

Where's my candle where's my bathtub where's Clare?

Just relax, love.

Fuck you.

There's my girl.

Mine. Do you hear me? *Mine.*

The glint of a syringe. Scissors.

I whipped my head back and forth on the pillow. Sucked my tongue so I wouldn't scream as the snip came.

"One more push."

No. Stay with me, lovey. Don't be—

Slip, slide, turn. Out.

Wiggly waily smear of limbs, all blood and squall.

I barely got a glimpse before they hustled her under her own bright lamp, laying her down in a plastic cot to rub her roughly, suctioning out her button nose and furious little mouth.

"Time of birth, thirteen forty-five."

My flight's scheduled moment of departure.

"Give her to me," I said, teeth chattering.

And, miracle of miracles, they did. Swaddled all snug like a jacket potato in foil, sporting a striped pink hat. Quiet now, her eyes never straying from mine all through my stitch-up.

For the next hour, we lay curled together, me with an ice pack on my sore parts, she in the crook of my arm. I sang her a ridiculous song about being the cutest calamari in the ocean, while Imogen took picture after picture with her mobile phone's camera and Gloria fed me bites of a cheeseburger I'd ordered up from the hospital kitchen. (Best meal of my flipping life, I kid you not.)

Little girl must have been hungry, too, 'cause she started rooting round, nuzzling me like, *Make with the goods!* Not like I had much on offer yet, but both birthing class and *Your You-Know-What Pregnancy* had been in agreement that those yellowy drips-and-drabs were "liquid gold," so I hiked my gown up straightaway.

"Stop."

I glanced over at the nurse. "What? It's good for her."

"We can't allow you until we've gotten back the results from your toxicology screen."

"Oh, you are freaking *kidding* me." Gloria, *I'm so not* in full force.

My lips trembled. "Only thing I've had is a hazelnut latte, I swear."

Against my gown, Squidlet whimpered and fretted.

"Shh, baby," I whispered, kissing the top of her head.

Nurse stood up. Walked over. Reached across the bed rails, arms outstretched. "I'll take her to the nursery for a feed."

And never bring her back?

Just say yes. You'll look even more dodgy if you don't.

"Okay," I said. "But only if she"—I pointed to Gloria—"goes with."

Frownypants sigh, followed by assent. My skin crawling, my fists curling, as they filed out.

Soon as the door closed, I fell onto Imogen, all silent howl.

"Easy, girlie," she said, patting my back. "You know Gloria won't let them pull any shit."

Sure enough, ten minutes later, back they came, Squidlet's pointy-capped head tucked under Gloria's chin. "Scrumptious, scrumptious thing," she cooed. "Let's get you back to your mum."

"Wait," I said. "Let Immi hold her." Just in ca—

Shh. Don't think it.

"All right, Auntie Imogen. Here you go." Delicate handover, Im looking delighted and terrified at once. "Steady her head. Just like that. Perfect."

Immi's eyes went damp. "God, she's so tiny."

"Who's my ickle Squidlet?"

Soon as she heard me, her face turned.

"She knows who *that* is," Gloria said, smiling.

Greedy, amazed, I reached hungrily for her. Cuddled her to my chest. Lay back and tucked my blanket round us both.

Voices in the hall. Footsteps. My nurse stood. Went to the door.

I glanced from Imogen to Gloria and back again.

"Im," I said hoarsely. "Go check."

She grabbed Gloria's hand. Squeezed it for reassurance.

Huge, almost comical steps. Arms pumping. Sneaky sneak, followed by a *joke's over* dart back to my bedside.

"What?" I said.

"Security."

My arms tightened round Squidlet. *No no no,* I mouthed, chin jerking.

Gloria rested her palm against my cheek. "Lesley."

Eye-squinch. Ceiling.

"Look at me, Lesley. *Look* at me."

Flicker.

It's happening, I mouthed again.

"You don't know that."

Airless throat. I wisped out speech. "It's gonna kill me."

She slid her hand up against my temple, holding me fast. "We won't let it." Sharp glance at Imogen. "Will we, Im?"

Immi's face was blank with terror. "N-no."

The nurse stepped back in, her features softened to pudding. "Lesley." First time she'd used my name in the four hours she'd kept watch. "There's a social worker here to see you."

"Don't need one," I said. "But thanks."

Her face flushed. "She's . . . she's from child protection."

I sat up. "Which team?"

"Islington."

Fuck oh fuck oh fuck.

"Papers," I managed. "Has she got any?"

"Hang on. I'll ask."

Soon as her back was turned, I motioned for Immi to unlatch the side rails on my bed. Fought to swing my legs over.

"Oh, no, you don't." Gloria put her hands on my shoulders.

"Let me up."

"Only if you tell me what you're planning to do."

Hide in the toilets. Jump out the window. Whatever it takes.

Door opened again. There she stood. Directress Butter-Up.

I shifted Squidlet into one elbow crook. Put up my palm to block Olivia's approach.

"Don't come near me," I said, like a desperate gun-brandisher. One of Those People, forever and ever, amen.

Olivia didn't move. Just handed the nurse a small sheaf.

As she brought it over, I slid back on the bed.

The page floated before my eyes. Couldn't touch it.

In re: Baby H.

My sleepsighing girl, rendered an initial.

The High Court judge's signature a smooth swirl.

I snatched it from the nurse and flung it across the room. Kamikaze paper airplane. Fuck that fuck that fucking fuck that.

Olivia bent down in her heels. Plucked the order from the floor. Straightened up and walked towards me.

"Don't do this," I heard Gloria whisper from the foot of the bed. "Please don't do this."

Imogen, sobbing into Gloria's shoulder.

I pressed my cheek to Squidlet's head.

"You brought me crisps and a soda when I ran away from home," I said. "Remember that girl." My voice broke. "Remember *me*."

Olivia's brows furrowed. Forehead line going deep. Mouth pinching into what looked like sorrow.

"Let's do it calmly," she said. "Gently. For your daughter's sake." Her voice tender. Almost reverent. *Your*.

Thank you, I almost said, but then she bent down, and my mouth watered with spit, and my eyes watered with rage. No more eager retriever, no more collaborative solutions. No more yes please sure absolutely whatever you'd like, here let me lift my skirt and lean across the desk so you can fuck me over even harder, no more no more no more, I'm done, do you hear me, done, so give me my—

My fist, aiming for her teeth.

My gray-fluffed feet, poised to kick the triangle between her legs.

My unbridled screams.

My forearm, swabbed with alcohol.

My wrists, laced into leather cuffs.

My ankles, spread and bound.

My sacred sweet shining thing, Margate funfair balloon, lifting, lifted, towards the ceiling, up and gone.

• • •

By the time they discharged me, bruised and staggering, it was almost midnight. I lay on the backseat with my head in Imogen's lap, moaning softly all the way back to the Kremskys'.

Jascha met us at the pavement, sleepless and solemn. I sat up just enough to reach for him, and he scooped me into his arms and carried me up the front steps.

Inside, the dogs barked and a wide-awake Sveta babbled. "How come Auntie Lesley's back? Why hasn't she got the big tummy anymore?" Her voice rose in panic. Her fingers tugged at her father's sleeve. "What's wrong? What happened to the baby? Tell me!"

"Shush. Let her rest." Curran, gently scooting her out of the way.

Jascha lay me down in the middle of his and Gloria's bed, and she and Imogen crawled in next to me, one on either side. Their hands soft on my lank hair. Their cool arms draped round my sweaty waist.

"Manky," I mumbled. "Sorry."

"Don't be."

"I'm going to bleed through your sheets."

"We've got extras, honey."

"Poison milk. They thought I had—"

"Arseholes. You have rockstar milk."

"I love you, Im."

"I love you, too. Now sleep."

An hour later, I jerked awake. Phantom pain. Frantic flail. "Where is she? Where?"

"Shh."

"Oh my God." Keening moan. "Oh my God."

The third time, Jascha came in with a glass of water and a Valium tablet.

"No. It'll hurt her." We could nurse at our next contact session. Maybe. If I stayed a good girl.

"Dr. P. says it's fine."

Well, then.

Swig. Candyfloss-spin. Fall.

Morning. Slits of sun through the drapes. How dare it.

The scent of eggs wafted from the kitchen. I'd have retched, if my guts weren't so worn.

Slow sit-up. Empty bed. Clean sheets.

I pressed the puckery mush of my deflated belly with my fingers.

Crazy little girl. Just imagining things.

My breasts felt hard as sandbags. Russian-game-show-hostess worthy.

I yawned and rubbed my eyes.

And then: another heat rush, another moist cascade-plunge.

I looked down at my shirt. Two giant circles of useless milk.

It's a lost cause, Smack-Talker Brain sighed.

Fuck off.

No, really. You know she's slurping down a bottle of formula in the arms of her loving foster mum right this minute. Having a swaddled, cuddly walk in the garden. Being rocked to sleep next to a lace-curtained window, snug as a bug. Tell me I'm not right.

You're a lying sack of shit.

I crawled off the bed. Stumbled towards the shower.

Medicine cabinet mirror gave me a gleaming wink. The haggard face in the glass crumpled.

Don't cry. It's better this way.

How can you even —

She won't mourn. She'll never remember.

You don't know that.

Let it go. Like breath.

No.

What? You don't want to sink into that warm water egg-bath?

Yeah, but —

Purple buds floating. Your tongue on Clare's chipped tooth. Dark hair, made darker.

I said no.

Her mouth. It'll drain all that sadness.

Oh my God please.

Lavender milk.

Help me.

You know what to do, Lesley-lovely.

I opened the cabinet. Reached for the aspirin bottle. Wrenched its top open, and stared inside.

Forty? Maybe?

Beggars can't be —

Plasticky bounce. Rain-spray of tablets, all over the tile.

Sputtering, I knelt fast (whoa! I could do that now!) to gather them in my palm.

That's it. No need to prolong the agony.

I pictured myself silent and shamed, sat down meekly before some family court wanker in a white wig, held captive to his diatribes as he reduced our mother-child bond to mere "letterbox contact." I saw myself praying for a Christmas card, a birthday wish, a single photo in a humble sleeve, anything, oh just a crumb, please. I imagined her becoming a Mulberry-pursed Mallorca girl with a pony and diamond-stud earrings.

No. A pensive, thoughtful creature, equal parts Victorian storybook and diffident anti-cool, sporting Doc Martens and hair gathered up in a graceful topknot. Wondering, asking, *What's my birth mum up to now?*

And then fuming, hurt-wracked, breathy with shock: *You mean she just killed herself? Didn't fight for me? Didn't even try?* Stomping up the stairs of her family's maisonette, shaking her head, willing herself not to cry, not to tremble. *God. Screw her.*

I willed myself not to cry. I willed myself not to tremble. Tightened the cap on the bottle of pills. Pulled myself up by the sink edge and set them back in the medicine cabinet, dusty but intact. Put on Gloria's garnet-colored silk robe and went downstairs into my family's cocooning embrace. Got online to research breast pumps. Rang Bradford Kamen and told him, "Be ruthless. I'm ready."

25

Six Months Later

Half a year old now, she is. Got so big, so fast, like a baby Buddha, rolling around on the floor, reaching for things. I bought her this toy that's like a model of a DNA molecule, pastel rainbow of colors that tumbles about the floor when she shoves it and rattles when she gives it a shake. Her eyes crinkling, her mouth opening in surprise, her little bum in the air as she lurches after it, loud, stubborn, squealy.

My man Bradford pushed for contact five days a week, but we had to settle for three. They're still letting me nurse, as long as I consent to drug tests. Which of course I do. Back in retriever mode, punctuated by the occasional grovel. *Pretty please, can we do a visit at a park? Bask in the rare summer sun?*

"Contact at our offices only, as per the order."

Right. Sure. You need to schedule us for a weekday midafternoon? Absolutely. Not an inconvenience. Whatever you think is best. Whatever it takes to make sure I can savor her while I still have time.

Thank God my new manager lets me nip out early, or else I'd never see my girl. Thanks to one of Dr. P.'s colleagues, I work for a mental health charity as a service user consultant now, advising Accident and Emergency nurses and university counseling services and GPs on how not to be arseholes when treating people who self-harm. (Yes, the irony boggles.)

At night, I hook the girls up to my pump for one last milking and lie down with my new talisman: a matrioshka doll Vera gave me, the itty-bittiest baby in the painted-wood bunch. My hand closed tight round it, all through my broken sleep.

I hate to say this, but I just want to be done.

The morning of our final hearing, I wear a silk blouse and the first skirt I've bought in years. Not only do I want to look tidy for court, but I also have to give a presentation for work beforehand, to a bunch of burnt-out psychiatrists whose energy has been sapped by treating "those bloody borderlines." (They don't use the phrase out loud, of course, but I can see the judgment in their exhausted eyes.)

"What's most important," I tell them, "is that you convey to your patients that they aren't fundamentally flawed. That there is hope for their lives in the face of their seemingly unbearable pain."

After the shrinks thank me for my time, I run down the hall and lock myself in the ladies' room and press one palm to my mouth while pounding the other against the toilet stall's divider, because it feels as though what used to be the buoyant, healing truth has turned into a superficial platitude that, if the rest of this day goes badly, will become a complete and utter lie.

I hurry across the road to Pret with my hand still smart-ing. Listlessly force down a few bites of a ham-and-Gruyère baguette while scrawling on a legal pad. Every five seconds, I get a good-luck text from somebody on my mobile. I know they're trying to rally me, but I can't bear the thought of my right to motherhood boiling down to nothing more than ca-pricious luck.

On my way to chuck my barely eaten sandwich in the bin, I bump into a woman who looks about my own mum's age. She gives me a small, wry smile, and gestures towards the front of my shirt, which bears an inkblot of leaked milk. "Never fails to let down on your lunch break, does it?"

My face goes hot. I start to blink. "Nope."

"It gets easier," she says. "Leaving them."

The entire tube ride back to Islington, I bury my face in my upstretched arm that clutches the ceiling rail so no one will see my tears.

At the entrance to the social services office, I wipe my eyes with my index fingers, hard. Breathe deep, blow it out. The last thing she needs to see, on what may be our last visit, is my shaky, scattered fear.

I go inside and plunk my messenger bag on the reception desk so the security guard can search it for blades and pill bottles. I should be offended, but honestly I'm just relieved I'm not required to drop my knickers.

He rifles through the mishmash: a copy of *The Dia-lectical Behavior Therapy Skills Workbook*, the legal pad, my

headphones, random bits and bobs from my breast pump.
"All clear."

Not yet, I think, and heft the bag back onto my shoulder,
pulling out my mobile to check the time.

Five past one. Shit. *Five* whole precious minutes lost.

I break into a run down the hall. Nearly against the
door marked *PARENTING ASSESSMENT CENTRE*. Step
back, and give what I hope sounds like a not-too-desperate
knock.

I never know which social worker I'm going to get as
my chaperone. Lots of times they send nervous trainees not
much older than I am, which strikes me as incredibly stupid.
I mean, if I'm such a danger, wouldn't they break out the big
supervisory guns? At least the trainees are women, though.
Couple times I've gotten a more senior male worker, which is
beyond awkward when I need to take my bra down to nurse.

The door opens now, and I silently curse my old complaints, and just about fall over in sickened disbelief, because
the worker du jour, on the most fraught day ever, is none
other than their biggest gun. Olivia.

Bad sign, Smack-Talker Brain warns. *More than bad. Ominous.*

"Hi," I force out. "Sorry I'm late."

*Idiot. You shouldn't have mentioned it. They'll call you "mater-
nally disengaged." Too busy slashing your arms up to show up.*

"It's all right," Olivia says quietly. "She just got dropped
off."

I've never met my daughter's foster mum. But I have to
give her props, whomever she is, because one day Squidlet
came in wearing the fuchsia Doc Martens Jascha bought her.

I edge past Olivia and sprint across the industrial carpet to where my girlie lies playing with her DNA molecule. Soon as I drop to my knees in front of her, her eyes widen and her breath huffs with excitement.

"Come here, you." I hoist her into my lap, standing her up so she can bounce.

She grabs my hair in both hands. Her drooly mouth grins.

"Oh, yeah," I say, grinning back. "Wednesday afternoon is the best, innit?"

By some miracle, I manage to keep my voice bright. And to her credit, Olivia manages to refrain from awkward small talk or, even worse, Big Talk about what she and I both know is coming up at half past three.

Instead, what she says is, "I figured you mightn't have had time for lunch today, so I brought you these." And then she gestures towards a vending-machine soda and packet of crisps on the sofa table, and my throat feels like it might burst from the lump swelling inside it.

"Thanks," I say, nonchalantly as humanly possible, and reach over for the drink.

Squidlet plops into my lap and commences batting at the can, trying to pull its tab before I do.

"No, no, no," I say, laughing. "You don't need this, trust me."

I take a deep swallow, then pass the soda back to Olivia. As I settle my spine against the bottom of the nearby couch, she hands me a pillow to soften the hard lean. "Thanks," I say, more softly, less nonchalantly, this time.

Squidlet pats my blouse, her palm mashing into the

dried milk stain. Her lips purse to let out a low hoot of anticipation.

I glance pointedly at Olivia. "My latest test came back clean."

She nods. "I know."

Of course she does. I unbutton my shirt just enough, and as if on cue, Squidlet rolls onto her side and dives in, her latched-on mouth powerful yet whispery. I'd been afraid nursing would feel creepy, but just as with her uterine gymnastics, the sensation was surprisingly tender and lovely when it came.

I watch her tiny jaws work and listen to the adorable *yep* sound of her swallows. She wriggles round at first, one leg kicking rhythmically against the couch leg, one hand twiddling my blouse buttons as the milk plummets, all reverent relief. At least I'm giving her *something* unequivocally good and pure.

Eventually her eyelids close, and her little feet tuck against my belly, and her gulps fade to sighs. My head nods in its own drowse. The rush of hormones always makes me feel a little spacey. Not in a bad way, not like ditching this world for the ceiling, just a yummy doze I could curl up inside forever.

I tip my head back. Shut my eyes. Can't look at the clock. Can't even look at her little face, much as I want to memorize it. So I just hold her near till she unlatches and I feel the satiated slump of her chin.

My eyes flicker back open. I sit up, suddenly self-conscious at being so exposed in front of Olivia, and scramble to hoist my slumbering girl onto my shoulder so it doesn't look like I'm suffocating her while covering my-self up.

Olivia's gaze on us stays steady, imbued with a softness I want to deride as pity, but have to admit looks more like compassion.

"That can't be comfortable down there," she says. "Why don't you hop up on the couch, and I'll fetch you two a blanket?"

Give her the brush-off. She's only being this nice because it's your final visit.

Shut up. You don't know that.

"Yes, please." I heave myself up from the floor, guard-ing the baby's head while my teeth grit at my back's wince, and settle into a corner of the couch, my whole body gratefully sinking. It's not a leather marshmallow like the one in the Victims' Services suite years ago, but it'll do.

With her back turned to me, Olivia goes over to a cup-board and opens it to reveal shelves stocked with nappies and formula cans and bins of small toys. As I watch her search the stacks of linens, I'm seized by a pair of shocking thoughts: *Is she giving me an out? Could we make a run for it?*

No, Wise Mind warns. *That won't help anyone.*

"Here you are." She returns with a fringed pastel throw that looks like the one Mum used to keep folded across the back of our old couch.

I try to reach for the blanket, but it's too hard to grab and tuck around me while holding so much snoozing dead weight, so Olivia drapes it lightly over both of us. I slide my feet up onto the couch and nestle on my side.

The clock above the door reads *1:35*.

I press my cheek to the top of my daughter's pale, wispy head. Whisper her name to her, over and over. Not her pregnancy nickname, not her courtroom pseudonym, but the true, full name I've given her, the one on her birth certificate, the one that her potential parents will be able to change soon as the adoption decree's ink dries.

Lulled by the mantra, I drift back into oxytocin drunkenness, its pull irresistible. I tuck the blanket tighter around us, like I did in the hospital right after I'd devoured my cheeseburger, right before Olivia marched in with the judgment that said she could take her from me.

My gaze flits up to the clock. *1:46.*

Fourteen minutes of fame left, laughs Smack-Talker Brain.

I think of my brave-as-fuck teenage self, pretending she was Flavor Flav just before the satellite eye clicked on at my dad's trial. I catch Olivia's eye, which blinks with equal parts solemnity and surveillance.

"Tell me when it's time," I tell her.

Downy fuzz, faint snores. My hand the maternal one beneath the makeshift duvet now, stroking the curve of her cheek. My mouth nuzzling her temple. The drift like an undertow.

When I slide out of it, Olivia doesn't have to inform me. My body knows what the clock reads. *1:59.*

I sit up slowly, one hand on Squidlet's back, the other cupping her skull. Olivia stands midway between the couch and the door.

"I don't want to wake her up," I say. "Can I just lay her

back down, or do I have to . . ." My words trail off as I picture the official handover.

"No, no, that's quite all right."

"I mean, I don't think she'll roll off or anything."

"She'll be fine, Lesley."

God, I hope so.

2:00. I ache to prolong this as long as I can, to push every mandated boundary, but I know that if I do, I'll be late to court.

So I set her down, and kiss her on the forehead, and smooth her blanket, and whisper, "Bye, darlin'," like I'm just popping back to work for a few hours and we'll be reunited by suppertime, playing it casual, not only because otherwise I'll break but also because I have to believe that that's exactly what will happen.

On my way out, I pluck the soda and the bag of crisps from the table. Ersatz supper tray for a sick little girl.

Olivia now stands sentry at the door. I wonder what she'll do after she closes it behind me. Slump to the floor? Ugly cry like Mum in that meeting room? Pick up my fretful daughter when she wakes and whisper, "Shh, there, there, we won't have to worry about *her* anymore, will we?"

However she reacts, it won't matter. What will matter is how I do.

"Take care of yourself, Lesley," she says softly. "Please."

Emotion Mind's ready to shoot back with a jacked-up *Quit underestimating me, bitch!*, but I rein it in, and nod, and promise. "I will."

• • •

In the corridor, I swig from the soda like I'm still that famished teenager, gulping the chemical syrup as though it's a flipping Valium cocktail. I left my Dr. P.–approved emergency stash at home. Still wanting to prove myself.

My hands shake so badly the drink slops down my shirt. I glimpse the glint of the tab's metal, picture it torn from the can to produce a jagged edge.

Smack-Talker Brain thinks that's an excellent start. I tell it fuck no, and rush home to grab a clean blouse and the Valium.

It's already started to kick in by the time I meet Gloria and Jascha in the corridor outside my assigned courtroom. When they beckon me over, I huddle in the space between them.

Jascha rubs my shoulder. "Immi's on her way."

Gloria takes my opposite hand. "You all right?"

I'm not, but I know what she's asking: *Are you safe?*

"Yeah," I say, because I am.

She looks relieved. Reaches up to tuck a strand of hair behind my ear.

"Umm, your blouse," Jascha says, and gestures towards my shirt's crooked line of hurriedly done-up buttons.

"Shit," I mutter as I see Bradford coming down the hall.

"Here." Gloria unknots her silk scarf from her neck and drapes it around mine. "This should cover it."

I think of her in the girls' bathroom at Hawthorn Hill, shrugging out of her own blouse in order to save my life. I think of my throbbing arm and dilated eyes and youthful, aching need that felt as though it would never be fulfilled.

"Thank you," I whisper.

Bradford's almost at my side now, ready to pull me into a private meeting.

"Just a second," Gloria says to him, as she finishes tying the scarf. Then she puts her hands on my suddenly tremory shoulders and kisses me on the forehead, softly as I did my daughter just before I left her, and says the words my mother should have said to me just before I testified at these courts six years ago:

"I love you. We'll be waiting right here."

In our consultation cubicle, I listen to Bradford's litany of encouragements. "I can't promise, but we've a new judge with a good reunification track record. You'll have options."

I don't think about them as he ushers me into the courtroom. I think of nothing. Zen till the end.

Breathe.

No cameras. No blinky eyes. No media allowed. Just the usual players: the children's guardian, the solicitors, the file folders that weigh more combined than my Squidlet.

Lord Justice enters.

Dear Screaming Women, dear bare lightbulb, dear ersatz vase.

Dear latte, dear Ulysses, dear soul cards.

Dear Smartie-crapping unicorn, dear candle, dear pudding token ring.

Dear Wise Mind, dear darkbright Vivaldi-Clash, dear everything that has brought me this far.

"This case has proved itself to be a most controversial one, with compelling arguments on both sides of the ledger. I shan't belabor its voluminous details, but will rather enumerate my judgment's most critical findings."

I stare down at the legal pad in my lap. Reread the phrase I'd written over and over during my halfhearted lunch at Pret:

NOT A FAILURE.

NOT A FAILURE.

NOT A FAILURE.

"It is my belief that Miss Holloway does have significant challenges in regards to her psychiatric stability, as per expert witness Dr. Paul Orton's assessment."

Breathe.

"And her ability to skillfully parent may very well be impacted by those challenges in future."

Breathe.

"Conversely, Miss Holloway has also shown herself to be proactive in managing her symptoms, resourceful in gathering supports about her, and possessed of a healthy self-awareness of her limitations—all qualities that decrease her safety risk."

Write that down. In calligraphy. I want to frame it.

"Such a risk, of course, is not nil, and certainly justifies social services' investigation, as well as its decision to create a child protection plan."

Breathe.

"In fact, I shall go on record as stating that I am in

favor of further concerted efforts to ensure the welfare of Baby H."

I clutch Bradford Kamen's arm.

"However, I also believe that the removal of Miss Holloway's child at birth was an utterly inappropriate and heavy-handed measure, taken in flagrant defiance of previous rulings set forth in the European High Court."

Come on, Brussels. Save me.

Excruciating pause.

"Therefore, it is my ruling that custody be returned to Miss Holloway, with the caveat that she be monitored by Children's Services for the foreseeable future."

I want to grin, but I can't. I want to sigh down till my shoulders drop, but they're stuck. Tense yet slack-jawed. It's like I've been slapped.

Are you deaf? *He just said yes.*

"Congratulations, Lesley."

Shake Bradford's hand, for fuck's sake. He made this happen.

My own hand shaking like Francesca's.

"It's all right. I know you're staggered."

Staggered, and staggering. He links his elbow through mine to walk me out, but I feel neither the shuffle of my feet nor the brush of his wool suit jacket against my arm.

In the corridor, it's like Sveta's adoption in reverse: Imogen screaming "Team Six Percent, baby!" in my ear; Jascha pulling me to his chest in a gentle hug as Bradford rambles on in debrief. "Landmark case . . . never thought . . . really should contact the media again."

"No," I say. "No more."

"But it's critical we —"

"You heard her," Gloria says, taking my hand and ducking me out of the throng.

In the ladies', I lean over the sink and splash cold-as-it-will-go water on my face while she massages my shoulders hard from behind.

"Feeling anything now?"

"Yeah." I look up at myself in the mirror. Gorgeous scarf. Strong face. "Like a fucking rockstar."

Mussels have barely hit our celebratory table at Belgo before more people start pouring in: Curran and Vera and Sveta, Sophie and Dr. P., and even Francesca, who's now back home and heaps mellower, stepped down to day rehab and a cane.

I'm just about to reach across Immi for a top-up on my steak frites when, through the front window, I glimpse Squidlet, being carried in by a bosomy auburn-haired lady I've never seen before.

My heart lurches. I wasn't expecting this so soon.

I scramble to my feet, almost knocking my chair into a waiter. As her minder brings her over, our table of ten bursts into applause.

It isn't till Squidlet startles at the sound, then leans her cheek into the woman's neck, that I realize: Not just a minder. Her foster mum.

"Diana," she says, jovial and matter-of-fact, and hands my girl over to me.

We sit together while I smooch on Squidlet, and she tells me about how she's been fostering for twenty years: not just adorable, easy-to-place babies but also special-needs kids and teens. Turns out she once had a girl come to her straight from Claymoor Lodge.

"How's she doing?" I say, my mouth full of pavlova.

"Quite well," she says, and pauses. "For her."

I pass Squidlet over to Sveta, who's been begging to hold her for the last hour, and watch as Diana gets out a small notepad. "I hope it's not too presumptuous of me, but I wrote you a list. Things she likes, little—"

I'm her fucking mother. I already know.

Or do I?

No. How can I? We've never spent more than two hours together at a time. Never left our bland-carpeted, supervised bubble.

What does she eat? Does she loathe her bath or love it? What makes her—

I swallow my pride. I say, "Please. Show me."

She goes down the facts, one by one—*Been a bit grumpy lately, but she might be cutting a tooth; down to one nap in the afternoon, the busy little monkey; adores the bath and pureed sweet potato.* And I sit next to her, full of gratitude and fear, thinking, *Oh my God, she's going to wish me luck and walk out and leave me here, and then I'm finally going to do this. I'm finally going to have to do this. Me.*

Not a fostering veteran, not a well-heeled couple with a live-in nanny, but me.

(*Careful what you wish for,* Smack-Talker Brain whispers.)

I tell it to shut its evil gob. I memorize the list. I hold Squidlet up for Diana to kiss good-bye, willing myself not to ponder this moment's could-have-been mirror image.

• • •

Back home, we get settled on our ex-heartburn pillows and have some milk while watching telly.

"See her?" I point to Nigella, who's making frittata with lots of cleavage-revealing egg-crack leans. "That's Mummy's wife. She just doesn't know it yet."

Squidlet gives a liquidy gulp of approval, then pulls away from my nipple with a grimace, her face crumpling like mine before the medicine cabinet the morning after she was born. I'm about to heave her over my shoulder for a burp when she lets out a thin, reedy wail that quickly ratchets up into a scream.

For the next hour, I walk her back and forth, taking all the steps I can in each direction of my studio, *one two three four five six seven eight nine ten, aaand* . . .

No rest. Her face scowling red, her eyes agonized slits.

I check her nappy. I feel her forehead. I hike my shirt up to my collarbone and unsnap my nursing bra, but she turns her cheek, all howling refusal.

See? Smack-Talker Brain mutters. *She doesn't even want you.*

Turn, pace, turn.

I cradle her against my shoulder. Bounce her a little. Glance at every pink object (*blanket, cardigan*) in the room.

Think, Leslyochka. Think.

Fever? No. Hungry? No. Poo? Thank God, no.

Her screams chalkboard scratches in my ear.

I bounce harder, higher. My arms cramp with her weight as a dark ribbon of thought unspools: *Shake her want to shake her want to shake her.*

But I don't.

I stop. Close my eyes. Clench my jaw. Ride out the wave. Now the sigh. Now the shoulder-drop. My teeth relax.

You idiot. Her *teeth*. The list. Remember?

I lay her down on my bed. Settle the pillows around her, close enough that she won't fall, but not so close as to smother.

Her fists pummel the air as I uncap the tube of anesthetic gel. I crook my sticky pinkie finger past her lower lip, smear the thick goop on her aching tooth-nubs.

For a moment she stops, stunned by the tingle, but then her mouth opens in delicate rage again.

Crap. I wipe the clear crud on the nearest pillow with a swipe. As I bring my hands up, their fingers curl into claws.

Breathe.

I push my shoulders down. Hoist her up again.

"*Ja znaiyu*, baby," I say. "I know."

Turn, pace, turn. Eventually I start singing to drown her out, oddball maternal jukebox, everything I can think of. Not long after "Sour Times," she starts rubbing her mouth against the seam of my shirt, like Clare only not, tiny tetchy moans.

"Little light, shining . . ."

I stroke her sweaty head. Feel and hear her snore's whistle-snort inhale. Turn-pace a few more rounds for good measure, then set her on the bed in her pillow nest again.

My unburdened arms shudder. I push my hair back from my head, hold it up in a painful ponytail.

("Miss Holloway has also shown herself to be proactive in managing her symptoms, resourceful in gathering supports about her, and possessed of a healthy self-awareness of her limitations.")

I take my mobile and go into the bathroom, keeping the door open. I sit down on the toilet lid, next to the cheerful turquoise curtain that hides a shower that hides a razor that I do not even consider using, and ring Gloria to tell her what just happened. "Smack-Talker Brain still says I'm Ainsley MacIntyre."

"Why? Just because you felt a less-than-charitable, seething-with-frustration impulse towards your own child?" She laughs. "Nice try."

"But—"

"What? It happens."

"To you?"

"Yeah, to me. And to every mother in the universe, if she's being honest."

"So I did okay."

"You did *fine*, sweetie. Tell Smack-Talker Brain to take a long jump off a short pier, and go snuggle that delicious girl of yours."

Soon as I crawl into bed, she rolls over against me, her pursed mouth suck-twitching in sleep. What about, I wonder?

Lavender milk. Sheep dreams.

I nestle her still-damp head atop my bad forearm. Close my eyes. Picture her at twelve, thirteen, fourteen, equal parts Victorian storybook and diffident anti-cool, wondering, asking, answered: every one of us etched on, brokenwhole, fragile, arise.

acknowledgments

This novel truly took a village to create, and I am profoundly and perpetually grateful to be surrounded by it.

Like Lesley, I owe my life to dialectical behavior therapy, and by extension to the compassionate wisdom of its founder, Dr. Marsha Linehan, and the tireless kindness of the staff of Portland DBT. Special thanks are also due to Catherine Barlow, M.D., who patiently guided me back to creative confidence, both during the writing of *Etched on Me* and the long but fruitful search to find it the right home.

That home would not have been found had it not been for the extraordinary persistence and faith of my agents, Jane Gelfman and Victoria Marini, who fiercely championed this dark horse of a literary comeback and guided it toward the wonderful team at Washington Square Press and Simon & Schuster.

Chief amongst them is my amazing editor, Sarah Cantin, who saw the beauty in the brutality, loved Lesley as much as I did, and helped me fine-tune her story's emotional resonance with astuteness and heart. It's been a delight and a privilege to work together.

I can wholly say the same for my MFA mentors and workshop leaders in the creative writing program at Antioch University Los Angeles:

Gayle Brandeis, who nurtured my fiction's poetry and my nervous foray back into graduate-level work.

Frank Gaspar, who gave me the wise (and hilarious, to my gallows sense of humor) dictate to "do more cutting!" (Scenes, that is.)

Program chair Steve Heller, who deserves a medal of honor for humoring all the despairing emails I sent him when my own Smack-Talker Brain was convinced I should stop writing altogether. (It was your sage advice to "rest, read, and don't push the story" that allowed me to prove it wrong.)

Alistair McCartney, who affirmed my accurate portrayal of UK bureaucracy (whew!).

Dodie Bellamy, who offered me a role model for writing queer, embodied, and on the edge.

Susan Taylor Chehak, whose reading list and workshops stretched my literary brain in ways I didn't know it could bend, and ignited it so quickly I couldn't take notes fast enough.

And, of course, Leonard Chang, who kicked my complacency to the curb, daring me to get real and finally let Lesley speak. This book is what it is because you leveled with me.

My Antiochian thanks wouldn't be complete without a shout-out to my MFA graduating class, the Carnelians, who are without a doubt the coolest, most talented, and most supportive cohort ever. (Go, Carnies!)

Yet more props go to my Tuesday-night critique group, the Tiny Tigers, who never tired of reading revisions of Chapter One over—and over, and over—again. Bless you, Cheri Lasota, Charity Heller, Wendy Grant, and Alissa Bohling.

Thanks also to my test readers, Lyla Wolfenstein, Jen Harris, Karen Compton, Jillian Schweitzer, and Allison McCarthy, for their feedback and cheerleading, and as always to my undergraduate mentor at Goucher College, Madison Smartt Bell, who never fails to come through with avuncular advice even over a decade later.

And to my "Dream Team" blurbers, Clare Allan, Jacquelyn Mitchard, Randy Susan Meyers, Amy Hatvany, and Erika Dreifus: Your early support and gorgeous praise for *Etched on Me* has left me humbled and thrilled in equal measure.

To Jennifer Morales and Arwyn Daemyir, the dearest of supporters, friends, and literary midwives: thank you for loving the Lesley-ness in me, and for helping make this book possible.

Finally, to my husband and daughter, Michael and Maya Luevane, the greatest motivators to "stay alive and show up" imaginable: Thank you for enduring the weeks I spent in L.A. for grad school, the nights I spent holed up in coffee shops, the twelve-hour days in which I wandered the world inside my head. You are the reason I'm still writing, and the reason I'm still here.

Jenn Crowell
July 2013
Forest Grove, Oregon

Etched on Me

Jenn Crowell

**A Washington Square Press
Readers Club Guide**

Questions and Topics for Discussion

1. How does Crowell use visual imagery to give the reader greater access into Lesley's psyche? For example, how did you understand the "ceiling" metaphor?

2. Discuss the importance of music to Lesley. How does its role in her life evolve as the novel progresses? You might also consider the role of music in your own life, and how your taste or relationship to it has evolved. Have certain types of music (or certain artists or playlists) been influential to you at specific moments in time?

3. How does the trip to Russia change Lesley's relationship with the Kremskys?

4. A poster that catches Lesley's eye in the social services office asserts "You CAN break the cycle of violence." What do you think this means for her — and what do you think the novel is saying about the possibility for second chances? How is the past shown to reverberate into the present within the narrative? Is this necessarily a bad thing?

5. Lesley acutely experiences both dissociation and embodiment throughout the novel. Discuss some examples of these as a group. How do instances of each also serve as coping mechanisms for Lesley, and how does embodiment, in particular, become a sign of growth and mechanism for her healing?

6. Turn to pages 47 and 48 and re-read Lesley's analysis of self-harm, and her explanation as to why she

does it. Do you think that causing deliberate physical injury to oneself, such as cutting, is different from other forms of self-inflicted harm (like addiction to harmful substances or eating disorders)? In what ways do you think we all engage in self-harm to some degree?

7. Did Lesley challenge your assumptions about sexual identity? If so, what surprised you? Why do you think she ultimately described her sexual orientation as "queer" to Dr. Orton, rather than "bisexual"? In your discussion, you might also consider the historically fraught conflation of a minority sexual identity with mental illness (for example, the *DSM*—the *Diagnostic and Statistical Manual of Mental Disorders*—labeled homosexuality as deviant behavior until as late as 1974).

8. Both Gloria and Lesley find that their identity as a mother enables them, in key moments, to draw upon a deeper reserve of strength than they otherwise felt they had. Can you find these instances in the text? Regardless of whether or not you are a mother, have you ever experienced something similar?

9. Did you think that Lesley should have contacted Declan once she discovered she was pregnant? What would you have done in her situation? You might also consider Lesley's attempt to flee the UK and travel to the United States. Did you empathize with her struggle to make that decision? Would you have taken that kind of risk?

10. Consider the women who take on maternal roles for Lesley. What is each character uniquely able to offer or teach her—and how do their influences manifest in her choices, and her own experience of motherhood? Conversely, what does Lesley offer or teach these women?

11. Aurelia and Clare are spectral presences in Lesley's subconscious throughout the novel. Why do you feel they haunt her as vividly as they do? In particular, why do you think Lesley seems more haunted by the ghost of her mother than that of her father? You might also consider whether there are people from your past who similarly "haunt" you, and what it is about those relationships that have stayed with you.

12. For many characters in *Etched on Me*—Sophie, Gloria and Jascha, Lesley, even Clare's parents— bringing a child into the world proves to be an uphill battle. Alternatively, Lesley's parents both fail her, in critical ways. With this in mind, what do you think the novel is ultimately saying about family?

13. The British system of health care and social services is clearly different from that of the United States. Do you agree with Imogen that the investigation into Lesley's fitness for parenthood is an example of "socialism gone awry"? Or does the case of Ainsley MacIntyre, and the possibility for other, similar scenarios, justify a certain level of scrutiny toward future mothers?

Enhance Your Reading Group

1. Crowell's first novel, *Necessary Madness*, is narrated by Gloria (from *Etched on Me*) and chronicles the aftermath of her first husband's death. Consider reading *Necessary Madness* as a group. How does it affect your view of Gloria's character in *Etched on Me*, or what added insight do you feel you have into her? Is there a character from *Etched on Me* that you would want to narrate a novel?

2. *Etched on Me* is inspired by a true story—that of Fran Lyon, a twenty-two-year-old British woman who fled her home country in 2007 when she was nearly eight months pregnant. UK social services had ordered that she would be forced to surrender custody of her child within minutes of giving birth, due to her mental health history (raped at fourteen, she had suffered depression and instances of self-harm during her adolescence). Despite receiving extensive treatment and being granted a clean bill of health from various psychiatric professionals, Lyon was still considered a risk to her unborn child. As a group, search online for newspaper articles that covered this story at the time it was unfolding, or go to www.youtube .com/watch?v=90q5kXlOW_g to watch a BBC interview with Lyon during her pregnancy.

3. DBT (dialectical behavior therapy) is a widely recognized form of psychotherapy used to treat individuals with BPD (borderline personality

disorder)—but it is also, as Gloria jokingly acknowledges, a fairly useful tool for anyone. Turn to pages 159 and 160 to read through Dr. P.'s description of the Rational Mind, Emotion Mind, and Wise Mind. Together, brainstorm some everyday, stressful situations in which applying these structures could be helpful to you. To learn more about DBT, visit: www.behaviorialtech.org and www.dbtselfhelp.com.

4. "Soul cards" are one of the hallmarks of Lesley's time on the Phoenix. Nominate one or two group members to bring old magazines to your meeting, and make your own soul card as you discuss *Etched on Me*. Share your creations at the end of the meeting, and see if they illuminate anything about your peers, or yourself, that you weren't expecting. To learn more about soul cards, visit the Soul Collage™ website at www.soulcollage.com.

5. Music has a constant presence throughout *Etched on Me*. Visit Jenn Crowell's website at www.jenncrowell.com to find a playlist of songs that are featured in the novel.